A Christmas Carol

AND OTHER CHRISTMAS TALES

A CHRISTMAS CAROL

AND OTHER CHRISTMAS TALES

BARNES & NOBLE

NEW YORK

This 2021 edition printed for Barnes & Noble Booksellers, Inc. by Sterling Publishing Co., Inc.

ISBN 978-1-4351-7045-2

Barnes & Noble Booksellers, Inc.
33 East 17th Street
New York, NY 10003

Manufactured in India

1 3 5 7 9 10 8 6 4 2

Cover design by Gina Bonanno
Book design by Kevin Ullrich
Endpapers by Bridgeman Images

CONTENTS

Poems

INTRODUCTION

Christmas means different things to different people. To some it is a holiday known for the merriment of parties, gift-giving, tree-trimming, and other traditional festivities. To others it is a time when families come together to count past blessings and look forward with hope to a new year of fulfillment. To still others, it is a season of benevolence and charity, in which kindness is extended not only to family and friends but to those who are less fortunate than themselves.

Writers and poets know that Christmas means all these things and more, and the best of them have commemorated the many aspects of the Yuletide season in works whose reading has become as much a part of the holiday as any other Christmas tradition. This colorfully illustrated holiday treasury brings together eleven stories and ten poems that celebrate the Christmas season and its wide variety of expressions.

The title tale is without question the best-known Christmas story in the English language. Charles Dickens published *A Christmas Carol* in 1843 to raise social awareness of the plight of the poor and neglected in Victorian England. The story was prefigured in Dickens's large body of work seven years earlier with the publication of "The Story of the Goblins Who Stole a Sexton." This serial sketch, collected as a chapter in *The Pickwick Papers*, tells of curmudgeonly and bibulous sexton Gabriel Grub, who one Christmas Eve is chastised by a clutch of graveyard goblins with visions of the genial and festive ways that most people celebrate the holiday. Dickens did not "invent" Christmas with *A Christmas Carol*, as he is sometimes credited, but his story's publication laid the groundwork for virtually every Christmas story written since. Through "my Carol" (as he referred to it), Dickens articulated what he hoped would be a universal appreciation of Christmas as "a good time; a kind, forgiving, charitable, pleasant time; the only time I know of, in the long calendar of the year, when men and women seem by one consent to open their shut-up hearts freely." The text of *A Christmas Carol*, as reprinted here, features the distinguished artwork of Arthur Rackham.

Many elements from *A Christmas Carol* trickled down into other writers' Christmas stories over the years. Festivities around the family home and hearth that punctuate Dickens's tale appear in L. M. Montgomery's "Christmas at Red Butte," the story of a young woman's generosity toward her siblings and the gifts greater than material goods that they all reap. The spirit of charity that motivates the reformed Scrooge to acts of kindness at the end of Dickens's tale translates into the acts of holiday gift-giving that bring joy to unfortunates faced with a joyless Christmas in Louisa May Alcott's "A Christmas Dream, and How It Came to Be True," a story that references Dickens's work explicitly.

"Old Christmas," by Washington Irving, began life as five separate sketches published in his collection *The Sketch Book* (1819–1820). Irving's account of traditional holiday celebrations in England and his suggestion of how many of them transferred across the pond to America proved so popular that he later published them as their own book, illustrated over the years by a number of different artists.

E. T. A. Hoffmann's "The Nutcracker and the Mouse King" (1816) predates Irving's tale by several years, and it has become, indirectly, one of the best-loved tales of the holiday season. In 1844, best-selling French author Alexandre Dumas adapted the story for young readers as *The History of a Nutcracker*. In the early 1890s, the Dumas rendition of the story was adapted for the now well-known stage ballet scored with the music of composer Pyotr Ilyich Tchaikovsky. Readers who know the story of *The Nutcracker* from the ballet will find the Hoffmann version somewhat different but no less a-sparkle with the magic that has made both classic Christmas fantasies. This printing of the story is illustrated with many images by George Bertall that appeared in the tale's 1847 translation into English, as well as with color plates by Czech artist Artuš Scheiner

Of course, it wouldn't be Christmas without Santa Claus! Katharine Carrington's "The Doll That Santa Claus Brought" hinges on the childhood dream of actually catching Santa red-handed as he delivers his Christmas gifts. And in "Kris Kringle and His Elves," B. McLoughlin walks readers through Santa's (aka Kris Kringle's) paces as he plans and executes his Christmas Eve travels.

And speaking of Santa, surely the most famous poem to celebrate the holiday is Clement Clarke Moore's "A Visit from St. Nicholas," which is reprinted here adorned with the artwork of Jessie Willcox Smith. First published in 1823, Moore's poem is responsible for much of the mythology that we associate with Santa today, from his physical looks to his magic ability to drive a present-laden sleigh drawn by reindeer through the air. This book's other poems address in miniature many of the same themes addressed in the stories: the decorating of the Christmas tree, the hanging of stockings at the fireplace, and the celebration of Christmas and its true spirit in song and veneration.

Like presents beneath the tree, the stories and poems in this volume are treats that capture the joyful spirit of the Christmas season and glow with the warmth of the holiday fireside. Although dressed in Yuletide trappings, they offer pleasures that can be enjoyed the whole year round.

STORIES

A CHRISTMAS CAROL

IN PROSE

Being a Ghost Story of Christmas

CHARLES DICKENS

Stave I
MARLEY'S GHOST

Marley was dead: to begin with. There is no doubt whatever about that. The register of his burial was signed by the clergyman, the clerk, the undertaker, and the chief mourner. Scrooge signed it: and Scrooge's name was good upon 'Change, for anything he chose to put his hand to. Old Marley was as dead as a door-nail.

Mind! I don't mean to say that I know, of my own knowledge, what there is particularly dead about a door-nail. I might have been inclined, myself, to regard a coffin-nail as the deadest piece of ironmongery in the trade. But the wisdom of our ancestors is in the simile; and my unhallowed hands shall not disturb it, or the Country's done for. You will therefore permit me to repeat, emphatically, that Marley was as dead as a door-nail.

4

Scrooge knew he was dead? Of course he did. How could it be otherwise? Scrooge and he were partners for I don't know how many years. Scrooge was his sole executor, his sole administrator, his sole assign, his sole residuary legatee, his sole friend, and sole mourner. And even Scrooge was not so dreadfully cut up by the sad event, but that he was an excellent man of business on the very day of the funeral, and solemnised it with an undoubted bargain.

The mention of Marley's funeral brings me back to the point I started from. There is no doubt that Marley was dead. This must be distinctly understood, or nothing wonderful can come of the story I am going to relate. If we were not perfectly convinced that Hamlet's Father died before the play began, there would be nothing more remarkable in his taking a stroll at night, in an easterly wind, upon his own ramparts, than there would be in any other middle-aged gentleman rashly turning out after dark in a breezy spot—say Saint Paul's Churchyard for instance—literally to astonish his son's weak mind.

Scrooge never painted out Old Marley's name. There it stood, years afterwards, above the warehouse door: Scrooge and Marley. The firm was known as Scrooge and Marley. Sometimes people new to the business called Scrooge Scrooge, and sometimes Marley, but he answered to both names. It was all the same to him.

Oh! but he was a tight-fisted hand at the grind-stone, Scrooge! a squeezing, wrenching, grasping, scraping, clutching, covetous, old sinner! Hard and sharp as flint, from which no steel had ever struck out generous fire; secret, and self-contained, and solitary as an oyster. The cold within him froze his old features, nipped his pointed nose, shrivelled his cheek, stiffened his gait; made his eyes red, his thin lips blue; and spoke out shrewdly in his grating voice. A frosty rime was on his head, and on his eyebrows, and his wiry chin. He carried his own low temperature always about with him; he iced his office in the dog-days; and didn't thaw it one degree at Christmas.

External heat and cold had little influence on Scrooge. No warmth could warm, no wintry weather chill him. No wind that blew was bitterer than he, no falling snow was more intent upon its purpose, no pelting rain less open to entreaty. Foul weather didn't know where to have him. The heaviest rain, and snow, and hail, and sleet, could boast of the advantage over him in only one respect. They often "came down" handsomely, and Scrooge never did.

Nobody ever stopped him in the street to say, with gladsome looks, "My dear Scrooge, how are you? When will you come to see me?" No beggars implored him to bestow a trifle, no children asked him what it was o'clock, no man or woman ever once in all his life inquired the way to such and such a place, of Scrooge. Even the blind men's dogs appeared to know him; and when they saw him coming on, would tug their owners into doorways and up courts; and then would wag their tails as though they said, "No eye at all is better than an evil eye, dark master!"

But what did Scrooge care! It was the very thing he liked. To edge his way along the crowded paths of life, warning all human sympathy to keep its distance, was what the knowing ones call "nuts" to Scrooge.

Once upon a time—of all the good days in the year, on Christmas Eve—old Scrooge sat busy in his counting-house. It was cold, bleak, biting weather: foggy withal: and he could hear the people in the court outside, go wheezing up and down, beating their hands upon their breasts, and stamping their feet upon the pavement stones to warm them. The city clocks had only just gone three, but it was quite dark already—it had not been light all day—and candles were flaring in the windows of the neighbouring offices, like ruddy smears upon the palpable brown air. The fog came pouring in at every chink and keyhole, and was so dense without, that although the court was of the narrowest, the houses opposite were mere phantoms. To see the dingy cloud come drooping down, obscuring everything, one might have thought that Nature lived hard by, and was brewing on a large scale.

The door of Scrooge's counting-house was open that he might keep his eye upon his clerk, who in a dismal little cell beyond, a sort of tank, was copying letters. Scrooge had a very small fire, but the clerk's fire was so very much smaller that it looked like one coal. But he couldn't replenish it, for Scrooge kept the coal-box in his own room; and so surely as the clerk came in with the shovel, the master predicted that it would be necessary for them to part. Wherefore the clerk put on his white comforter, and tried to warm himself at the candle; in which effort, not being a man of a strong imagination, he failed.

"A merry Christmas, uncle! God save you!" cried a cheerful voice. It was the voice of Scrooge's nephew, who came upon him so quickly that this was the first intimation he had of his approach.

"Bah!" said Scrooge, "Humbug!"

He had so heated himself with rapid walking in the fog and frost, this nephew of Scrooge's, that he was all in a glow; his face was ruddy and handsome; his eyes sparkled, and his breath smoked again.

"Christmas a humbug, uncle!" said Scrooge's nephew. "You don't mean that, I am sure?"

"I do," said Scrooge. "Merry Christmas! what right have you to be merry? what right have you to be merry? You're poor enough."

"Come, then," returned the nephew gaily. "What right have you to be dismal? what right have you to be morose? You're rich enough."

Scrooge having no better answer ready on the spur of the moment, said, "Bah!" again; and followed it up with "Humbug."

"Don't be cross, uncle!" said the nephew.

"What else can I be," returned the uncle, "when I live in such a world of fools as this? Merry Christmas! Out upon merry Christmas! What's Christmas time to you but a time for paying bills without money; a time for finding yourself a year older, but not an hour richer; a time for balancing your books and having every item in 'em through a round dozen of months presented dead against you? If I could work my will," said Scrooge indignantly, "every idiot who goes about with 'Merry Christmas' on his lips, should be boiled with his own pudding, and buried with a stake of holly through his heart. He should!"

"Uncle!" pleaded the nephew.

"Nephew!" returned the uncle sternly, "keep Christmas in your own way, and let me keep it in mine."

"Keep it!" repeated Scrooge's nephew. "But you don't keep it."

"Let me leave it alone, then," said Scrooge. "Much good may it do you! Much good it has ever done you!"

"There are many things from which I might have derived good, by which I have not profited, I dare say," returned the nephew. "Christmas among the rest. But I am sure I have always thought of Christmas time, when it has come round—apart from the veneration due to its sacred name and origin, if anything belonging to it can be apart from that—as a good time; a kind, forgiving, charitable, pleasant time; the only time I know of, in the long calendar of the year, when men and women seem by one consent to open their shut-up hearts freely, and to think of people below them as if they really were fellow-passengers to the grave, and not another race of creatures bound on other journeys. And therefore, uncle, though it has never put a scrap of gold or silver in my pocket, I believe that it *has* done me good, and *will* do me good; and I say, God bless it!"

The clerk in the tank involuntarily applauded. Becoming immediately sensible of the impropriety, he poked the fire, and extinguished the last frail spark for ever.

"Let me hear another sound from *you*," said Scrooge, "and you'll keep your Christmas by losing your situation! You're quite a powerful speaker, sir," he added, turning to his nephew. "I wonder you don't go into Parliament."

"Don't be angry, uncle. Come! Dine with us to-morrow."

Scrooge said that he would see him—yes, indeed he did. He went the whole length of the expression, and said that he would see him in that extremity first.

"But why?" cried Scrooge's nephew. "Why?"

"Why did you get married?" said Scrooge.

"Because I fell in love."

"Because you fell in love!" growled Scrooge, as if that were the only one thing in the world more ridiculous than a merry Christmas. "Good afternoon!"

"Nay, uncle, but you never came to see me before that happened. Why give it as a reason for not coming now?"

"Good afternoon," said Scrooge.

"I want nothing from you; I ask nothing of you; why cannot we be friends?"

"Good afternoon," said Scrooge.

"I am sorry, with all my heart, to find you so resolute. We have never had any quarrel, to which I have been a party. But I have made the trial in homage to Christmas, and I'll keep my Christmas humour to the last. So A Merry Christmas, uncle!"

"Good afternoon!" said Scrooge.

"And A Happy New Year!"

"Good afternoon!" said Scrooge.

His nephew left the room without an angry word, notwithstanding. He stopped at the outer door to bestow the greetings of the season on the clerk, who, cold as he was, was warmer than Scrooge; for he returned them cordially.

"There's another fellow," muttered Scrooge; who overheard him: "my clerk, with fifteen shillings a week, and a wife and family, talking about a merry Christmas. I'll retire to Bedlam."

This lunatic, in letting Scrooge's nephew out, had let two other people in. They were portly gentlemen, pleasant to behold, and now stood, with their hats off, in Scrooge's office. They had books and papers in their hands, and bowed to him.

"Scrooge and Marley's, I believe," said one of the gentlemen, referring to his list. "Have I the pleasure of addressing Mr. Scrooge, or Mr. Marley?"

"Mr. Marley has been dead these seven years," Scrooge replied. "He died seven years ago, this very night."

"We have no doubt his liberality is well represented by his surviving partner," said the gentleman, presenting his credentials.

It certainly was; for they had been two kindred spirits. At the ominous word "liberality," Scrooge frowned, and shook his head, and handed the credentials back.

"At this festive season of the year, Mr. Scrooge," said the gentleman, taking up a pen, "it is more than usually desirable that we should make some slight provision for the Poor and destitute, who suffer greatly at the present time. Many thousands are in want of common necessaries; hundreds of thousands are in want of common comforts, sir."

"Are there no prisons?" asked Scrooge.

"Plenty of prisons," said the gentleman, laying down the pen again.

"And the Union workhouses?" demanded Scrooge. "Are they still in operation?"

"They are. Still," returned the gentleman, "I wish I could say they were not."

"The Treadmill and the Poor Law are in full vigour, then?" said Scrooge.

"Both very busy, sir."

"Oh! I was afraid, from what you said at first, that something had occurred to stop them in their useful course," said Scrooge. "I'm very glad to hear it."

"Under the impression that they scarcely furnish Christian cheer of mind or body to the multitude," returned the gentleman, "a few of us are endeavouring to raise a fund to buy the Poor some meat and drink, and means of warmth. We choose this time, because it is a time, of all others, when Want is keenly felt, and Abundance rejoices. What shall I put you down for?"

"Nothing!" Scrooge replied.

"You wish to be anonymous?"

"I wish to be left alone," said Scrooge. "Since you ask me what I wish, gentlemen, that is my answer. I don't make merry myself at Christmas and I can't afford to make idle people merry. I help to support the establishments I have mentioned—they cost enough; and those who are badly off must go there."

"Many can't go there; and many would rather die."

"If they would rather die," said Scrooge, "they had better do it, and decrease the surplus population. Besides—excuse me—I don't know that."

"But you might know it," observed the gentleman.

"It's not my business," Scrooge returned. "It's enough for a man to understand his own business, and not to interfere with other people's. Mine occupies me constantly. Good afternoon, gentlemen!"

Seeing clearly that it would be useless to pursue their point, the gentlemen withdrew. Scrooge resumed his labours with an improved opinion of himself, and in a more facetious temper than was usual with him.

Meanwhile the fog and darkness thickened so, that people ran about with flaring links, proffering their services to go before horses in carriages, and conduct them on their way. The ancient tower of a church, whose gruff old bell was always peeping slily down at

Scrooge out of a Gothic window in the wall, became invisible, and struck the hours and quarters in the clouds, with tremulous vibrations afterwards as if its teeth were chattering in its frozen head up there. The cold became intense. In the main street, at the corner of the court, some labourers were repairing the gas-pipes, and had lighted a great fire in a brazier, round which a party of ragged men and boys were gathered: warming their hands and winking their eyes before the blaze in rapture. The water-plug being left in solitude, its overflowings sullenly congealed, and turned to misanthropic ice. The brightness of the shops where holly sprigs and berries crackled in the lamp heat of the windows, made pale faces ruddy as they passed. Poulterers' and grocers' trades became a splendid joke: a glorious pageant, with which it was next to impossible to believe that such dull principles as bargain and sale had anything to do. The Lord Mayor, in the stronghold of the mighty Mansion House, gave orders to his fifty cooks and butlers to keep Christmas as a Lord Mayor's household should; and even the little tailor, whom he had fined five shillings on the previous Monday for being drunk and bloodthirsty in the streets, stirred up to-morrow's pudding in his garret, while his lean wife and the baby sallied out to buy the beef.

Foggier yet, and colder. Piercing, searching, biting cold. If the good Saint Dunstan had but nipped the Evil Spirit's nose with a touch of such weather as that, instead of using his familiar weapons, then indeed he would have roared to lusty purpose. The owner of one scant young nose, gnawed and mumbled by the hungry cold as bones are gnawed by dogs, stooped down at Scrooge's keyhole to regale him with a Christmas carol: but at the first sound of—

"God bless you, merry gentleman!
May nothing you dismay!"

Scrooge seized the ruler with such energy of action, that the singer fled in terror, leaving the keyhole to the fog and even more congenial frost.

At length the hour of shutting up the counting-house arrived. With an ill-will Scrooge dismounted from his stool, and tacitly admitted the fact to the expectant clerk in the Tank, who instantly snuffed his candle out, and put on his hat.

"You'll want all day to-morrow, I suppose?" said Scrooge.

"If quite convenient, sir."

"It's not convenient," said Scrooge, "and it's not fair. If I was to stop half-a-crown for it, you'd think yourself ill-used, I'll be bound?"

The clerk smiled faintly.

"And yet," said Scrooge, "you don't think *me* ill-used, when I pay a day's wages for no work."

The clerk observed that it was only once a year.

"A poor excuse for picking a man's pocket every twenty-fifth of December!" said Scrooge, buttoning his great-coat to the chin. "But I suppose you must have the whole day. Be here all the earlier next morning."

The clerk promised that he would; and Scrooge walked out with a growl. The office was closed in a twinkling, and the clerk, with the long ends of his white comforter dangling below his waist (for he boasted no great-coat), went down a slide on Cornhill, at the end of a lane of boys, twenty times, in honour of its being Christmas Eve, and then ran home to Camden Town as hard as he could pelt, to play at blindman's-buff.

Scrooge took his melancholy dinner in his usual melancholy tavern; and having read all the newspapers, and beguiled the rest of the evening with his banker's-book, went home to bed. He lived in chambers which had once belonged to his deceased partner. They were a gloomy suite of rooms, in a lowering pile of building up a yard, where it had so little business to be, that one could scarcely help fancying it must have run there when it was a young house, playing at hide-and-seek with other houses, and forgotten the way out again. It was old enough now, and dreary enough, for nobody lived in it but Scrooge, the other rooms being all let out as offices. The yard was so dark that even Scrooge, who knew its every stone, was fain to grope with his hands. The fog and frost so hung about the black old gateway of the house, that it seemed as if the Genius of the Weather sat in mournful meditation on the threshold.

Now, it is a fact, that there was nothing at all particular about the knocker on the door, except that it was very large. It is also a fact, that Scrooge had seen it, night and morning, during his whole residence in that place; also that Scrooge had as little of what is called fancy about him as any man in the City of London, even including—which is a bold word—the corporation, aldermen, and livery. Let it also be borne in mind that

Scrooge had not bestowed one thought on Marley, since his last mention of his seven years' dead partner that afternoon. And then let any man explain to me, if he can, how it happened that Scrooge, having his key in the lock of the door, saw in the knocker, without its undergoing any intermediate process of change—not a knocker, but Marley's face.

Marley's face. It was not in impenetrable shadow as the other objects in the yard were, but had a dismal light about it, like a bad lobster in a dark cellar. It was not angry or ferocious, but looked at Scrooge as Marley used to look: with ghostly spectacles turned up on its ghostly forehead. The hair was curiously stirred, as if by breath or hot air; and, though the eyes were wide open, they were perfectly motionless. That, and its livid colour, made it horrible; but its horror seemed to be in spite of the face and beyond its control, rather than a part of its own expression.

As Scrooge looked fixedly at this phenomenon, it was a knocker again.

To say that he was not startled, or that his blood was not conscious of a terrible sensation to which it had been a stranger from infancy, would be untrue. But he put his hand upon the key he had relinquished, turned it sturdily, walked in, and lighted his candle.

He *did* pause, with a moment's irresolution, before he shut the door; and he *did* look cautiously behind it first, as if he half expected to be terrified with the sight of Marley's pigtail sticking out into the hall. But there was nothing on the back of the door, except the screws and nuts that held the knocker on, so he said "Pooh, pooh!" and closed it with a bang.

The sound resounded through the house like thunder. Every room above, and every cask in the wine-merchant's cellars below, appeared to have a separate peal of echoes of its own. Scrooge was not a man to be frightened by echoes. He fastened the door, and walked across the hall, and up the stairs; slowly too: trimming his candle as he went.

You may talk vaguely about driving a coach-and-six up a good old flight of stairs, or through a bad young Act of Parliament; but I mean to say you might have got a hearse up that staircase, and taken it broadwise, with the splinter-bar towards the wall and the door towards the balustrades: and done it easy. There was plenty of width for that, and room to spare; which is perhaps the reason why Scrooge thought he saw a locomotive hearse going on before him in the gloom. Half-a-dozen gas-lamps out of the street wouldn't have lighted the entry too well, so you may suppose that it was pretty dark with Scrooge's dip.

Up Scrooge went, not caring a button for that. Darkness is cheap, and Scrooge liked it. But before he shut his heavy door, he walked through his rooms to see that all was right. He had just enough recollection of the face to desire to do that.

Sitting-room, bed-room, lumber-room. All as they should be. Nobody under the table, nobody under the sofa; a small fire in the grate; spoon and basin ready; and the little saucepan of gruel (Scrooge had a cold in his head) upon the hob. Nobody under the bed; nobody in the closet; nobody in his dressing-gown, which was hanging up in a suspicious attitude against the wall. Lumber-room as usual. Old fire-guard, old shoes, two fish-baskets, washing-stand on three legs, and a poker.

Quite satisfied, he closed his door, and locked himself in; double-locked himself in, which was not his custom. Thus secured against surprise, he took off his cravat; put on his dressing-gown and slippers, and his nightcap; and sat down before the fire to take his gruel.

It was a very low fire indeed; nothing on such a bitter night. He was obliged to sit close to it, and brood over it, before he could extract the least sensation of warmth from such a handful of fuel. The fireplace was an old one, built by some Dutch merchant long ago, and paved all round with quaint Dutch tiles, designed to illustrate the Scriptures. There were Cains and Abels, Pharaoh's daughters; Queens of Sheba, Angelic messengers descending through the air on clouds like feather-beds, Abrahams, Belshazzars, Apostles putting off to sea in butter-boats, hundreds of figures to attract his thoughts; and yet that face of Marley, seven years dead, came like the ancient Prophet's rod, and swallowed up the whole. If each smooth tile had been a blank at first, with power to shape some picture on its surface from the disjointed fragments of his thoughts, there would have been a copy of old Marley's head on every one.

"Humbug!" said Scrooge; and walked across the room.

After several turns, he sat down again. As he threw his head back in the chair, his glance happened to rest upon a bell, a disused bell, that hung in the room, and communicated for some purpose now forgotten with a chamber in the highest story of the building. It was with great astonishment, and with a strange, inexplicable dread, that as he looked, he saw this bell begin to swing. It swung so softly in the outset that it scarcely made a sound; but soon it rang out loudly, and so did every bell in the house.

This might have lasted half a minute, or a minute, but it seemed an hour. The bells ceased as they had begun, together. They were succeeded by a clanking noise, deep down below; as if some person were dragging a heavy chain over the casks in the wine-merchant's cellar. Scrooge then remembered to have heard that ghosts in haunted houses were described as dragging chains.

The cellar-door flew open with a booming sound, and then he heard the noise much louder, on the floors below; then coming up the stairs; then coming straight towards his door.

"It's humbug still!" said Scrooge. "I won't believe it."

His colour changed though, when, without a pause, it came on through the heavy door, and passed into the room before his eyes. Upon its coming in, the dying flame leaped up, as though it cried, "I know him; Marley's Ghost!" and fell again.

The same face: the very same. Marley in his pigtail, usual waistcoat, tights and boots; the tassels on the latter bristling, like his pigtail, and his coat-skirts, and the hair upon his head. The chain he drew was clasped about his middle. It was long, and wound about him like a tail; and it was made (for Scrooge observed it closely) of cash-boxes, keys, padlocks, ledgers, deeds, and heavy purses wrought in steel. His body was transparent; so that Scrooge, observing him, and looking through his waistcoat, could see the two buttons on his coat behind.

Scrooge had often heard it said that Marley had no bowels, but he had never believed it until now.

No, nor did he believe it even now. Though he looked the phantom through and through, and saw it standing before him; though he felt the chilling influence of its death-cold eyes; and marked the very texture of the folded kerchief bound about its head and chin, which wrapper he had not observed before; he was still incredulous, and fought against his senses.

"How now!" said Scrooge, caustic and cold as ever. "What do you want with me?"

"Much!"—Marley's voice, no doubt about it.

"Who are you?"

"Ask me who I *was*."

"Who *were* you then?" said Scrooge, raising his voice. "You're particular, for a shade." He was going to say "to a shade," but substituted this, as more appropriate.

"In life I was your partner, Jacob Marley."

"Can you—can you sit down?" asked Scrooge, looking doubtfully at him.

"I can."

"Do it, then."

Scrooge asked the question, because he didn't know whether a ghost so transparent might find himself in a condition to take a chair; and felt that in the event of its being impossible, it might involve the necessity of an embarrassing explanation. But the ghost sat down on the opposite side of the fireplace, as if he were quite used to it.

"You don't believe in me," observed the Ghost.

"I don't," said Scrooge.

"What evidence would you have of my reality beyond that of your senses?"

"I don't know," said Scrooge.

"Why do you doubt your senses?"

"Because," said Scrooge, "a little thing affects them. A slight disorder of the stomach makes them cheats. You may be an undigested bit of beef, a blot of mustard, a crumb of cheese, a fragment of an underdone potato. There's more of gravy than of grave about you, whatever you are!"

Scrooge was not much in the habit of cracking jokes, nor did he feel, in his heart, by any means waggish then. The truth is, that he tried to be smart, as a means of distracting his own attention, and keeping down his terror; for the spectre's voice disturbed the very marrow in his bones.

To sit, staring at those fixed glazed eyes, in silence for a moment, would play, Scrooge felt, the very deuce with him. There was something very awful, too, in the spectre's being provided with an infernal atmosphere of its own. Scrooge could not feel it himself, but this was clearly the case; for though the Ghost sat perfectly motionless, its hair, and skirts, and tassels, were still agitated as by the hot vapour from an oven.

"You see this toothpick?" said Scrooge, returning quickly to the charge, for the reason just assigned; and wishing, though it were only for a second, to divert the vision's stony gaze from himself.

"I do," replied the Ghost.

"You are not looking at it," said Scrooge.

"But I see it," said the Ghost, "notwithstanding."

"Well!" returned Scrooge, "I have but to swallow this, and be for the rest of my days persecuted by a legion of goblins, all of my own creation. Humbug, I tell you—humbug!"

At this the spirit raised a frightful cry, and shook its chain with such a dismal and appalling noise, that Scrooge held on tight to his chair, to save himself from falling in a swoon. But how much greater was his horror, when the phantom taking off the bandage round its head, as if it were too warm to wear indoors, its lower jaw dropped down upon its breast!

Scrooge fell upon his knees, and clasped his hands before his face.

"Mercy!" he said. "Dreadful apparition, why do you trouble me?"

"Man of the worldly mind!" replied the Ghost, "do you believe in me or not?"

"I do," said Scrooge. "I must. But why do spirits walk the earth, and why do they come to me?"

"It is required of every man," the Ghost returned, "that the spirit within him should walk abroad among his fellowmen, and travel far and wide; and if that spirit goes not forth in life, it is condemned to do so after death. It is doomed to wander through the world—oh, woe is me!—and witness what it cannot share, but might have shared on earth, and turned to happiness!"

Again the spectre raised a cry, and shook its chain and wrung its shadowy hands.

"You are fettered," said Scrooge, trembling. "Tell me why?"

"I wear the chain I forged in life," replied the Ghost. "I made it link by link, and yard by yard; I girded it on of my own free will, and of my own free will I wore it. Is its pattern strange to *you*?"

Scrooge trembled more and more.

"Or would you know," pursued the Ghost, "the weight and length of the strong coil you bear yourself? It was full as heavy and as long as this, seven Christmas Eves ago. You have laboured on it, since. It is a ponderous chain!"

Scrooge glanced about him on the floor, in the expectation of finding himself surrounded by some fifty or sixty fathoms of iron cable: but he could see nothing.

"Jacob," he said, imploringly. "Old Jacob Marley, tell me more. Speak comfort to me, Jacob!"

"I have none to give," the Ghost replied. "It comes from other regions, Ebenezer Scrooge, and is conveyed by other ministers, to other kinds of men. Nor can I tell you what I would. A very little more is all permitted to me. I cannot rest, I cannot stay, I cannot linger anywhere. My spirit never walked beyond our counting-house—mark me!—in life my spirit never roved beyond the narrow limits of our money-changing hole; and weary journeys lie before me!"

It was a habit with Scrooge, whenever he became thoughtful, to put his hands in his breeches pockets. Pondering on what the Ghost had said, he did so now, but without lifting up his eyes, or getting off his knees.

"You must have been very slow about it, Jacob," Scrooge observed, in a business-like manner, though with humility and deference.

"Slow!" the Ghost repeated.

"Seven years dead," mused Scrooge. "And travelling all the time!"

"The whole time," said the Ghost. "No rest, no peace. Incessant torture of remorse."

"You travel fast?" said Scrooge.

"On the wings of the wind," replied the Ghost.

"You might have got over a great quantity of ground in seven years," said Scrooge.

The Ghost, on hearing this, set up another cry, and clanked its chain so hideously in the dead silence of the night, that the Ward would have been justified in indicting it for a nuisance.

"Oh! captive, bound, and double-ironed," cried the phantom, "not to know, that ages of incessant labour by immortal creatures, for this earth must pass into eternity before the good of which it is susceptible is all developed. Not to know that any Christian spirit working kindly in its little sphere, whatever it may be, will find its mortal life too short for its vast means of usefulness. Not to know that no space of regret can make amends for one life's opportunity misused! Yet such was I! Oh! such was I!"

"But you were always a good man of business, Jacob," faltered Scrooge, who now began to apply this to himself.

"Business!" cried the Ghost, wringing its hands again. "Mankind was my business. The common welfare was my business; charity, mercy, forbearance, and benevolence, were, all, my business. The dealings of my trade were but a drop of water in the comprehensive ocean of my business!"

It held up its chain at arm's length, as if that were the cause of all its unavailing grief, and flung it heavily upon the ground again.

"At this time of the rolling year," the spectre said, "I suffer most. Why did I walk through crowds of fellow-beings with my eyes turned down, and never raise them to that blessed Star which led the Wise Men to a poor abode! Were there no poor homes to which its light would have conducted *me!*"

Scrooge was very much dismayed to hear the spectre going on at this rate, and began to quake exceedingly.

"Hear me!" cried the Ghost. "My time is nearly gone."

"I will," said Scrooge. "But don't be hard upon me! Don't be flowery, Jacob! Pray!"

"How it is that I appear before you in a shape that you can see, I may not tell. I have sat invisible beside you many and many a day."

It was not an agreeable idea. Scrooge shivered, and wiped the perspiration from his brow.

"That is no light part of my penance," pursued the Ghost. "I am here to-night to warn you, that you have yet a chance and hope of escaping my fate. A chance and hope of my procuring, Ebenezer."

"You were always a good friend to me," said Scrooge. "Thank'ee!"

"You will be haunted," resumed the Ghost, "by Three Spirits."

Scrooge's countenance fell almost as low as the Ghost's had done.

"Is that the chance and hope you mentioned, Jacob?" he demanded, in a faltering voice.

"It is."

"I—I think I'd rather not," said Scrooge.

"Without their visits," said the Ghost, "you cannot hope to shun the path I tread. Expect the first to-morrow, when the bell tolls One."

"Couldn't I take 'em all at once, and have it over, Jacob?" hinted Scrooge.

"Expect the second on the next night at the same hour. The third upon the next night when the last stroke of Twelve has ceased to vibrate. Look to see me no more; and look that, for your own sake, you remember what has passed between us!"

When it had said these words, the spectre took its wrapper from the table, and bound it round its head, as before. Scrooge knew this, by the smart sound its teeth made, when the jaws were brought together by the bandage. He ventured to raise his eyes again, and found his supernatural visitor confronting him in an erect attitude, with its chain wound over and about its arm.

The apparition walked backward from him; and at every step it took, the window raised itself a little, so that when the spectre reached it, it was wide open. It beckoned Scrooge to approach, which he did. When they were within two paces of each other, Marley's Ghost held up its hand, warning him to come no nearer. Scrooge stopped.

Not so much in obedience, as in surprise and fear: for on the raising of the hand, he became sensible of confused noises in the air; incoherent sounds of lamentation and

regret; wailings inexpressibly sorrowful and self-accusatory. The spectre, after listening for a moment, joined in the mournful dirge; and floated out upon the bleak, dark night.

Scrooge followed to the window: desperate in his curiosity. He looked out.

The air was filled with phantoms, wandering hither and thither in restless haste, and moaning as they went. Every one of them wore chains like Marley's Ghost; some few (they might be guilty governments) were linked together; none were free. Many had been personally known to Scrooge in their lives. He had been quite familiar with one old ghost, in a white waistcoat, with a monstrous iron safe attached to its ankle, who cried piteously at being unable to assist a wretched woman with an infant, whom it saw below, upon a door-step. The misery with them all was, clearly, that they sought to interfere, for good, in human matters, and had lost the power for ever.

Whether these creatures faded into mist, or mist enshrouded them, he could not tell. But they and their spirit voices faded together; and the night became as it had been when he walked home.

Scrooge closed the window, and examined the door by which the Ghost had entered. It was double-locked, as he had locked it with his own hands, and the bolts were undisturbed. He tried to say "Humbug!" but stopped at the first syllable. And being, from the emotion he had undergone, or the fatigues of the day, or his glimpse of the Invisible World, or the dull conversation of the Ghost, or the lateness of the hour, much in need of repose; went straight to bed, without undressing, and fell asleep upon the instant.

Stave II
The First of the Three Spirits

When Scrooge awoke, it was so dark, that looking out of bed, he could scarcely distinguish the transparent window from the opaque walls of his chamber. He was endeavouring to pierce the darkness with his ferret eyes, when the chimes of a neighbouring church struck the four quarters. So he listened for the hour.

To his great astonishment the heavy bell went on from six to seven, and from seven to eight, and regularly up to twelve; then stopped. Twelve! It was past two when he went to bed. The clock was wrong. An icicle must have got into the works. Twelve!

He touched the spring of his repeater, to correct this most preposterous clock. Its rapid little pulse beat twelve: and stopped.

"Why, it isn't possible," said Scrooge, "that I can have slept through a whole day and far into another night. It isn't possible that anything has happened to the sun, and this is twelve at noon!"

The idea being an alarming one, he scrambled out of bed, and groped his way to the window. He was obliged to rub the frost off with the sleeve of his dressing-gown before he could see anything; and could see very little then. All he could make out was, that it was still very foggy and extremely cold, and that there was no noise of people running to and fro, and making a great stir, as there unquestionably would have been if night had beaten off bright day, and taken possession of the world. This was a great relief, because "three days after sight of this First of Exchange pay to Mr. Ebenezer Scrooge or his order," and so forth, would have become a mere United States' security if there were no days to count by.

Scrooge went to bed again, and thought, and thought, and thought it over and over and over, and could make nothing of it. The more he thought, the more perplexed he was; and the more he endeavoured not to think, the more he thought. Marley's Ghost bothered him exceedingly. Every time he resolved within himself, after mature inquiry, that it was all a dream, his mind flew back again, like a strong spring released, to its first position, and presented the same problem to be worked all through, "Was it a dream or not?"

Scrooge lay in this state until the chime had gone three quarters more, when he remembered, on a sudden, that the Ghost had warned him of a visitation when the bell tolled one. He resolved to lie awake until the hour was passed; and, considering that he could no more go to sleep than go to Heaven, this was perhaps the wisest resolution in his power.

The quarter was so long, that he was more than once convinced he must have sunk into a doze unconsciously, and missed the clock. At length it broke upon his listening ear.

"Ding, dong!"

"A quarter past," said Scrooge, counting.

"Ding, dong!"

"Half past!" said Scrooge.

"Ding, dong!"

"A quarter to it," said Scrooge.

"Ding, dong!"

"The hour itself," said Scrooge, triumphantly, "and nothing else!"

He spoke before the hour bell sounded, which it now did with a deep, dull, hollow, melancholy One. Light flashed up in the room upon the instant, and the curtains of his bed were drawn.

The curtains of his bed were drawn aside, I tell you, by a hand. Not the curtains at his feet, nor the curtains at his back, but those to which his face was addressed. The curtains of his bed were drawn aside; and Scrooge, starting up into a half-recumbent attitude, found himself face to face with the unearthly visitor who drew them: as close to it as I am now to you, and I am standing in the spirit at your elbow.

It was a strange figure—like a child: yet not so like a child as like an old man, viewed through some supernatural medium, which gave him the appearance of having receded from the view, and being diminished to a child's proportions. Its hair, which hung about its neck and down its back, was white as if with age; and yet the face had not a wrinkle in it, and the tenderest bloom was on the skin. The arms were very long and muscular; the hands the same, as if its hold were of uncommon strength. Its legs and feet, most delicately formed, were, like those upper members, bare. It wore a tunic of the purest white; and round its waist was bound a lustrous belt, the sheen of which was beautiful. It held a branch of fresh green holly in its hand; and, in singular contradiction of that wintry emblem, had its dress trimmed with summer flowers. But the strangest thing about it was, that from the crown of its head there sprung a bright clear jet of light, by which all this was visible; and which was doubtless the occasion of its using, in its duller moments, a great extinguisher for a cap, which it now held under its arm.

Even this, though, when Scrooge looked at it with increasing steadiness, was *not* its strangest quality. For as its belt sparkled and glittered now in one part and now in another, and what was light one instant, at another time was dark, so the figure itself fluctuated in its distinctness: being now a thing with one arm, now with one leg, now with twenty legs, now a pair of legs without a head, now a head without a body: of which dissolving parts, no outline would be visible in the dense gloom wherein they melted away. And in the very wonder of this, it would be itself again; distinct and clear as ever.

"Are you the Spirit, sir, whose coming was foretold to me?" asked Scrooge.

"I am!"

The voice was soft and gentle. Singularly low, as if instead of being so close beside him, it were at a distance.

"Who, and what are you?" Scrooge demanded.

"I am the Ghost of Christmas Past."

"Long Past?" inquired Scrooge: observant of its dwarfish stature.

"No. Your past."

Perhaps, Scrooge could not have told anybody why, if anybody could have asked him; but he had a special desire to see the Spirit in his cap; and begged him to be covered.

"What!" exclaimed the Ghost, "would you so soon put out, with worldly hands, the light I give? Is it not enough that you are one of those whose passions made this cap, and force me through whole trains of years to wear it low upon my brow!"

Scrooge reverently disclaimed all intention to offend or any knowledge of having wilfully "bonneted" the Spirit at any period of his life. He then made bold to inquire what business brought him there.

"Your welfare!" said the Ghost.

Scrooge expressed himself much obliged, but could not help thinking that a night of unbroken rest would have been more conducive to that end. The Spirit must have heard him thinking, for it said immediately:

"Your reclamation, then. Take heed!"

It put out its strong hand as it spoke, and clasped him gently by the arm.

"Rise! and walk with me!"

It would have been in vain for Scrooge to plead that the weather and the hour were not adapted to pedestrian purposes; that bed was warm, and the thermometer a long way below freezing; that he was clad but lightly in his slippers, dressing-gown, and nightcap; and that he had a cold upon him at that time. The grasp, though gentle as a woman's hand, was not to be resisted. He rose: but finding that the Spirit made towards the window, clasped his robe in supplication.

"I am a mortal," Scrooge remonstrated, "and liable to fall."

"Bear but a touch of my hand *there*," said the Spirit, laying it upon his heart, "and you shall be upheld in more than this!"

As the words were spoken, they passed through the wall, and stood upon an open country road, with fields on either hand. The city had entirely vanished. Not a vestige of it was to be seen. The darkness and the mist had vanished with it, for it was a clear, cold, winter day, with snow upon the ground.

"Good Heaven!" said Scrooge, clasping his hands together, as he looked about him. "I was bred in this place. I was a boy here!"

The Spirit gazed upon him mildly. Its gentle touch, though it had been light and instantaneous, appeared still present to the old man's sense of feeling. He was conscious of a thousand odours floating in the air, each one connected with a thousand thoughts, and hopes, and joys, and cares long, long, forgotten!

"Your lip is trembling," said the Ghost. "And what is that upon your cheek?"

Scrooge muttered, with an unusual catching in his voice, that it was a pimple; and begged the Ghost to lead him where he would.

"You recollect the way?" inquired the Spirit.

"Remember it!" cried Scrooge with fervour; "I could walk it blindfold."

"Strange to have forgotten it for so many years!" observed the Ghost. "Let us go on."

They walked along the road, Scrooge recognising every gate, and post, and tree; until a little market-town appeared in the distance, with its bridge, its church, and winding river. Some shaggy ponies now were seen trotting towards them with boys upon their backs, who called to other boys in country gigs and carts, driven by farmers. All these boys were in great spirits, and shouted to each other, until the broad fields were so full of merry music, that the crisp air laughed to hear it!

"These are but shadows of the things that have been," said the Ghost. "They have no consciousness of us."

The jocund travellers came on; and as they came, Scrooge knew and named them every one. Why was he rejoiced beyond all bounds to see them! Why did his cold eye glisten, and his heart leap up as they went past! Why was he filled with gladness when he heard them give each other Merry Christmas, as they parted at cross-roads and bye-ways, for their several homes! What was merry Christmas to Scrooge? Out upon merry Christmas! What good had it ever done to him?

"The school is not quite deserted," said the Ghost. "A solitary child, neglected by his friends, is left there still."

Scrooge said he knew it. And he sobbed.

They left the high-road, by a well-remembered lane, and soon approached a mansion of dull red brick, with a little weathercock-surmounted cupola, on the roof, and a bell hanging in it. It was a large house, but one of broken fortunes; for the spacious offices were little used, their walls were damp and mossy, their windows broken, and their gates decayed. Fowls clucked and strutted in the stables; and the coach-houses and sheds were over-run with grass. Nor was it more retentive of its ancient state, within; for entering the dreary hall, and glancing through the open doors of many rooms, they found them poorly furnished, cold, and vast. There was an earthy savour in the air, a chilly bareness in the place, which associated itself somehow with too much getting up by candle-light, and not too much to eat.

They went, the Ghost and Scrooge, across the hall, to a door at the back of the house. It opened before them, and disclosed a long, bare, melancholy room, made barer still by lines of plain deal forms and desks. At one of these a lonely boy was reading near a feeble fire; and Scrooge sat down upon a form, and wept to see his poor forgotten self as he used to be.

Not a latent echo in the house, not a squeak and scuffle from the mice behind the panelling, not a drip from the half-thawed water-spout in the dull yard behind, not a sigh among the leafless boughs of one despondent poplar, not the idle swinging of an empty store-house door, no, not a clicking in the fire, but fell upon the heart of Scrooge with a softening influence, and gave a freer passage to his tears.

The Spirit touched him on the arm, and pointed to his younger self, intent upon his reading. Suddenly a man, in foreign garments: wonderfully real and distinct to look at: stood outside the window, with an axe stuck in his belt, and leading by the bridle an ass laden with wood.

"Why, it's Ali Baba!" Scrooge exclaimed in ecstasy. "It's dear old honest Ali Baba! Yes, yes, I know! One Christmas time, when yonder solitary child was left here all alone, he *did* come, for the first time, just like that. Poor boy! And Valentine," said Scrooge, "and his wild brother, Orson; there they go! And what's his name, who was put down in his drawers, asleep, at the Gate of Damascus; don't you see him! And the Sultan's Groom turned upside down by the Genii; there he is upon his head! Serve him right. I'm glad of it. What business had *he* to be married to the Princess!"

To hear Scrooge expending all the earnestness of his nature on such subjects, in a most extraordinary voice between laughing and crying; and to see his heightened and excited face; would have been a surprise to his business friends in the city, indeed.

"There's the Parrot!" cried Scrooge. "Green body and yellow tail, with a thing like a lettuce growing out of the top of his head; there he is! Poor Robin Crusoe, he called him, when he came home again after sailing round the island. 'Poor Robin Crusoe, where have you been, Robin Crusoe?' The man thought he was dreaming, but he wasn't. It was the Parrot, you know. There goes Friday, running for his life to the little creek! Halloa! Hoop! Halloo!"

Then, with a rapidity of transition very foreign to his usual character, he said, in pity for his former self, "Poor boy!" and cried again.

"I wish," Scrooge muttered, putting his hand in his pocket, and looking about him, after drying his eyes with his cuff: "but it's too late now."

"What is the matter?" asked the Spirit.

"Nothing," said Scrooge. "Nothing. There was a boy singing a Christmas Carol at my door last night. I should like to have given him something: that's all."

The Ghost smiled thoughtfully, and waved its hand: saying as it did so, "Let us see another Christmas!"

Scrooge's former self grew larger at the words, and the room became a little darker and more dirty. The panels shrunk, the windows cracked; fragments of plaster fell out of the ceiling, and the naked laths were shown instead; but how all this was brought about, Scrooge knew no more than you do. He only knew that it was quite correct; that everything had happened so; that there he was, alone again, when all the other boys had gone home for the jolly holidays.

He was not reading now, but walking up and down despairingly. Scrooge looked at the Ghost, and with a mournful shaking of his head, glanced anxiously towards the door.

It opened; and a little girl, much younger than the boy, came darting in, and putting her arms about his neck, and often kissing him, addressed him as her "Dear, dear brother."

"I have come to bring you home, dear brother!" said the child, clapping her tiny hands, and bending down to laugh. "To bring you home, home, home!"

"Home, little Fan?" returned the boy.

"Yes!" said the child, brimful of glee. "Home, for good and all. Home, for ever and ever. Father is so much kinder than he used to be, that home's like Heaven! He spoke so gently to me one dear night when I was going to bed, that I was not afraid to ask him once more if you might come home; and he said Yes, you should; and sent me in a coach to bring you. And you're to be a man!" said the child, opening her eyes, "and are never to come back here; but first, we're to be together all the Christmas long, and have the merriest time in all the world."

"You are quite a woman, little Fan!" exclaimed the boy.

She clapped her hands and laughed, and tried to touch his head; but being too little, laughed again, and stood on tiptoe to embrace him. Then she began to drag him, in her childish eagerness, towards the door; and he, nothing loth to go, accompanied her.

A terrible voice in the hall cried, "Bring down Master Scrooge's box, there!" and in the hall appeared the school-master himself, who glared on Master Scrooge with a ferocious condescension, and threw him into a dreadful state of mind by shaking hands with him. He then conveyed him and his sister into the veriest old well of a shivering best-parlour that ever was seen, where the maps upon the wall, and the celestial and terrestrial globes in the windows, were waxy with cold. Here he produced a decanter of curiously light wine, and a block of curiously heavy cake, and administered instalments of those dainties to the young people: at the same time, sending out a meagre servant to offer a glass of "something" to the postboy, who answered that he thanked the gentleman, but if it was the same tap as he had tasted before, he had rather not. Master Scrooge's trunk being by this time tied on to the top of the chaise, the children bade the schoolmaster good-bye right willingly; and getting into it, drove gaily down the garden-sweep: the quick wheels dashing the hoar-frost and snow from off the dark leaves of the evergreens like spray.

"Always a delicate creature, whom a breath might have withered," said the Ghost. "But she had a large heart!"

"So she had," cried Scrooge. "You're right. I will not gainsay it, Spirit. God forbid!"

"She died a woman," said the Ghost, "and had, as I think, children."

"One child," Scrooge returned.

"True," said the Ghost. "Your nephew!"

Scrooge seemed uneasy in his mind; and answered briefly, "Yes."

Although they had but that moment left the school behind them, they were now in the busy thoroughfares of a city, where shadowy passengers passed and repassed; where shadowy carts and coaches battled for the way, and all the strife and tumult of a real city were. It was made plain enough, by the dressing of the shops, that here too it was Christmas time again; but it was evening, and the streets were lighted up.

The Ghost stopped at a certain warehouse door, and asked Scrooge if he knew it.

"Know it!" said Scrooge. "Was I apprenticed here!"

They went in. At sight of an old gentleman in a Welsh wig, sitting behind such a high desk, that if he had been two inches taller he must have knocked his head against the ceiling, Scrooge cried in great excitement:

"Why, it's old Fezziwig! Bless his heart; it's Fezziwig alive again!"

Old Fezziwig laid down his pen, and looked up at the clock, which pointed to the hour of seven. He rubbed his hands; adjusted his capacious waistcoat; laughed all over himself, from his shoes to his organ of benevolence; and called out in a comfortable, oily, rich, fat, jovial voice:

"Yo ho, there! Ebenezer! Dick!"

Scrooge's former self, now grown a young man, came briskly in, accompanied by his fellow-'prentice.

"Dick Wilkins, to be sure!" said Scrooge to the Ghost. "Bless me, yes. There he is. He was very much attached to me, was Dick. Poor Dick! Dear, dear!"

"Yo ho, my boys!" said Fezziwig. "No more work to-night. Christmas Eve, Dick. Christmas, Ebenezer! Let's have the shutters up," cried old Fezziwig, with a sharp clap of his hands, "before a man can say Jack Robinson!"

You wouldn't believe how those two fellows went at it! They charged into the street with the shutters—one, two, three—had 'em up in their places—four, five, six—barred 'em and pinned 'em—seven, eight, nine—and came back before you could have got to twelve, panting like race-horses.

"Hilli-ho!" cried old Fezziwig, skipping down from the high desk, with wonderful agility. "Clear away, my lads, and let's have lots of room here! Hilli-ho, Dick! Chirrup, Ebenezer!"

Clear away! There was nothing they wouldn't have cleared away, or couldn't have cleared away, with old Fezziwig looking on. It was done in a minute. Every movable was packed off, as if it were dismissed from public life for evermore; the floor was swept and watered, the lamps were trimmed, fuel was heaped upon the fire; and the warehouse was as snug, and warm, and dry, and bright a ball-room, as you would desire to see upon a winter's night.

In came a fiddler with a music-book, and went up to the lofty desk, and made an orchestra of it, and tuned like fifty stomach-aches. In came Mrs. Fezziwig, one vast substantial smile. In came the three Miss Fezziwigs, beaming and lovable. In came the six young followers whose hearts they broke. In came all the young men and women employed in the business. In came the housemaid, with her cousin, the baker. In came the cook, with her brother's particular friend, the milkman. In came the boy from over the way, who was suspected of not having board enough from his master; trying to hide himself behind the girl from next door but one, who was proved to have had her ears pulled by her mistress. In they all came, one after another; some shyly, some boldly, some gracefully, some awkwardly, some pushing, some pulling; in they all came, any-how and everyhow. Away they all went, twenty couple at once; hands half round and back again the other way; down the middle and up again; round and round in various stages of affectionate grouping; old top couple always turning up in the wrong place; new top couple starting off again, as soon as they got there; all top couples at last, and not a bottom one to help them! When this result was brought about, old Fezziwig, clapping his hands to stop the dance, cried out, "Well done!" and the fiddler plunged his hot face into a pot of porter, especially provided for that purpose. But scorning rest, upon his reappearance, he instantly began again, though there were no dancers yet, as if the other fiddler had been carried home, exhausted, on a shutter, and he were a brand-new man resolved to beat him out of sight, or perish.

There were more dances, and there were forfeits, and more dances, and there was cake, and there was negus, and there was a great piece of Cold Roast, and there was a great piece of Cold Boiled, and there were mince-pies, and plenty of beer. But the great effect of the evening came after the Roast and Boiled, when the fiddler (an artful dog, mind! The sort of man who knew his business better than you or I could have told it him!) struck up "Sir Roger de Coverley." Then old Fezziwig stood out to dance with Mrs. Fezziwig. Top couple, too; with a good stiff piece of work cut out for them; three or four and twenty pair of partners; people who were not to be trifled with; people who *would* dance, and had no notion of walking.

But if they had been twice as many—ah, four times—old Fezziwig would have been a match for them, and so would Mrs. Fezziwig. As to *her*, she was worthy to be his partner in every sense of the term. If that's not high praise, tell me higher, and I'll use it. A positive light appeared to issue from Fezziwig's calves. They shone in every part of the dance like moons. You couldn't have predicted, at any given time, what would have become of them next. And when old Fezziwig and Mrs. Fezziwig had gone all through the dance; advance and retire, both hands to your partner, bow and curtsey, corkscrew, thread-the-needle, and back again to your place; Fezziwig "cut"—cut so deftly, that he appeared to wink with his legs, and came upon his feet again without a stagger.

When the clock struck eleven, this domestic ball broke up. Mr. and Mrs. Fezziwig took their stations, one on either side of the door, and shaking hands with every person individually as he or she went out, wished him or her a Merry Christmas. When everybody had retired but the two 'prentices, they did the same to them; and thus the cheerful voices died away, and the lads were left to their beds; which were under a counter in the back-shop.

During the whole of this time, Scrooge had acted like a man out of his wits. His heart and soul were in the scene, and with his former self. He corroborated everything, remembered everything, enjoyed everything, and underwent the strangest agitation. It was not until now, when the bright faces of his former self and Dick were turned from them, that he remembered the Ghost, and became conscious that it was looking full upon him, while the light upon its head burnt very clear.

"A small matter," said the Ghost, "to make these silly folks so full of gratitude."

"Small!" echoed Scrooge.

The Spirit signed to him to listen to the two apprentices, who were pouring out their hearts in praise of Fezziwig: and when he had done so, said,

"Why! Is it not? He has spent but a few pounds of your mortal money: three or four perhaps. Is that so much that he deserves this praise?"

"It isn't that," said Scrooge, heated by the remark, and speaking unconsciously like his former, not his latter, self. "It isn't that, Spirit. He has the power to render us happy or unhappy; to make our service light or burdensome; a pleasure or a toil. Say that his power lies in words and looks; in things so slight and insignificant that it is impossible to add and count 'em up: what then? The happiness he gives, is quite as great as if it cost a fortune."

He felt the Spirit's glance, and stopped.

"What is the matter?" asked the Ghost.

"Nothing particular," said Scrooge.

"Something, I think?" the Ghost insisted.

"No," said Scrooge, "No. I should like to be able to say a word or two to my clerk just now. That's all."

His former self turned down the lamps as he gave utterance to the wish; and Scrooge and the Ghost again stood side by side in the open air.

"My time grows short," observed the Spirit. "Quick!"

This was not addressed to Scrooge, or to any one whom he could see, but it produced an immediate effect. For again Scrooge saw himself. He was older now; a man in the prime of life. His face had not the harsh and rigid lines of later years; but it had begun to wear the signs of care and avarice. There was an eager, greedy, restless motion in the eye, which showed the passion that had taken root, and where the shadow of the growing tree would fall.

He was not alone, but sat by the side of a fair young girl in a mourning-dress: in whose eyes there were tears, which sparkled in the light that shone out of the Ghost of Christmas Past.

"It matters little," she said, softly. "To you, very little. Another idol has displaced me; and if it can cheer and comfort you in time to come, as I would have tried to do, I have no just cause to grieve."

"What Idol has displaced you?" he rejoined.

"A golden one."

"This is the even-handed dealing of the world!" he said. "There is nothing on which it is so hard as poverty; and there is nothing it professes to condemn with such severity as the pursuit of wealth!"

"You fear the world too much," she answered, gently. "All your other hopes have merged into the hope of being beyond the chance of its sordid reproach. I have seen your nobler aspirations fall off one by one, until the master-passion, Gain, engrosses you. Have I not?"

"What then?" he retorted. "Even if I have grown so much wiser, what then? I am not changed towards you."

She shook her head.

"Am I?"

"Our contract is an old one. It was made when we were both poor and content to be so, until, in good season, we could improve our worldly fortune by our patient industry. You *are* changed. When it was made, you were another man."

"I was a boy," he said impatiently.

"Your own feeling tells you that you were not what you are," she returned. "I am. That which promised happiness when we were one in heart, is fraught with misery now that we are two. How often and how keenly I *have* thought of this, I will not say. It is enough that I have thought of it, and can release you."

"Have I ever sought release?"

"In words. No. Never."

"In what, then?"

"In a changed nature; in an altered spirit; in another atmosphere of life; another Hope as its great end. In everything that made my love of any worth or value in your sight. If this had never been between us," said the girl, looking mildly, but with steadiness, upon him; "tell me, would you seek me out and try to win me now? Ah, no!"

He seemed to yield to the justice of this supposition, in spite of himself. But he said with a struggle, "You think not."

"I would gladly think otherwise if I could," she answered, "Heaven knows! When *I* have learned a Truth like this, I know how strong and irresistible it must be. But if you were free to-day, to-morrow, yesterday, can even I believe that you would choose a dowerless girl—you who, in your very confidence with her, weigh everything by Gain: or, choosing her, if for a moment you were false enough to your one guiding principle to do so, do I not know that your repentance and regret would surely follow? I do; and I release you. With a full heart, for the love of him you once were."

He was about to speak; but with her head turned from him, she resumed.

"You may—the memory of what is past half makes me hope you will— have pain in this. A very, very brief time, and you will dismiss the recollection of it, gladly, as an unprofitable dream, from which it happened well that you awoke. May you be happy in the life you have chosen!"

She left him, and they parted.

"Spirit!" said Scrooge, "show me no more! Conduct me home. Why do you delight to torture me?"

"One shadow more!" exclaimed the Ghost.

"No more!" cried Scrooge. "No more. I don't wish to see it. Show me no more!"

But the relentless Ghost pinioned him in both his arms, and forced him to observe what happened next.

They were in another scene and place; a room, not very large or handsome, but full of comfort. Near to the winter fire sat a beautiful young girl, so like that last that Scrooge believed it was the same, until he saw *her*, now a comely matron, sitting opposite her daughter. The noise in this room was perfectly tumultuous, for there were more children there, than Scrooge in his agitated state of mind could count; and, unlike the celebrated herd in the poem, they were not forty children conducting themselves like one, but every child was conducting itself like forty. The consequences were uproarious beyond belief; but no one seemed to care; on the contrary, the mother and daughter laughed heartily, and enjoyed it very much; and the latter, soon beginning to mingle in the sports, got pillaged by the young brigands most ruthlessly. What would I not have given to be one of them! Though I never could have been so rude, no, no! I wouldn't for the wealth of all the world have crushed that braided hair, and torn it down; and for the precious little shoe, I wouldn't have plucked it off, God bless my soul! to save my life. As to measuring her waist in sport, as they did, bold young brood, I couldn't have done it; I should have expected my arm to have grown round it for a punishment, and never come straight again. And yet I should have dearly liked, I own, to have touched her lips; to have questioned her, that she might have opened them; to have looked upon the lashes of her downcast eyes, and never raised a blush; to have let loose waves of hair, an inch of which would be a keepsake beyond price: in short, I should have liked, I do confess, to have had the lightest licence of a child, and yet to have been man enough to know its value.

But now a knocking at the door was heard, and such a rush immediately ensued that she with laughing face and plundered dress was borne towards it the centre of a flushed and boisterous group, just in time to greet the father, who came home attended by a man laden with Christmas toys and presents. Then the shouting and the struggling,

and the onslaught that was made on the defenceless porter! The scaling him with chairs for ladders to dive into his pockets, despoil him of brown-paper parcels, hold on tight by his cravat, hug him round his neck, pommel his back, and kick his legs in irrepressible affection! The shouts of wonder and delight with which the development of every package was received! The terrible announcement that the baby had been taken in the act of putting a doll's frying-pan into his mouth, and was more than suspected of having swallowed a fictitious turkey, glued on a wooden platter! The immense relief of finding this a false alarm! The joy, and gratitude, and ecstasy! They are all indescribable alike. It is enough that by degrees the children and their emotions got out of the parlour, and by one stair at a time, up to the top of the house; where they went to bed, and so subsided.

And now Scrooge looked on more attentively than ever, when the master of the house, having his daughter leaning fondly on him, sat down with her and her mother at his own fireside; and when he thought that such another creature, quite as graceful and as full of promise, might have called him father, and been a spring-time in the haggard winter of his life, his sight grew very dim indeed.

"Belle," said the husband, turning to his wife with a smile, "I saw an old friend of yours this afternoon."

"Who was it?"

"Guess!"

"How can I? Tut, don't I know?" she added in the same breath, laughing as he laughed. "Mr. Scrooge."

"Mr. Scrooge it was. I passed his office window; and as it was not shut up, and he had a candle inside, I could scarcely help seeing him. His partner lies upon the point of death, I hear; and there he sat alone. Quite alone in the world, I do believe."

"Spirit!" said Scrooge in a broken voice, "remove me from this place."

"I told you these were shadows of the things that have been," said the Ghost. "That they are what they are, do not blame me!"

"Remove me!" Scrooge exclaimed, "I cannot bear it!"

He turned upon the Ghost, and seeing that it looked upon him with a face, in which in some strange way there were fragments of all the faces it had shown him, wrestled with it.

"Leave me! Take me back. Haunt me no longer!"

In the struggle, if that can be called a struggle in which the Ghost with no visible resistance on its own part was undisturbed by any effort of its adversary, Scrooge observed that its light was burning high and bright; and dimly connecting that with its influence over him, he seized the extinguisher-cap, and by a sudden action pressed it down upon its head.

The Spirit dropped beneath it, so that the extinguisher covered its whole form; but though Scrooge pressed it down with all his force, he could not hide the light: which streamed from under it, in an unbroken flood upon the ground.

He was conscious of being exhausted, and overcome by an irresistible drowsiness; and, further, of being in his own bed-room. He gave the cap a parting squeeze, in which his hand relaxed; and had barely time to reel to bed, before he sank into a heavy sleep.

STAVE III
THE SECOND OF THE THREE SPIRITS

Awaking in the middle of a prodigiously tough snore, and sitting up in bed to get his thoughts together, Scrooge had no occasion to be told that the bell was again upon the stroke of One. He felt that he was restored to consciousness in the right nick of time, for the especial purpose of holding a conference with the second messenger despatched to him through Jacob Marley's intervention. But finding that he turned uncomfortably cold when he began to wonder which of his curtains this new spectre would draw back, he put them every one aside with his own hands; and lying down again, established a sharp look-out all round the bed. For he wished to challenge the Spirit on the moment of its appearance, and did not wish to be taken by surprise, and made nervous.

Gentlemen of the free-and-easy sort, who plume themselves on being acquainted with a move or two, and being usually equal to the time-of-day, express the wide range of their capacity for adventure by observing that they are good for anything from pitch-and-toss to manslaughter; between which opposite extremes, no doubt, there lies a tolerably wide and comprehensive range of subjects. Without venturing for Scrooge quite as hardily as this, I don't mind calling on you to believe that he was ready for a good broad field of strange appearances, and that nothing between a baby and rhinoceros would have astonished him very much.

Now, being prepared for almost anything, he was not by any means prepared for nothing; and, consequently, when the Bell struck One, and no shape appeared, he was taken with a violent fit of trembling. Five minutes, ten minutes, a quarter of an hour went by, yet nothing came. All this time, he lay upon his bed, the very core and centre of a blaze of ruddy light, which streamed upon it when the clock proclaimed the hour; and which, being only light, was more alarming than a dozen ghosts, as he was powerless to make out what it meant, or would be at; and was sometimes apprehensive that he might be at that very moment an interesting case of spontaneous combustion, without having the consolation of knowing it. At last, however, he began to think—as you or I would have thought at first; for it is always the person not in the predicament who knows what ought to have been done in it, and would unquestionably have done it too—at last, I say, he began to think that the source and secret of this ghostly light might be in the adjoining room, from whence, on further tracing it, it seemed to shine. This idea taking full possession of his mind, he got up softly and shuffled in his slippers to the door.

The moment Scrooge's hand was on the lock, a strange voice called him by his name, and bade him enter. He obeyed.

It was his own room. There was no doubt about that. But it had undergone a surprising transformation. The walls and ceiling were so hung with living green, that it looked a perfect grove; from every part of which, bright gleaming berries glistened. The crisp leaves of holly, mistletoe, and ivy reflected back the light, as if so many little mirrors had been scattered there; and such a mighty blaze went roaring up the chimney, as that dull petrification of a hearth had never known in Scrooge's time, or Marley's, or for many and many a winter season gone. Heaped up on the floor, to form a kind of throne, were turkeys, geese, game, poultry, brawn, great joints of meat, sucking-pigs, long wreaths of sausages, mince-pies, plum-puddings, barrels of oysters, red-hot chestnuts, cherry-cheeked apples, juicy oranges, luscious pears, immense twelfth-cakes, and seething bowls of punch, that made the chamber dim with their delicious steam. In easy state upon this couch, there sat a jolly Giant, glorious to see; who bore a glowing torch, in shape not unlike Plenty's horn, and held it up, high up, to shed its light on Scrooge, as he came peeping round the door.

"Come in!" exclaimed the Ghost. "Come in! and know me better, man!"

Scrooge entered timidly, and hung his head before this Spirit. He was not the dogged Scrooge he had been; and though the Spirit's eyes were clear and kind, he did not like to meet them.

"I am the Ghost of Christmas Present," said the Spirit. "Look upon me!"

Scrooge reverently did so. It was clothed in one simple green robe, or mantle, bordered with white fur. This garment hung so loosely on the figure, that its capacious breast was bare, as if disdaining to be warded or concealed by any artifice. Its feet, observable beneath the ample folds of the garment, were also bare; and on its head it wore no other covering than a holly wreath, set here and there with shining icicles. Its dark brown curls were long and free; free as its genial face, its sparkling eye, its open hand, its cheery voice, its unconstrained demeanour, and its joyful air. Girded round its middle was an antique scabbard; but no sword was in it, and the ancient sheath was eaten up with rust.

"You have never seen the like of me before!" exclaimed the Spirit.

"Never," Scrooge made answer to it.

"Have never walked forth with the younger members of my family; meaning (for I am very young) my elder brothers born in these later years?" pursued the Phantom.

"I don't think I have," said Scrooge. "I am afraid I have not. Have you had many brothers, Spirit?"

"More than eighteen hundred," said the Ghost.

"A tremendous family to provide for!" muttered Scrooge.

The Ghost of Christmas Present rose.

"Spirit," said Scrooge submissively, "conduct me where you will. I went forth last night on compulsion, and I learnt a lesson which is working now. To-night, if you have aught to teach me, let me profit by it."

"Touch my robe!"

Scrooge did as he was told, and held it fast.

Holly, mistletoe, red berries, ivy, turkeys, geese, game, poultry, brawn, meat, pigs, sausages, oysters, pies, puddings, fruit, and punch, all vanished instantly. So did the room, the fire, the ruddy glow, the hour of night, and they stood in the city streets on Christmas morning, where (for the weather was severe) the people made a rough, but brisk and not unpleasant kind of music, in scraping the snow from the pavement in front of their dwellings, and from the tops of their houses, whence it was mad delight to the boys to see it come plumping down into the road below, and splitting into artificial little snow-storms.

The house fronts looked black enough, and the windows blacker, contrasting with the smooth white sheet of snow upon the roofs, and with the dirtier snow upon the ground; which last deposit had been ploughed up in deep furrows by the heavy wheels of carts and waggons; furrows that crossed and re-crossed each other hundreds of times where the great streets branched off, and made intricate channels, hard to trace in the thick yellow mud and icy water. The sky was gloomy, and the shortest streets were choked up with a dingy mist, half thawed, half frozen, whose heavier particles descended in a shower of sooty atoms, as if all the chimneys in Great Britain had, by one consent, caught fire, and were blazing away to their dear hearts' content. There was nothing very cheerful in the climate or the town, and yet was there an air of cheerfulness abroad that the clearest summer air and brightest summer sun might have endeavoured to diffuse in vain.

For, the people who were shovelling away on the housetops were jovial and full of glee; calling out to one another from the parapets, and now and then exchanging a facetious snowball—better-natured missile far than many a wordy jest—laughing heartily if it went right and not less heartily if it went wrong. The poulterers' shops were still half open, and the fruiterers' were radiant in their glory. There were great, round, pot-bellied baskets of chestnuts, shaped like the waistcoats of jolly old gentlemen, lolling at the doors, and tumbling out into the street in their apoplectic opulence. There were ruddy, brown-faced, broad-girthed Spanish Onions, shining in the fatness of their growth like Spanish Friars, and winking from their shelves in wanton slyness at the girls as they went by, and glanced demurely at the hung-up mistletoe. There were pears and apples, clustered high in blooming pyramids; there were bunches of grapes, made, in the shop-keepers' benevolence to dangle from conspicuous hooks, that people's mouths might water gratis as they passed; there were piles of filberts, mossy and brown, recalling, in their fragrance, ancient walks among the woods, and pleasant shufflings ankle deep through withered leaves; there were Norfolk Biffins, squat and swarthy, setting off the yellow of the oranges and lemons, and, in the great compactness of their juicy persons, urgently entreating and beseeching to be carried home in paper bags and eaten after dinner. The very gold and silver fish, set forth among these choice fruits in a bowl, though members of a dull and stagnant-blooded race, appeared to know that there was something going on; and, to a fish, went gasping round and round their little world in slow and passionless excitement.

The Grocers'! oh, the Grocers'! nearly closed, with perhaps two shutters down, or one; but through those gaps such glimpses! It was not alone that the scales descending on the counter made a merry sound, or that the twine and roller parted company so briskly, or that the canisters were rattled up and down like juggling tricks, or even that the blended scents of tea and coffee were so grateful to the nose, or even that the raisins were so plentiful and rare, the almonds so extremely white, the sticks of cinnamon so long and straight, the other spices so delicious, the candied fruits so caked and spotted with molten sugar as to make the coldest lookers-on feel faint and subsequently bil-ious. Nor was it that the figs were moist and pulpy, or that the French plums blushed in modest tartness from their highly-decorated boxes, or that everything was good to eat and in its Christmas dress; but the customers were all so hurried and so eager in the hopeful promise of the day, that they tumbled up against each other at the door, crash-ing their wicker baskets wildly, and left their purchases upon the counter, and came running back to fetch them, and committed hundreds of the like mistakes, in the best humour possible; while the Grocer and his people were so frank and fresh that the pol-ished hearts with which they fastened their aprons behind might have been their own, worn outside for general inspection, and for Christmas daws to peck at if they chose.

But soon the steeples called good people all, to church and chapel, and away they came, flocking through the streets in their best clothes, and with their gayest faces. And at the same time there emerged from scores of bye-streets, lanes, and nameless turnings, innumerable people, carrying their dinners to the bakers' shops. The sight of these poor revellers appeared to interest the Spirit very much, for he stood with Scrooge beside him in a baker's doorway, and taking off the covers as their bearers passed, sprinkled incense on their dinners from his torch. And it was a very uncommon kind of torch, for once or twice when there were angry words between some dinner-carriers who had jostled each other, he shed a few drops of water on them from it, and their good humour was restored directly. For they said, it was a shame to quarrel upon Christmas Day. And so it was! God love it, so it was!

In time the bells ceased, and the bakers were shut up; and yet there was a genial shadowing forth of all these dinners and the progress of their cooking, in the thawed blotch of wet above each baker's oven; where the pavement smoked as if its stones were cooking too.

"Is there a peculiar flavour in what you sprinkle from your torch?" asked Scrooge.

"There is. My own."

"Would it apply to any kind of dinner on this day?" asked Scrooge.

"To any kindly given. To a poor one most."

"Why to a poor one most?" asked Scrooge.

"Because it needs it most."

"Spirit," said Scrooge, after a moment's thought, "I wonder you, of all the beings in the many worlds about us, should desire to cramp these people's opportunities of innocent enjoyment."

"I!" cried the Spirit.

"You would deprive them of their means of dining every seventh day, often the only day on which they can be said to dine at all," said Scrooge. "Wouldn't you?"

"I!" cried the Spirit.

"You seek to close these places on the Seventh Day?" said Scrooge. "And it comes to the same thing."

"*I* seek!" exclaimed the Spirit.

"Forgive me if I am wrong. It has been done in your name, or at least in that of your family," said Scrooge.

"There are some upon this earth of yours," returned the Spirit, "who lay claim to know us, and who do their deeds of passion, pride, ill-will, hatred, envy, bigotry, and selfishness in our name, who are as strange to us and all our kith and kin, as if they had never lived. Remember that, and charge their doings on themselves, not us."

Scrooge promised that he would; and they went on, invisible, as they had been before, into the suburbs of the town. It was a remarkable quality of the Ghost (which Scrooge had observed at the baker's), that notwithstanding his gigantic size, he could accommodate himself to any place with ease; and that he stood beneath a low roof quite as gracefully and like a supernatural creature, as it was possible he could have done in any lofty hall.

And perhaps it was the pleasure the good Spirit had in showing off this power of his, or else it was his own kind, generous, hearty nature, and his sympathy with all poor men, that led him straight to Scrooge's clerk's; for there he went, and took Scrooge with him, holding to his robe; and on the threshold of the door the Spirit smiled, and stopped to bless Bob Cratchit's dwelling with the sprinkling of his torch. Think of that! Bob had but fifteen "Bob" a-week himself; he pocketed on Saturdays but fifteen copies of his Christian name; and yet the Ghost of Christmas Present blessed his four-roomed house!

Then up rose Mrs. Cratchit, Cratchit's wife, dressed out but poorly in a twice-turned gown, but brave in ribbons, which are cheap and make a goodly show for sixpence; and she laid the cloth, assisted by Belinda Cratchit, second of her daughters, also brave in ribbons; while Master Peter Cratchit plunged a fork into the saucepan of potatoes, and getting the corners of his monstrous shirt collar (Bob's private property, conferred upon his son and heir in honour of the day) into his mouth, rejoiced to find himself so gallantly attired, and yearned to show his linen in the fashionable Parks. And now two smaller Cratchits, boy and girl, came tearing in, screaming that outside the baker's they had smelt the goose, and known it for their own; and basking in luxurious thoughts of sage and onion, these young Cratchits danced about the table, and exalted Master Peter Cratchit to the skies, while he (not proud, although his collars nearly choked him) blew the fire, until the slow potatoes bubbling up, knocked loudly at the saucepan-lid to be let out and peeled.

"Whatever has ever got your precious father then?" said Mrs. Cratchit. "And your brother, Tiny Tim! And Martha warn't as late last Christmas Day by half-an-hour?"

"Here's Martha, mother!" said a girl, appearing as she spoke.

"Here's Martha, mother!" cried the two young Cratchits. "Hurrah! There's *such* a goose, Martha!"

"Why, bless your heart alive, my dear, how late you are!" said Mrs. Cratchit, kissing her a dozen times, and taking off her shawl and bonnet for her with officious zeal.

"We'd a deal of work to finish up last night," replied the girl, "and had to clear away this morning, mother!"

"Well! Never mind so long as you are come," said Mrs. Cratchit. "Sit ye down before the fire, my dear, and have a warm, Lord bless ye!"

"No, no! There's father coming," cried the two young Cratchits, who were everywhere at once. "Hide, Martha, hide!"

So Martha hid herself, and in came little Bob, the father, with at least three feet of comforter exclusive of the fringe, hanging down before him; and his threadbare clothes darned up and brushed, to look seasonable; and Tiny Tim upon his shoulder. Alas for Tiny Tim, he bore a little crutch, and had his limbs supported by an iron frame!

"Why, where's our Martha?" cried Bob Cratchit, looking round.

"Not coming," said Mrs. Cratchit.

"Not coming!" said Bob, with a sudden declension in his high spirits; for he had been Tim's blood horse all the way from church, and had come home rampant. "Not coming upon Christmas Day!"

Martha didn't like to see him disappointed, if it were only in joke; so she came out prematurely from behind the closet door, and ran into his arms, while the two young Cratchits hustled Tiny Tim, and bore him off into the wash-house, that he might hear the pudding singing in the copper.

"And how did little Tim behave?" asked Mrs. Cratchit, when she had rallied Bob on his credulity, and Bob had hugged his daughter to his heart's content.

"As good as gold," said Bob, "and better. Somehow he gets thoughtful, sitting by himself so much, and thinks the strangest things you ever heard. He told me, coming home, that he hoped the people saw him in the church, because he was a cripple, and it might be pleasant to them to remember upon Christmas Day, who made lame beggars walk, and blind men see."

Bob's voice was tremulous when he told them this, and trembled more when he said that Tiny Tim was growing strong and hearty.

His active little crutch was heard upon the floor, and back came Tiny Tim before another word was spoken, escorted by his brother and sister to his stool before the fire; and while Bob, turning up his cuffs—as if, poor fellow, they were capable of being made more shabby—compounded some hot mixture in a jug with gin and lemons, and stirred it round and round and put it on the hob to simmer; Master Peter, and the two ubiquitous young Cratchits went to fetch the goose, with which they soon returned in high procession.

Such a bustle ensued that you might have thought a goose the rarest of all birds; a feathered phenomenon, to which a black swan was a matter of course—and in truth it was something very like it in that house. Mrs. Cratchit made the gravy (ready beforehand in a little saucepan) hissing hot; Master Peter mashed the potatoes with incredible vigour; Miss Belinda sweetened up the apple-sauce; Martha dusted the hot plates; Bob took Tiny Tim beside him in a tiny corner at the table; the two young Cratchits set

chairs for everybody, not forgetting themselves, and mounting guard upon their posts, crammed spoons into their mouths, lest they should shriek for goose before their turn came to be helped. At last the dishes were set on, and grace was said. It was succeeded by a breathless pause, as Mrs. Cratchit, looking slowly all along the carving-knife, prepared to plunge it in the breast; but when she did, and when the long expected gush of stuffing issued forth, one murmur of delight arose all round the board, and even Tiny Tim, excited by the two young Cratchits, beat on the table with the handle of his knife, and feebly cried Hurrah!

There never was such a goose. Bob said he didn't believe there ever was such a goose cooked. Its tenderness and flavour, size and cheapness, were the themes of universal admiration. Eked out by apple-sauce and mashed potatoes, it was a sufficient dinner for the whole family; indeed, as Mrs. Cratchit said with great delight (surveying one small atom of a bone upon the dish), they hadn't ate it all at last! Yet every one had had enough, and the youngest Cratchits in particular, were steeped in sage and onion to the eyebrows! But now, the plates being changed by Miss Belinda, Mrs. Cratchit left the room alone—too nervous to bear witnesses—to take the pudding up and bring it in.

Suppose it should not be done enough! Suppose it should break in turning out! Suppose somebody should have got over the wall of the back-yard, and stolen it, while they were merry with the goose—a supposition at which the two young Cratchits became livid! All sorts of horrors were supposed.

Hallo! A great deal of steam! The pudding was out of the copper. A smell like a washing-day! That was the cloth. A smell like an eating-house and a pastrycook's next door to each other, with a laundress's next door to that! That was the pudding! In half a minute Mrs. Cratchit entered—flushed, but smiling proudly—with the pudding, like a speckled cannon-ball, so hard and firm, blazing in half of half-a-quartern of ignited brandy, and bedight with Christmas holly stuck into the top.

Oh, a wonderful pudding! Bob Cratchit said, and calmly too, that he regarded it as the greatest success achieved by Mrs. Cratchit since their marriage. Mrs. Cratchit said that now the weight was off her mind, she would confess she had had her doubts about the quantity of flour. Everybody had something to say about it, but nobody said or thought it was at all a small pudding for a large family. It would have been flat heresy to do so. Any Cratchit would have blushed to hint at such a thing.

At last the dinner was all done, the cloth was cleared, the

hearth swept, and the fire made up. The compound in the jug being tasted, and considered perfect, apples and oranges were put upon the table, and a shovel-full of chestnuts on the fire. Then all the Cratchit family drew round the hearth, in what Bob Cratchit called a circle, meaning half a one; and at Bob Cratchit's elbow stood the family display of glass. Two tumblers, and a custard-cup without a handle.

These held the hot stuff from the jug, however, as well as golden goblets would have done; and Bob served it out with beaming looks, while the chestnuts on the fire sputtered and cracked noisily. Then Bob proposed:

"A Merry Christmas to us all, my dears. God bless us!"

Which all the family re-echoed.

"God bless us every one!" said Tiny Tim, the last of all.

He sat very close to his father's side upon his little stool. Bob held his withered little hand in his, as if he loved the child, and wished to keep him by his side, and dreaded that he might be taken from him.

"Spirit," said Scrooge, with an interest he had never felt before, "tell me if Tiny Tim will live."

"I see a vacant seat," replied the Ghost, "in the poor chimney-corner, and a crutch without an owner, carefully preserved. If these shadows remain unaltered by the Future, the child will die."

"No, no," said Scrooge. "Oh, no, kind Spirit! say he will be spared."

"If these shadows remain unaltered by the Future, none other of my race," returned the Ghost, "will find him here. What then? If he be like to die, he had better do it, and decrease the surplus population."

Scrooge hung his head to hear his own words quoted by the Spirit, and was overcome with penitence and grief.

"Man," said the Ghost, "if man you be in heart, not adamant, forbear that wicked cant until you have discovered What the surplus is, and Where it is. Will you decide what men shall live, what men shall die? It may be, that in the sight of Heaven, you are more worthless and less fit to live than millions like this poor man's child. Oh God! to hear the Insect on the leaf pronouncing on the too much life among his hungry brothers in the dust!"

Scrooge bent before the Ghost's rebuke, and trembling cast his eyes upon the ground. But he raised them speedily, on hearing his own name.

"Mr. Scrooge!" said Bob; "I'll give you Mr. Scrooge, the Founder of the Feast!"

"The Founder of the Feast indeed!" cried Mrs. Cratchit, reddening. "I wish I had him here. I'd give him a piece of my mind to feast upon, and I hope he'd have a good appetite for it."

"My dear," said Bob, "the children! Christmas Day."

"It should be Christmas Day, I am sure," said she, "on which one drinks the health of such an odious, stingy, hard, unfeeling man as Mr. Scrooge. You know he is, Robert! Nobody knows it better than you do, poor fellow!"

"My dear," was Bob's mild answer, "Christmas Day."

"I'll drink his health for your sake and the Day's," said Mrs. Cratchit, "not for his. Long life to him! A merry Christmas and a happy new year! He'll be very merry and very happy, I have no doubt!"

The children drank the toast after her. It was the first of their proceedings which had no heartiness. Tiny Tim drank it last of all, but he didn't care twopence for it. Scrooge was the Ogre of the family. The mention of his name cast a dark shadow on the party, which was not dispelled for full five minutes.

After it had passed away, they were ten times merrier than before, from the mere relief of Scrooge the Baleful being done with. Bob Cratchit told them how he had a situation in his eye for Master Peter, which would bring in, if obtained, full five-and-sixpence weekly. The two young Cratchits laughed tremendously at the idea of Peter's being a man of business; and Peter himself looked thoughtfully at the fire from between his collars, as if he were deliberating what particular investments he should favour when he came into the receipt of that bewildering income. Martha, who was a poor apprentice at a milliner's, then told them what kind of work she had to do, and how many hours she worked at a stretch, and how she meant to lie abed to-morrow morning for a good long rest; to-morrow being a holiday she passed at home. Also how she had seen a countess and a lord some days before, and how the lord "was much about as tall as Peter"; at which Peter pulled up his collars so high that you couldn't have seen his head if you had been there. All this time the chestnuts and the jug went round and round; and by-and-bye they had a song, about a lost child travelling in the snow, from Tiny Tim, who had a plaintive little voice, and sang it very well indeed.

There was nothing of high mark in this. They were not a handsome family; they were not well dressed; their shoes were far from being water-proof; their clothes were scanty; and Peter might have known, and very likely did, the inside of a pawnbroker's. But, they were happy, grateful, pleased with one another, and contented with the time; and when they faded, and looked happier yet in the bright sprinklings of the Spirit's torch at parting, Scrooge had his eye upon them, and especially on Tiny Tim, until the last.

By this time it was getting dark, and snowing pretty heavily; and as Scrooge and the Spirit went along the streets, the brightness of the roaring fires in kitchens, parlours, and all sorts of rooms, was wonderful. Here, the flickering of the blaze showed preparations for a cosy dinner, with hot plates baking through and through before the fire, and deep red curtains, ready to be drawn to shut out cold and darkness. There all the children of the house were running out into the snow to meet their married sisters, brothers, cousins, uncles, aunts, and be the first to greet them. Here, again, were shadows on the window-blind of guests assembling; and there a group of handsome girls, all hooded and fur-booted, and all chattering at once, tripped lightly off to some near neighbour's house; where, woe upon the single man who saw them enter—artful witches, well they knew it—in a glow!

But, if you had judged from the numbers of people on their way to friendly gatherings, you might have thought that no one was at home to give them welcome when they got there, instead of every house expecting company, and piling up its fires half-chimney high. Blessings on it, how the Ghost exulted! How it bared its breadth of breast, and opened its capacious palm, and floated on, outpouring, with a generous hand, its bright and harmless mirth on everything within its reach! The very lamplighter, who ran on before, dotting the dusky street with specks of light, and who was dressed to spend the evening somewhere, laughed out loudly as the Spirit passed, though little kenned the lamplighter that he had any company but Christmas!

And now, without a word of warning from the Ghost, they stood upon a bleak and desert moor, where monstrous masses of rude stone were cast about, as though it were the burial-place of giants; and water spread itself wheresoever it listed, or would have done so, but for the frost that held it prisoner; and nothing grew but moss and furze, and coarse rank grass. Down in the west the setting sun had left a streak of fiery red, which glared upon the desolation for an instant, like a sullen eye, and frowning lower, lower, lower yet, was lost in the thick gloom of darkest night.

"What place is this?" asked Scrooge.

"A place where Miners live, who labour in the bowels of the earth," returned the Spirit. "But they know me. See!"

A light shone from the window of a hut, and swiftly they advanced towards it. Passing through the wall of mud and stone, they found a cheerful company assembled round a glowing fire. An old, old man and woman, with their children and their children's children, and another generation beyond that, all decked out gaily in their holiday attire. The old man, in a voice that seldom rose above the howling of the wind upon the barren waste, was singing them a Christmas song—it had been a very old song when he was a boy—and from time to time they all joined in the chorus. So surely as they raised their voices, the old man got quite blithe and loud; and so surely as they stopped, his vigour sank again.

The Spirit did not tarry here, but bade Scrooge hold his robe, and passing on above the moor, sped—whither? Not to sea? To sea. To Scrooge's horror, looking back, he saw the last of the land, a frightful range of rocks, behind them; and his ears were deafened by the thundering of water, as it rolled and roared, and raged among the dreadful caverns it had worn, and fiercely tried to undermine the earth.

Built upon a dismal reef of sunken rocks, some league or so from shore, on which the waters chafed and dashed, the wild year through, there stood a solitary lighthouse. Great heaps of sea-weed clung to its base, and storm-birds—born of the wind one might suppose, as sea-weed of the water—rose and fell about it, like the waves they skimmed.

But even here, two men who watched the light had made a fire, that through the loophole in the thick stone wall shed out a ray of brightness on the awful sea. Joining their horny hands over the rough table at which they sat, they wished each other Merry Christmas in their can of grog; and one of them: the elder, too, with his face all damaged and scarred with hard weather, as the figure-head of an old ship might be: struck up a sturdy song that was like a Gale in itself.

Again the Ghost sped on, above the black and heaving sea—on, on—until, being far away, as he told Scrooge, from any shore, they lighted on a ship. They stood beside the helmsman at the wheel, the look-out in the bow, the officers who had the watch; dark, ghostly figures in their several stations; but every man among them hummed a Christmas tune, or had a Christmas thought, or spoke below his breath to his companion of some bygone Christmas Day, with homeward hopes belonging to it. And every man on board, waking or sleeping, good or bad, had had a kinder word for another on that day than on any day in the year; and had shared to some extent in its festivities; and had remembered those he cared for at a distance, and had known that they delighted to remember him.

It was a great surprise to Scrooge, while listening to the moaning of the wind, and thinking what a solemn thing it was to move on through the lonely darkness over an unknown abyss, whose depths were secrets as profound as Death: it was a great surprise to Scrooge, while thus engaged, to hear a hearty laugh. It was a much greater surprise to Scrooge to recognise it as his own nephew's and to find himself in a bright, dry, gleaming room, with the Spirit standing smiling by his side, and looking at that same nephew with approving affability!

"Ha, ha!" laughed Scrooge's nephew. "Ha, ha, ha!"

If you should happen, by any unlikely chance, to know a man more blest in a laugh than Scrooge's nephew, all I can say is, I should like to know him too. Introduce him to me, and I'll cultivate his acquaintance.

It is a fair, even-handed, noble adjustment of things, that while there is infection in disease and sorrow, there is nothing in the world so irresistibly contagious as laughter and good-humour. When Scrooge's nephew laughed in this way: holding his sides, rolling his head, and twisting his face into the most extravagant contortions: Scrooge's niece, by marriage, laughed as heartily as he. And their assembled friends being not a bit behindhand, roared out lustily.

"Ha, ha! Ha, ha, ha, ha!"

"He said that Christmas was a humbug, as I live!" cried Scrooge's nephew. "He believed it too!"

"More shame for him, Fred!" said Scrooge's niece, indignantly. Bless those women; they never do anything by halves. They are always in earnest.

She was very pretty: exceedingly pretty. With a dimpled, surprised-looking, capital face; a ripe little mouth, that seemed made to be kissed—as no doubt it was; all kinds of good little dots about her chin, that melted into one another when she laughed; and the sunniest pair of eyes you ever saw in any little creature's head. Altogether she was what you would have called provoking, you know; but satisfactory, too. Oh, perfectly satisfactory.

"He's a comical old fellow," said Scrooge's nephew, "that's the truth: and not so pleasant as he might be. However, his offences carry their own punishment, and I have nothing to say against him."

"I'm sure he is very rich, Fred," hinted Scrooge's niece. "At least you always tell *me* so."

"What of that, my dear!" said Scrooge's nephew. "His wealth is of no use to him. He don't do any good with it. He don't make himself comfortable with it. He hasn't the satisfaction of thinking—ha, ha, ha!—that he is ever going to benefit Us with it."

"I have no patience with him," observed Scrooge's niece. Scrooge's niece's sisters, and all the other ladies, expressed the same opinion.

"Oh, I have!" said Scrooge's nephew. "I am sorry for him; I couldn't be angry with him if I tried. Who suffers by his ill whims! Himself, always. Here, he takes it into his head to dislike us, and he won't come and dine with us. What's the consequence? He don't lose much of a dinner."

"Indeed, I think he loses a very good dinner," interrupted Scrooge's niece. Everybody else said the same, and they must be allowed to have been competent judges, because they had just had dinner; and, with the dessert upon the table, were clustered round the fire, by lamplight.

"Well! I'm very glad to hear it," said Scrooge's nephew, "because I haven't great faith in these young housekeepers. What do *you* say, Topper?"

Topper had clearly got his eye upon one of Scrooge's niece's sisters, for he answered that a bachelor was a wretched outcast, who had no right to express an opinion on the subject. Whereat Scrooge's niece's sister—the plump one with the lace tucker: not the one with the roses—blushed.

"Do go on, Fred," said Scrooge's niece, clapping her hands. "He never finishes what he begins to say! He is such a ridiculous fellow!"

Scrooge's nephew revelled in another laugh, and as it was impossible to keep the infection off; though the plump sister tried hard to do it with aromatic vinegar; his example was unanimously followed.

"I was only going to say," said Scrooge's nephew, "that the consequence of his taking a dislike to us, and not making merry with us, is, as I think, that he loses some pleasant moments, which could do him no harm. I am sure he loses pleasanter companions than he can find in his own thoughts, either in his mouldy old office, or his dusty chambers. I mean to give him the same chance every year, whether he likes it or not, for I pity him. He may rail at Christmas till he dies, but he can't help thinking better of it—I defy him—if he finds me going there, in good temper, year after year, and saying Uncle Scrooge, how are you? If it only puts him in the vein to leave his poor clerk fifty pounds, *that's* something; and I think I shook him yesterday."

It was their turn to laugh now at the notion of his shaking Scrooge. But being thoroughly good-natured, and not much caring what they laughed at, so that they laughed at any rate, he encouraged them in their merriment, and passed the bottle joyously.

After tea, they had some music. For they were a musical family, and knew what they were about, when they sung a Glee or Catch, I can assure you: especially Topper, who could growl away in the bass like a good one, and never swell the large veins in his forehead, or get red in the face over it. Scrooge's niece played well upon the harp; and played among other tunes a simple little air (a mere nothing: you might learn to whistle it in two minutes), which had been familiar to the child who fetched Scrooge from the boarding-school, as he had been reminded by the Ghost of Christmas Past. When this strain of music sounded, all the things that Ghost had shown him, came upon his mind; he softened more and more; and thought that if he could have listened to it often, years ago, he might have cultivated the kindnesses of life for his own happiness with his own hands, without resorting to the sexton's spade that buried Jacob Marley.

But they didn't devote the whole evening to music. After a while they played at forfeits; for it is good to be children sometimes, and never better than at Christmas, when its mighty Founder was a child himself. Stop! There was first a game at blind-man's buff. Of course there was. And I no more believe Topper was really blind than I believe he had eyes in his boots. My opinion is, that it was a done thing between him and Scrooge's nephew; and that the Ghost of Christmas Present knew it. The way he went after that plump sister in the lace tucker, was an outrage on the credulity of human nature. Knocking down the fire-irons, tumbling over the chairs, bumping against the piano, smothering himself among the curtains, wherever she went, there went he! He always knew where the plump sister was. He wouldn't catch anybody else. If you had fallen up against him (as some of them did), on purpose, he would have made a feint of endeavouring to seize you, which would have been an affront to your understanding, and would instantly have sidled off in the direction of the plump sister. She often cried out that it wasn't fair; and it really was not. But when at last, he caught her; when, in spite of all her silken rustlings, and her rapid flutterings past him, he got her into a corner whence there was no escape; then his conduct was the most execrable. For his pretending not to know her; his pretending that it was necessary to touch her head-dress, and further to assure himself of her identity by pressing a certain ring upon her finger, and a certain chain about her neck; was vile, monstrous! No doubt she told him her opinion of it, when, another blind-man being in office, they were so very confidential together, behind the curtains.

Scrooge's niece was not one of the blind-man's buff party, but was made comfortable with a large chair and a footstool, in a snug corner, where the Ghost and Scrooge were close behind her. But she joined in the forfeits, and loved her love to admiration with all the letters of the alphabet. Likewise at the game of How, When, and Where, she was very great, and to the secret joy of Scrooge's nephew, beat her sisters hollow: though they were sharp girls too, as Topper could have told you. There might have been twenty people there, young and old, but they all played, and so did Scrooge; for wholly forgetting in the interest he had in what was going on, that his voice made no sound in their ears, he sometimes came out with his guess quite loud, and very often guessed quite right, too; for the sharpest needle, best Whitechapel, warranted not to cut in the eye, was not sharper than Scrooge; blunt as he took it in his head to be.

The Ghost was greatly pleased to find him in this mood, and looked upon him with such favour, that he begged like a boy to be allowed to stay until the guests departed. But this the Spirit said could not be done.

"Here is a new game," said Scrooge. "One half hour, Spirit, only one!"

It was a Game called Yes and No, where Scrooge's nephew had to think of something, and the rest must find out what; he only answering to their questions yes or no, as the case was. The brisk fire of questioning to which he was exposed, elicited from him that he was thinking of an animal, a live animal, rather a disagreeable animal, a savage animal, an animal that growled and grunted sometimes, and talked sometimes, and lived in London, and walked about the streets, and wasn't made a show of, and wasn't led by anybody, and didn't live in a menagerie, and was never killed in a market, and was not a horse, or an ass, or a cow, or a bull, or a tiger, or a dog, or a pig, or a cat, or a bear. At every fresh question that was put to him, this nephew burst into a fresh roar of laughter; and was so inexpressibly tickled, that he was obliged to get up off the sofa and stamp. At last the plump sister, falling into a similar state, cried out:

"I have found it out! I know what it is, Fred! I know what it is!"

"What is it?" cried Fred.

"It's your Uncle Scro-o-o-o-oge!"

Which it certainly was. Admiration was the universal sentiment, though some objected that the reply to "Is it a bear?" ought to have been "Yes"; inasmuch as an answer in the negative was sufficient to have diverted their thoughts from Mr. Scrooge, supposing they had ever had any tendency that way.

"He has given us plenty of merriment, I am sure," said Fred, "and it would be ungrateful not to drink his health. Here is a glass of mulled wine ready to our hand at the moment; and I say, 'Uncle Scrooge!'"

"Well! Uncle Scrooge!" they cried.

"A Merry Christmas and a Happy New Year to the old man, whatever he is!" said Scrooge's nephew. "He wouldn't take it from me, but may he have it, nevertheless. Uncle Scrooge!"

Uncle Scrooge had imperceptibly become so gay and light of heart, that he would have pledged the unconscious company in return, and thanked them in an inaudible speech, if the Ghost had given him time. But the whole scene passed off in the breath of the last word spoken by his nephew; and he and the Spirit were again upon their travels.

Much they saw, and far they went, and many homes they visited, but always with a happy end. The Spirit stood beside sick beds, and they were cheerful; on foreign lands, and they were close at home; by struggling men, and they were patient in their greater hope; by poverty, and it was rich. In almshouse, hospital, and jail, in misery's every refuge, where vain man in his little brief authority had not made fast the door, and barred the Spirit out, he left his blessing, and taught Scrooge his precepts.

It was a long night, if it were only a night; but Scrooge had his doubts of this, because the Christmas Holidays appeared to be condensed into the space of time they passed together. It was strange, too, that while Scrooge remained unaltered in his outward form, the Ghost grew older, clearly older. Scrooge had observed this change, but never spoke of it, until they left a children's Twelfth Night party, when, looking at the Spirit as they stood together in an open place, he noticed that its hair was grey.

"Are spirits' lives so short?" asked Scrooge.

"My life upon this globe, is very brief," replied the Ghost. "It ends to-night."

"To-night!" cried Scrooge.

"To-night at midnight. Hark! The time is drawing near."

The chimes were ringing the three quarters past eleven at that moment.

"Forgive me if I am not justified in what I ask," said Scrooge, looking intently at the Spirit's robe, "but I see something strange, and not belonging to yourself, protruding from your skirts. Is it a foot or a claw?"

"It might be a claw, for the flesh there is upon it," was the Spirit's sorrowful reply. "Look here."

From the foldings of its robe, it brought two children; wretched, abject, frightful, hideous, miserable. They knelt down at its feet, and clung upon the outside of its garment.

"Oh, Man! look here. Look, look, down here!" exclaimed the Ghost.

They were a boy and girl. Yellow, meagre, ragged, scowling, wolfish; but prostrate, too, in their humility. Where graceful youth should have filled their features out, and touched them with its freshest tints, a stale and shrivelled hand, like that of age, had pinched, and twisted them, and pulled them into shreds. Where angels might have sat enthroned, devils lurked, and glared out menacing. No change, no degradation, no perversion of humanity, in any grade, through all the mysteries of wonderful creation, has monsters half so horrible and dread.

Scrooge started back, appalled. Having them shown to him in this way, he tried to say they were fine children, but the words choked themselves, rather than be parties to a lie of such enormous magnitude.

"Spirit! are they yours?" Scrooge could say no more.

"They are Man's," said the Spirit, looking down upon them. "And they cling to me, appealing from their fathers. This boy is Ignorance. This girl is Want. Beware them both, and all of their degree, but most of all beware this boy, for on his brow I see that written which is Doom, unless the writing be erased. Deny it!" cried the Spirit, stretching out its hand towards the city. "Slander those who tell it ye! Admit it for your factious purposes, and make it worse. And bide the end!"

"Have they no refuge or resource?" cried Scrooge.

"Are there no prisons?" said the Spirit, turning on him for the last time with his own words. "Are there no workhouses?"

The bell struck twelve.

Scrooge looked about him for the Ghost, and saw it not. As the last stroke ceased to vibrate, he remembered the prediction of old Jacob Marley, and lifting up his eyes, beheld a solemn Phantom, draped and hooded, coming, like a mist along the ground, towards him.

Stave IV
The Last of the Spirits

The Phantom slowly, gravely, silently, approached. When it came near him, Scrooge bent down upon his knee; for in the very air through which this Spirit moved it seemed to scatter gloom and mystery.

It was shrouded in a deep black garment, which concealed its head, its face, its form, and left nothing of it visible save one outstretched hand. But for this it would have been difficult to detach its figure from the night, and separate it from the darkness by which it was surrounded.

He felt that it was tall and stately when it came beside him, and that its mysterious presence filled him with a solemn dread. He knew no more, for the Spirit neither spoke nor moved.

"I am in the presence of the Ghost of Christmas Yet To Come?" said Scrooge.

The Spirit answered not, but pointed onward with its hand.

"You are about to show me shadows of the things that have not happened, but will happen in the time before us," Scrooge pursued. "Is that so, Spirit?"

The upper portion of the garment was contracted for an instant in its folds, as if the Spirit had inclined its head. That was the only answer he received.

Although well used to ghostly company by this time, Scrooge feared the silent shape so much that his legs trembled beneath him, and he found that he could hardly stand when he prepared to follow it. The Spirit paused a moment, as observing his condition, and giving him time to recover.

But Scrooge was all the worse for this. It thrilled him with a vague uncertain horror, to know that behind the dusky shroud, there were ghostly eyes intently fixed upon him, while he, though he stretched his own to the utmost, could see nothing but a spectral hand and one great heap of black.

"Ghost of the Future!" he exclaimed, "I fear you more than any spectre I have seen. But as I know your purpose is to do me good, and as I hope to live to be another man from what I was, I am prepared to bear you company, and do it with a thankful heart. Will you not speak to me?"

It gave him no reply. The hand was pointed straight before them.

"Lead on!" said Scrooge. "Lead on! The night is waning fast, and it is precious time to me, I know. Lead on, Spirit!"

The Phantom moved away as it had come towards him. Scrooge followed in the shadow of its dress, which bore him up, he thought, and carried him along.

They scarcely seemed to enter the city; for the city rather seemed to spring up about them, and encompass them of its own act. But there they were, in the heart of it; on 'Change, amongst the merchants; who hurried up and down, and chinked the money in their pockets, and conversed in groups, and looked at their watches, and trifled thoughtfully with their great gold seals; and so forth, as Scrooge had seen them often.

The Spirit stopped beside one little knot of business men. Observing that the hand was pointed to them, Scrooge advanced to listen to their talk.

"No," said a great fat man with a monstrous chin, "I don't know much about it, either way. I only know he's dead."

"When did he die?" inquired another.

"Last night, I believe."

"Why, what was the matter with him?" asked a third, taking a vast quantity of snuff out of a very large snuff-box. "I thought he'd never die."

"God knows," said the first, with a yawn.

"What has he done with his money?" asked a red-faced gentleman with a pendulous excrescence on the end of his nose, that shook like the gills of a turkey-cock.

"I haven't heard," said the man with the large chin, yawning again. "Left it to his company, perhaps. He hasn't left it to *me*. That's all I know."

This pleasantry was received with a general laugh.

"It's likely to be a very cheap funeral," said the same speaker; "for upon my life I don't know of anybody to go to it. Suppose we make up a party and volunteer?"

"I don't mind going if a lunch is provided," observed the gentleman with the excrescence on his nose. "But I must be fed, if I make one."

Another laugh.

"Well, I am the most disinterested among you, after all," said the first speaker, "for I never wear black gloves, and I never eat lunch. But I'll offer to go, if anybody else will. When I come to think of it, I'm not at all sure that I wasn't his most particular friend; for we used to stop and speak whenever we met. Bye, bye!"

Speakers and listeners strolled away, and mixed with other groups. Scrooge knew the men, and looked towards the Spirit for an explanation.

The Phantom glided on into a street. Its finger pointed to two persons meeting. Scrooge listened again, thinking that the explanation might lie here.

He knew these men, also, perfectly. They were men of business: very wealthy, and of great importance. He had made a point always of standing well in their esteem: in a business point of view, that is; strictly in a business point of view.

"How are you?" said one.

"How are you?" returned the other.

"Well!" said the first. "Old Scratch has got his own at last, hey?"

"So I am told," returned the second. "Cold, isn't it?"

"Seasonable for Christmas time. You're not a skater, I suppose?"

"No. No. Something else to think of. Good morning!"

Not another word. That was their meeting, their conversation, and their parting.

Scrooge was at first inclined to be surprised that the Spirit should attach importance to conversations apparently so trivial; but feeling assured that they must have some hidden purpose, he set himself to consider what it was likely to be. They could scarcely be supposed to have any bearing on the death of Jacob, his old partner, for that was Past, and this Ghost's province was the Future. Nor could he think of any one immediately connected with himself, to whom he could apply them. But nothing doubting that to whomsoever they applied they had some latent moral for his own improvement, he resolved to treasure up every word he heard, and everything he saw; and especially to observe the shadow of himself when it appeared. For he had an expectation that the conduct of his future self would give him the clue he missed, and would render the solution of these riddles easy.

He looked about in that very place for his own image; but another man stood in his accustomed corner, and though the clock pointed to his usual time of day for being there, he saw no likeness of himself among the multitudes that poured in through the Porch. It gave him little surprise, however; for he had been revolving in his mind a change of life, and thought and hoped he saw his new-born resolutions carried out in this.

Quiet and dark, beside him stood the Phantom, with its outstretched hand. When he roused himself from his thoughtful quest, he fancied from the turn of the hand, and its situation in reference to himself, that the Unseen Eyes were looking at him keenly. It made him shudder, and feel very cold.

They left the busy scene, and went into an obscure part of the town, where Scrooge had never penetrated before, although he recognised its situation, and its bad repute. The ways were foul and narrow; the shops and houses wretched; the people half-naked, drunken, slipshod, ugly. Alleys and archways, like so many cesspools, disgorged their offences of smell, and dirt, and life, upon the straggling streets; and the whole quarter reeked with crime, with filth, and misery.

Far in this den of infamous resort, there was a low-browed, beetling shop, below a pent-house roof, where iron, old rags, bottles, bones, and greasy offal, were bought. Upon the floor within, were piled up heaps of rusty keys, nails, chains, hinges, files, scales, weights, and refuse iron of all kinds. Secrets that few would like to scrutinise were bred and hidden in mountains of unseemly rags, masses of corrupted fat, and sepulchres of bones. Sitting in among the wares he dealt in, by a charcoal stove, made of old bricks, was a grey-haired rascal, nearly seventy years of age; who had screened himself from the cold air without, by a frousy curtaining of miscellaneous tatters, hung upon a line; and smoked his pipe in all the luxury of calm retirement.

Scrooge and the Phantom came into the presence of this man, just as a woman with a heavy bundle slunk into the shop. But she had scarcely entered, when another woman, similarly laden, came in too; and she was closely followed by a man in faded black, who was no less startled by the sight of them, than they had been upon the recognition of each other. After a short period of blank astonishment, in which the old man with the pipe had joined them, they all three burst into a laugh.

"Let the charwoman alone to be the first!" cried she who had entered first. "Let the laundress alone to be the second; and let the undertaker's man alone to be the third. Look here, old Joe, here's a chance! If we haven't all three met here without meaning it!"

"You couldn't have met in a better place," said old Joe, removing his pipe from his mouth. "Come into the parlour. You were made free of it long ago, you know; and the other two an't strangers. Stop till I shut the door of the shop. Ah! How it skreeks! There an't such a rusty bit of metal in the place as its own hinges, I believe; and I'm sure there's no such old bones here, as mine. Ha, ha! We're all suitable to our calling, we're well matched. Come into the parlour. Come into the parlour."

The parlour was the space behind the screen of rags. The old man raked the fire together with an old stair-rod, and having trimmed his smoky lamp (for it was night), with the stem of his pipe, put it in his mouth again.

While he did this, the woman who had already spoken threw her bundle on the floor, and sat down in a flaunting manner on a stool; crossing her elbows on her knees, and looking with a bold defiance at the other two.

"What odds then! What odds, Mrs. Dilber?" said the woman. "Every person has a right to take care of themselves. *He* always did."

"That's true, indeed!" said the laundress. "No man more so."

"Why then, don't stand staring as if you was afraid, woman; who's the wiser? We're not going to pick holes in each other's coats, I suppose?"

"No, indeed!" said Mrs. Dilber and the man together. "We should hope not."

"Very well, then!" cried the woman. "That's enough. Who's the worse for the loss of a few things like these? Not a dead man, I suppose."

"No, indeed," said Mrs. Dilber, laughing.

"If he wanted to keep 'em after he was dead, a wicked old screw," pursued the woman, "why wasn't he natural in his lifetime? If he had been, he'd have had somebody to look after him when he was struck with Death, instead of lying gasping out his last there, alone by himself."

"It's the truest word that ever was spoke," said Mrs. Dilber. "It's a judgment on him."

"I wish it was a little heavier judgment," replied the woman; "and it should have been, you may depend upon it, if I could have laid my hands on anything else. Open that bundle, old Joe, and let me know the value of it. Speak out plain. I'm not afraid to be the first, nor afraid for them to see it. We know pretty well that we were helping ourselves, before we met here, I believe. It's no sin. Open the bundle, Joe."

But the gallantry of her friends would not allow of this; and the man in faded black, mounting the breach first, produced his plunder. It was not extensive. A seal or two, a pencil-case, a pair of sleeve-buttons, and a brooch of no great value, were all. They were severally examined and appraised by old Joe, who chalked the sums he was disposed to give for each, upon the wall, and added them up into a total when he found there was nothing more to come.

"That's your account," said Joe, "and I wouldn't give another sixpence, if I was to be boiled for not doing it. Who's next?"

Mrs. Dilber was next. Sheets and towels, a little wearing apparel, two old-fashioned silver teaspoons, a pair of sugar-tongs, and a few boots. Her account was stated on the wall in the same manner.

"I always give too much to ladies. It's a weakness of mine, and that's the way I ruin myself," said old Joe. "That's your account. If you asked me for another penny, and made it an open question, I'd repent of being so liberal and knock off half-a-crown."

"And now undo *my* bundle, Joe," said the first woman.

Joe went down on his knees for the greater convenience of opening it, and having unfastened a great many knots, dragged out a large and heavy roll of some dark stuff.

"What do you call this?" said Joe. "Bed-curtains!"

"Ah!" returned the woman, laughing and leaning forward on her crossed arms. "Bed-curtains!"

"You don't mean to say you took 'em down, rings and all, with him lying there?" said Joe.

"Yes I do," replied the woman. "Why not?"

"You were born to make your fortune," said Joe, "and you'll certainly do it."

"I certainly shan't hold my hand, when I can get anything in it by reaching it out, for the sake of such a man as He was, I promise you, Joe," returned the woman coolly. "Don't drop that oil upon the blankets, now."

"His blankets?" asked Joe.

"Whose else's do you think?" replied the woman. "He isn't likely to take cold without 'em, I dare say."

"I hope he didn't die of anything catching? Eh?" said old Joe, stopping in his work, and looking up.

"Don't you be afraid of that," returned the woman. "I an't so fond of his company that I'd loiter about him for such things, if he did. Ah! you may look through that shirt till your eyes ache; but you won't find a hole in it, nor a threadbare place. It's the best he had, and a fine one too. They'd have wasted it, if it hadn't been for me."

"What do you call wasting of it?" asked old Joe.

"Putting it on him to be buried in, to be sure," replied the woman with a laugh. "Somebody was fool enough to do it, but I took it off again. If calico an't good enough for such a purpose, it isn't good for anything. It's quite as becoming to the body. He can't look uglier than he did in that one."

Scrooge listened to this dialogue in horror. As they sat grouped about their spoil, in the scanty light afforded by the old man's lamp, he viewed them with a detestation and disgust, which could hardly have been greater, though they had been obscene demons, marketing the corpse itself.

"Ha, ha!" laughed the same woman, when old Joe, producing a flannel bag with money in it, told out their several gains upon the ground. "This is the end of it, you see! He frightened every one away from him when he was alive, to profit us when he was dead! Ha, ha, ha!"

"Spirit!" said Scrooge, shuddering from head to foot. "I see, I see. The case of this unhappy man might be my own. My life tends that way, now. Merciful Heaven, what is this!"

He recoiled in terror, for the scene had changed, and now he almost touched a bed: a bare, uncurtained bed: on which, beneath a ragged sheet, there lay a something covered up, which, though it was dumb, announced itself in awful language.

The room was very dark, too dark to be observed with any accuracy, though Scrooge glanced round it in obedience to a secret impulse, anxious to know what kind of room it was. A pale light, rising in the outer air, fell straight upon the bed; and on it, plundered and bereft, unwatched, unwept, uncared for, was the body of this man.

Scrooge glanced towards the Phantom. Its steady hand was pointed to the head. The cover was so carelessly adjusted that the slightest raising of it, the motion of a finger upon Scrooge's part, would have disclosed the face. He thought of it, felt how easy it would be to do, and longed to do it; but had no more power to withdraw the veil than to dismiss the spectre at his side.

Oh cold, cold, rigid, dreadful Death, set up thine altar here, and dress it with such terrors as thou hast at thy command: for this is thy dominion! But of the loved, revered, and honoured head, thou canst not turn one hair to thy dread purposes, or make one feature odious. It is not that the hand is heavy and will fall down when released; it is not that the heart and pulse are still; but that the hand WAS open, generous, and true; the heart brave, warm, and tender; and the pulse a man's. Strike, Shadow, strike! And see his good deeds springing from the wound, to sow the world with life immortal!

No voice pronounced these words in Scrooge's ears, and yet he heard them when he looked upon the bed. He thought, if this man could be raised up now, what would be his foremost thoughts? Avarice, hard-dealing, griping cares? They have brought him to a rich end, truly!

He lay, in the dark empty house, with not a man, a woman, or a child, to say that he was kind to me in this or that, and for the memory of one kind word I will be kind to him. A cat was tearing at the door, and there was a sound of gnawing rats beneath the hearth-stone. What *they* wanted in the room of death, and why they were so restless and disturbed, Scrooge did not dare to think.

"Spirit!" he said, "this is a fearful place. In leaving it, I shall not leave its lesson, trust me. Let us go!"

Still the Ghost pointed with an unmoved finger to the head.

"I understand you," Scrooge returned, "and I would do it, if I could. But I have not the power, Spirit. I have not the power."

Again it seemed to look upon him.

"If there is any person in the town, who feels emotion caused by this man's death," said Scrooge quite agonised, "show that person to me, Spirit, I beseech you!"

The Phantom spread its dark robe before him for a moment, like a wing; and withdrawing it, revealed a room by daylight, where a mother and her children were.

She was expecting some one, and with anxious eagerness; for she walked up and down the room; started at every sound; looked out from the window; glanced at the clock; tried, but in vain, to work with her needle; and could hardly bear the voices of the children in their play.

At length the long-expected knock was heard. She hurried to the door, and met her husband; a man whose face was careworn and depressed, though he was young. There was a remarkable expression in it now; a kind of serious delight of which he felt ashamed, and which he struggled to repress.

He sat down to the dinner that had been hoarding for him by the fire; and when she asked him faintly what news (which was not until after a long silence), he appeared embarrassed how to answer.

"Is it good?" she said, "or bad?"—to help him.

"Bad," he answered.

"We are quite ruined?"

"No. There is hope yet, Caroline."

"If *he* relents," she said, amazed, "there is! Nothing is past hope, if such a miracle has happened."

"He is past relenting," said her husband. "He is dead."

She was a mild and patient creature if her face spoke truth; but she was thankful in her soul to hear it, and she said so, with clasped hands. She prayed forgiveness the next moment, and was sorry; but the first was the emotion of her heart.

"What the half-drunken woman whom I told you of last night, said to me, when I tried to see him and obtain a week's delay; and what I thought was a mere excuse to avoid me; turns out to have been quite true. He was not only very ill, but dying, then."

"To whom will our debt be transferred?"

"I don't know. But before that time we shall be ready with the money; and even though we were not, it would be a bad fortune indeed to find so merciless a creditor in his successor. We may sleep to-night with light hearts, Caroline!"

Yes. Soften it as they would, their hearts were lighter. The children's faces, hushed and clustered round to hear what they so little understood, were brighter; and it was a happier house for this man's death! The only emotion that the Ghost could show him, caused by the event, was one of pleasure.

"Let me see some tenderness connected with a death," said Scrooge; "or that dark chamber, Spirit, which we left just now, will be for ever present to me."

The Ghost conducted him through several streets familiar to his feet; and as they went along, Scrooge looked here and there to find himself, but nowhere was he to be seen. They entered poor Bob Cratchit's house; the dwelling he had visited before; and found the mother and the children seated round the fire.

Quiet. Very quiet. The noisy little Cratchits were as still as statues in one corner, and sat looking up at Peter, who had a book before him. The mother and her daughters were engaged in sewing. But surely they were very quiet!

"'And He took a child, and set him in the midst of them.'"

Where had Scrooge heard those words? He had not dreamed them. The boy must have read them out, as he and the Spirit crossed the threshold. Why did he not go on?

The mother laid her work upon the table, and put her hand up to her face.

"The colour hurts my eyes," she said.

The colour? Ah, poor Tiny Tim!

"They're better now again," said Cratchit's wife. "It makes them weak by candle-light; and I wouldn't show weak eyes to your father when he comes home, for the world. It must be near his time."

"Past it rather," Peter answered, shutting up his book. "But I think he has walked a little slower than he used, these few last evenings, mother."

They were very quiet again. At last she said, and in a steady, cheerful voice, that only faltered once:

"I have known him walk with—I have known him walk with Tiny Tim upon his shoulder, very fast indeed."

"And so have I," cried Peter. "Often."

"And so have I," exclaimed another. So had all.

"But he was very light to carry," she resumed, intent upon her work, "and his father loved him so, that it was no trouble: no trouble. And there is your father at the door!"

She hurried out to meet him; and little Bob in his comforter—he had need of it, poor fellow—came in. His tea was ready for him on the hob, and they all tried who should help him to it most. Then the two young Cratchits got upon his knees and laid, each child a little cheek, against his face, as if they said, "Don't mind it, father. Don't be grieved!"

Bob was very cheerful with them, and spoke pleasantly to all the family. He looked at the work upon the table, and praised the industry and speed of Mrs. Cratchit and the girls. They would be done long before Sunday, he said.

"Sunday! You went to-day, then, Robert?" said his wife.

"Yes, my dear," returned Bob. "I wish you could have gone. It would have done you good to see how green a place it is. But you'll see it often. I promised him that I would walk there on a Sunday. My little, little child!" cried Bob. "My little child!"

He broke down all at once. He couldn't help it. If he could have helped it, he and his child would have been farther apart perhaps than they were.

He left the room, and went up stairs into the room above, which was lighted cheerfully, and hung with Christmas. There was a chair set close beside the child, and there were signs of some one having been there, lately. Poor Bob sat down in it, and when he had thought a little and composed himself, he kissed the little face. He was reconciled to what had happened, and went down again quite happy.

They drew about the fire, and talked; the girls and mother working still. Bob told them of the extraordinary kindness of Mr. Scrooge's nephew, whom he had scarcely seen but once, and who, meeting him in the street that day, and seeing that he looked a little—"just a little down you know," said Bob, inquired what had happened to distress him. "On which," said Bob, "for he is the pleasantest-spoken gentleman you ever heard, I told him. 'I am heartily sorry for it, Mr. Cratchit,' he said, 'and heartily sorry for your good wife.' By the bye, how he ever knew *that*, I don't know."

"Knew what, my dear?"

"Why, that you were a good wife," replied Bob.

"Everybody knows that!" said Peter.

"Very well observed, my boy!" cried Bob. "I hope they do. 'Heartily sorry,' he said, 'for your good wife. If I can be of service to you in any way,' he said, giving me his card, 'that's where I live. Pray come to me.' Now, it wasn't," cried Bob, "for the sake of anything he might be able to do for us, so much as for his kind way, that this was quite delightful. It really seemed as if he had known our Tiny Tim, and felt with us."

"I'm sure he's a good soul!" said Mrs. Cratchit.

"You would be surer of it, my dear," returned Bob, "if you saw and spoke to him. I shouldn't be at all surprised—mark what I say!—if he got Peter a better situation."

"Only hear that, Peter," said Mrs. Cratchit.

"And then," cried one of the girls, "Peter will be keeping company with some one, and setting up for himself."

"Get along with you!" retorted Peter, grinning.

"It's just as likely as not," said Bob, "one of these days; though there's plenty of time for that, my dear. But however and whenever we part from one another, I am sure we shall none of us forget poor Tiny Tim—shall we—or this first parting that there was among us?"

"Never, father!" cried they all.

"And I know," said Bob, "I know, my dears, that when we recollect how patient and how mild he was; although he was a little, little child; we shall not quarrel easily among ourselves, and forget poor Tiny Tim in doing it."

"No, never, father!" they all cried again.

"I am very happy," said little Bob, "I am very happy!"

Mrs. Cratchit kissed him, his daughters kissed him, the two young Cratchits kissed him, and Peter and himself shook hands. Spirit of Tiny Tim, thy childish essence was from God!

"Spectre," said Scrooge, "something informs me that our parting moment is at hand. I know it, but I know not how. Tell me what man that was whom we saw lying dead?"

The Ghost of Christmas Yet To Come conveyed him, as before—though at a different time, he thought: indeed, there seemed no order in these latter visions, save that they were in the Future—into the resorts of business men, but showed him not himself. Indeed, the Spirit did not stay for anything, but went straight on, as to the end just now desired, until besought by Scrooge to tarry for a moment.

"This court," said Scrooge, "through which we hurry now, is where my place of occupation is, and has been for a length of time. I see the house. Let me behold what I shall be, in days to come!"

The Spirit stopped; the hand was pointed elsewhere.

"The house is yonder," Scrooge exclaimed. "Why do you point away?"

The inexorable finger underwent no change.

Scrooge hastened to the window of his office, and looked in. It was an office still, but not his. The furniture was not the same, and the figure in the chair was not himself. The Phantom pointed as before.

He joined it once again, and wondering why and whither he had gone, accompanied it until they reached an iron gate. He paused to look round before entering.

A churchyard. Here, then; the wretched man whose name he had now to learn, lay underneath the ground. It was a worthy place. Walled in by houses; overrun by grass and weeds, the growth of vegetation's death, not life; choked up with too much burying; fat with repleted appetite. A worthy place!

The Spirit stood among the graves, and pointed down to One. He advanced towards it trembling. The Phantom was exactly as it had been, but he dreaded that he saw new meaning in its solemn shape.

"Before I draw nearer to that stone to which you point," said Scrooge, "answer me one question. Are these the shadows of the things that Will be, or are they shadows of things that May be, only?"

Still the Ghost pointed downward to the grave by which it stood.

"Men's courses will foreshadow certain ends, to which, if persevered in, they must lead," said Scrooge. "But if the courses be departed from, the ends will change. Say it is thus with what you show me!"

The Spirit was immovable as ever.

Scrooge crept towards it, trembling as he went; and following the finger, read upon the stone of the neglected grave his own name, EBENEZER SCROOGE.

"Am *I* that man who lay upon the bed?" he cried, upon his knees.

The finger pointed from the grave to him, and back again.

"No, Spirit! Oh no, no!"

The finger still was there.

"Spirit!" he cried, tight clutching at its robe, "hear me! I am not the man I was. I will not be the man I must have been but for this intercourse. Why show me this, if I am past all hope!"

For the first time the hand appeared to shake.

"Good Spirit," he pursued, as down upon the ground he fell before it: "Your nature intercedes for me, and pities me. Assure me that I yet may change these shadows you have shown me, by an altered life!"

The kind hand trembled.

"I will honour Christmas in my heart, and try to keep it all the year. I will live in the Past, the Present, and the Future. The Spirits of all Three shall strive within me. I will not shut out the lessons that they teach. Oh, tell me I may sponge away the writing on this stone!"

In his agony, he caught the spectral hand. It sought to free itself, but he was strong in his entreaty, and detained it. The Spirit, stronger yet, repulsed him.

Holding up his hands in a last prayer to have his fate reversed, he saw an alteration in the Phantom's hood and dress. It shrunk, collapsed, and dwindled down into a bedpost.

STAVE V
THE END OF IT

Yes! and the bedpost was his own. The bed was his own, the room was his own. Best and happiest of all, the Time before him was his own, to make amends in!

"I will live in the Past, the Present, and the Future!" Scrooge repeated, as he scrambled out of bed. "The Spirits of all Three shall strive within me. Oh Jacob Marley! Heaven, and the Christmas Time be praised for this! I say it on my knees, old Jacob; on my knees!"

He was so fluttered and so glowing with his good intentions, that his broken voice would scarcely answer to his call. He had been sobbing violently in his conflict with the Spirit, and his face was wet with tears.

"They are not torn down," cried Scrooge, folding one of his bed-curtains in his arms, "they are not torn down, rings and all. They are here—I am here—the shadows of the things that would have been, may be dispelled. They will be. I know they will!"

His hands were busy with his garments all this time; turning them inside out, putting them on upside down, tearing them, mislaying them, making them parties to every kind of extravagance.

"I don't know what to do!" cried Scrooge, laughing and crying in the same breath; and making a perfect Laocoön of himself with his stockings. "I am as light as a feather, I am as happy as an angel, I am as merry as a schoolboy. I am as giddy as a drunken man. A merry Christmas to everybody! A happy New Year to all the world. Hallo here! Whoop! Hallo!"

He had frisked into the sitting-room, and was now standing there: perfectly winded.

"There's the saucepan that the gruel was in!" cried Scrooge, starting off again, and going round the fireplace. "There's the door, by which the Ghost of Jacob Marley entered! There's the corner where the Ghost of Christmas Present, sat! There's the window where I saw the wandering Spirits! It's all right, it's all true, it all happened. Ha ha ha!"

Really, for a man who had been out of practice for so many years, it was a splendid laugh, a most illustrious laugh. The father of a long, long line of brilliant laughs!

"I don't know what day of the month it is!" said Scrooge. "I don't know how long I've been among the Spirits. I don't know anything. I'm quite a baby. Never mind. I don't care. I'd rather be a baby. Hallo! Whoop! Hallo here!"

He was checked in his transports by the churches ringing out the lustiest peals he had ever heard. Clash, clang, hammer; ding, dong, bell. Bell, dong, ding; hammer, clang, clash! Oh, glorious. Glorious!

Running to the window, he opened it, and put out his head. No fog, no mist; clear, bright, jovial, stirring, cold; cold, piping for the blood to dance to; Golden sunlight; Heavenly sky; sweet fresh air; merry bells. Oh, glorious. Glorious!

"What's to-day!" cried Scrooge, calling downward to a boy in Sunday clothes, who perhaps had loitered in to look about him.

"Eh?" returned the boy, with all his might of wonder.

"What's to-day, my fine fellow?" said Scrooge.

"To-day!" replied the boy. "Why, CHRISTMAS DAY."

"It's Christmas Day!" said Scrooge to himself. "I haven't missed it. The Spirits have done it all in one night. They can do anything they like. Of course they can. Of course they can. Hallo, my fine fellow!"

"Hallo!" returned the boy.

"Do you know the Poulterer's, in the next street but one, at the corner?" Scrooge inquired.

"I should hope I did," replied the lad.

"An intelligent boy!" said Scrooge. "A remarkable boy! Do you know whether they've sold the prize Turkey that was hanging up there?—Not the little prize Turkey: the big one?"

"What, the one as big as me?" returned the boy.

"What a delightful boy!" said Scrooge. "It's a pleasure to talk to him. Yes, my buck!"

"It's hanging there now," replied the boy.

"Is it?" said Scrooge. "Go and buy it."

"Walk-ER!" exclaimed the boy.

"No, no," said Scrooge, "I am in earnest. Go and buy it, and tell 'em to bring it here, that I may give them the direction where to take it. Come back with the man, and I'll give you a shilling. Come back with him in less than five minutes and I'll give you half-a-crown!"

The boy was off like a shot. He must have had a steady hand at a trigger who could have got a shot off half so fast.

"I'll send it to Bob Cratchit's!" whispered Scrooge, rubbing his hands, and splitting with a laugh. "He sha'n't know who sends it. It's twice the size of Tiny Tim. Joe Miller never made such a joke as sending it to Bob's will be!"

The hand in which he wrote the address was not a steady one, but write it he did, somehow, and went down stairs to open the street door, ready for the coming of the poulterer's man. As he stood there, waiting his arrival, the knocker caught his eye.

"I shall love it, as long as I live!" cried Scrooge, patting it with his hand. "I scarcely ever looked at it before. What an honest expression it has in its face! It's a wonderful knocker!—Here's the Turkey! Hallo! Whoop! How are you! Merry Christmas!"

It *was* a Turkey! He never could have stood upon his legs, that bird. He would have snapped 'em short off in a minute, like sticks of sealing-wax.

"Why, it's impossible to carry that to Camden Town," said Scrooge. "You must have a cab."

The chuckle with which he said this, and the chuckle with which he paid for the Turkey, and the chuckle with which he paid for the cab, and the chuckle with which he recompensed the boy, were only to be exceeded by the chuckle with which he sat down breathless in his chair again, and chuckled till he cried.

Shaving was not an easy task, for his hand continued to shake very much; and shaving requires attention, even when you don't dance while you are at it. But if he had cut the end of his nose off, he would have put a piece of sticking-plaister over it, and been quite satisfied.

He dressed himself "all in his best," and at last got out into the streets. The people were by this time pouring forth, as he had seen them with the Ghost of Christmas Present; and walking with his hands behind him, Scrooge regarded every one with a delighted smile. He looked so irresistibly pleasant, in a word, that three or four good-humoured fellows said, "Good morning, sir! A merry Christmas to you!" And Scrooge said often afterwards, that of all the blithe sounds he had ever heard, those were the blithest in his ears.

He had not gone far, when coming on towards him he beheld the portly gentleman, who had walked into his counting-house the day before, and said, "Scrooge and Marley's, I believe?" It sent a pang across his heart to think how this old gentleman would look upon him when they met; but he knew what path lay straight before him, and he took it.

"My dear sir," said Scrooge, quickening his pace, and taking the old gentleman by both his hands.

"How do you do? I hope you succeeded yesterday. It was very kind of you. A merry Christmas to you, sir!"

"Mr. Scrooge?"

"Yes," said Scrooge. "That is my name, and I fear it may not be pleasant to you. Allow me to ask your pardon. And will you have the goodness"—here Scrooge whispered in his ear.

"Lord bless me!" cried the gentleman, as if his breath were taken away. "My dear Mr. Scrooge, are you serious?"

"If you please," said Scrooge. "Not a farthing less. A great many back-payments are included in it, I assure you. Will you do me that favour?"

"My dear sir," said the other, shaking hands with him. "I don't know what to say to such munifi—"

"Don't say anything, please," retorted Scrooge. "Come and see me. Will you come and see me?"

"I will!" cried the old gentleman. And it was clear he meant to do it.

"Thank'ee," said Scrooge. "I am much obliged to you. I thank you fifty times. Bless you!"

He went to church, and walked about the streets, and watched the people hurrying to and fro, and patted children on the head, and questioned beggars, and looked down into the kitchens of houses, and up to the windows, and found that everything could yield him pleasure. He had never dreamed that any walk—that anything—could give him so much happiness. In the afternoon he turned his steps towards his nephew's house.

He passed the door a dozen times, before he had the courage to go up and knock. But he made a dash, and did it:

"Is your master at home, my dear?" said Scrooge to the girl. Nice girl! Very.

"Yes, sir."

"Where is he, my love?" said Scrooge.

"He's in the dining-room, sir, along with mistress. I'll show you up stairs, if you please."

"Thank'ee. He knows me," said Scrooge, with his hand already on the dining-room lock. "I'll go in here, my dear."

He turned it gently, and sidled his face in, round the door. They were looking at the table (which was spread out in great array); for these young housekeepers are always nervous on such points, and like to see that everything is right.

"Fred!" said Scrooge.

Dear heart alive, how his niece by marriage started! Scrooge had forgotten, for the moment, about her sitting in the corner with the footstool, or he wouldn't have done it, on any account.

"Why bless my soul!" cried Fred, "who's that?"

"It's I. Your uncle Scrooge. I have come to dinner. Will you let me in, Fred?"

Let him in! It is a mercy he didn't shake his arm off. He was at home in five minutes. Nothing could be heartier. His niece looked just the same. So did Topper when *he* came. So did the plump sister when she came. So did every one when *they* came. Wonderful party, wonderful games, wonderful unanimity, won-der-ful happiness!

But he was early at the office next morning. Oh, he was early there. If he could only be there first, and catch Bob Cratchit coming late! That was the thing he had set his heart upon.

And he did it; yes, he did! The clock struck nine. No Bob. A quarter past. No Bob. He was full eighteen minutes and a half behind his time. Scrooge sat with his door wide open, that he might see him come into the Tank.

His hat was off, before he opened the door; his comforter too. He was on his stool in a jiffy; driving away with his pen, as if he were trying to overtake nine o'clock.

"Hallo!" growled Scrooge, in his accustomed voice, as near as he could feign it. "What do you mean by coming here at this time of day?"

"I am very sorry, sir," said Bob. "I *am* behind my time."

"You are?" repeated Scrooge. "Yes. I think you are. Step this way, sir, if you please."

"It's only once a year, sir," pleaded Bob, appearing from the Tank. "It shall not be repeated. I was making rather merry yesterday, sir."

"Now, I'll tell you what, my friend," said Scrooge, "I am not going to stand this sort of thing any longer. And therefore," he continued, leaping from his stool, and giving Bob such a dig in the waistcoat that he staggered back into the Tank again: "and therefore I am about to raise your salary!"

Bob trembled, and got a little nearer to the ruler. He had a momentary idea of knocking Scrooge down with it, holding him, and calling to the people in the court for help and a strait-waistcoat.

"A merry Christmas, Bob!" said Scrooge, with an earnestness that could not be mistaken, as he clapped him on the back. "A merrier Christmas, Bob, my good fellow, than I have given you, for many a year! I'll raise your salary, and endeavour to assist your struggling family, and we will discuss your affairs this very afternoon,

over a Christmas bowl of smoking bishop, Bob! Make up the fires, and buy another coal-scuttle before you dot another i, Bob Cratchit!"

Scrooge was better than his word. He did it all, and infinitely more; and to Tiny Tim, who did NOT die, he was a second father. He became as good a friend, as good a master, and as good a man, as the good old city knew, or any other good old city, town, or borough, in the good old world. Some people laughed to see the alteration in him, but he let them laugh, and little heeded them; for he was wise enough to know that nothing ever happened on this globe, for good, at which some people did not have their fill of laughter in the outset; and knowing that such as these would be blind anyway, he thought it quite as well that they should wrinkle up their eyes in grins, as have the malady in less attractive forms. His own heart laughed: and that was quite enough for him.

He had no further intercourse with Spirits, but lived upon the Total Abstinence Principle, ever afterwards; and it was always said of him, that he knew how to keep Christmas well, if any man alive possessed the knowledge. May that be truly said of us, and all of us! And so, as Tiny Tim observed, God bless Us, Every One!

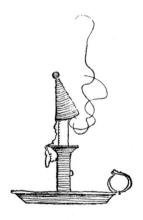

THE DOLL THAT SANTA CLAUS BROUGHT

KATHARINE CARRINGTON

On the stoop of a city house stood a little girl. Her thoughts were filled with Santa Claus, and the wonderful things he would bring her.

But Maude was thinking more of Santa Claus himself than of his gifts, and a determination to see the dear old man who loved children so, and who had been so kind to her, filled her little head. And in its wake came the determination to see him that very night. "For," thought Maude, "so kind an old gentleman will not really be displeased with me for wanting to thank him for the toys he has brought." And she smiled to think how astonished papa would be in the morning when she told him what Santa Claus had said.

So she went into the library, where papa sat smoking, and waiting to bid his little girl good night. Together they hung the Christmas stocking, and the little heart beat fast as she pictured Santa Claus standing where her father stood, on the hearth-rug just —opposite the great window.

She went to bed dreaming of the coming interview, and meaning to lie awake until Santa Claus came; but soon the waking dreams became real ones, and Maude slept in her cozy little bed.

* * * * *

In another quarter of the great city, a squalid quarter where Maude had never been, lived a ragged, hungry little girl, who had never heard of Santa Claus until to-day. Her home was a basement room, scantily furnished, and unheated; but as she stood on the step, cold, hunger, everything was forgotten in the rapture that had been imparted to her by a dirty little urchin, as cold and hungry as herself. For Maggie had listened with bated breath while he told her about a wonderful old man named Santa Claus, who had lived for hundreds of years, and who loved children so that he had a mysterious workshop where he made beautiful toys for them. And Bob had told her that this very night Santa Claus would harness his reindeer to his sleigh, and would ride through the snow to the city, bringing something to every child. "Even to us, Maggie; to you and to me! Only you must hang up yer stockin', or he won't know as you wants anythink, and then he won't stop."

And Maggie was in raptures. Perhaps he would bring her a doll! And head and heart were so full of the pictured dolly that she did not see her tired father, who had been all day unsuccessfully seeking work.

He spoke to her, and she started, and remembered how cold it was, and that there was almost nothing to eat in the house, and she went quickly and helped prepare the scanty meal, and when he had sat down to it she told him. The great news could be kept no longer. And when he looked at her so sadly, she was too absorbed in thoughts of Santa Claus to notice it. She sat on the old, broken-down stool, and pictured to herself a doll.

"And *there* is where she will stand!" she said; "and she will have golding curls, and a red gownd with a long trail, like the one I seen in the shop, and a big hat with a white feather sweepin' round it, and lace on her gownd, and a string of gold beads on her neck, and red shoes and stockin's. And oh, when I wakes in the morning, *there* she will stand! And I will call her Evangerliner, and it will be grand—just grand!" and Maggie clapped her blue little hands and danced for joy.

Her father sat very still, and she went on with her talk: "And I must take off my stockin' and hang it up by a pin to the wall, or he will think I don't want anythink. That foot will be dretful cold to-night, but I ain't got no other stockin's, and I can stand it for just one night."

And off came the ragged stocking, and Maggie pinned it up against the wall, where it would greet her opening eyes; then, running quickly to her bed, pulled the thin quilt over her, and shut her eyes tight, that morning might come the sooner.

The man sat for a time with his head in his hands, the great tears falling between his fingers, and when he raised his head his eyes were hard. Taking his hat, he walked out of the house. He went directly to the rich quarter of the city. As he tramped along, his attention was arrested by the soft glow of firelight shining through an unshaded window. He drew near and looked in, and something seemed to grip his throat, for there, directly facing him in the glare of the firelight, among a multitude of books and toys, stood the doll of Maggie's imagination—"red gownd, sweepin' feather, gold necklace," and all, just as Maggie had pictured her!

* * * * *

Maude opened her bright eyes and sat up in bed to listen. Yes! There was certainly a noise in the library. Santa Claus had come! So, with beating heart, she slipped out of bed very quietly, and crept down the stairway, and, opening the door of the library, tripped softly in. Yes, there he was! Books and toys were grouped about the hearth, and he was bending over a big doll in a long red frock.

"Oh, Mr. Santa Claus," she said, "I want to thank you for all the pretty things you have brought me; and please do not be angry with me, dear Mr. Santa Claus, because I love you so!"

The figure holding the doll stood erect and wheeled about.

"Why!" cried Maude, "are you Santa Claus? I didn't know Santa Claus looked like that! I thought he was fat and rosy and jolly; and you are thin and poor-looking, and your eyes—your eyes frighten me! Oh, if you please, Santa Claus, don't be angry! I am very sorry, and I didn't know you would mind what I said. I didn't think!"

The color came into the man's face, and he said in a low, shamed voice: "I ain't angry, little girl; only I was just thinkin' of takin' this 'ere doll to another little girl as ain't got no doll. But I won't, if you'll just be quiet and not call anybody."

"No," said Maude; "I won't call my father, because I know you don't like people to see you. That doll is just lovely, but you may have it, if you will give it to that little girl who has no doll, for I have a great many, you know. And are you going now, and may I see you go, and will you go up the chimney? I never supposed Santa Claus could look like you, or that he would talk like you, either. I think I am sorry I saw you," and tears came into the earnest eyes, "because I loved you so much before. But I will try to like you, Santa Claus, because you are so good."

The man's face grew red again as the child spoke, and he hesitated; but his eyes fell on the dainty stocking crammed with Christmas goodies, and he thought of that other stocking, hanging thin and empty opposite Maggie's bed, and he walked with the doll in his arms toward the window.

"Oh," cried Maude, "are you going—and out of the window? I thought you would go up the chimney! I thought Santa Claus always went up the chimney!" and Maude was ready to cry again.

But the man was gone. He had climbed out of the window, and was lost in the darkness without.

Feeling queer and frightened, Maude turned without a glance at the toys scattered over the carpet, and crept back to bed, where she sobbed herself to sleep.

The next morning Mr. Page was much disturbed by the open window and the missing doll, as well as by Maude's listlessness over her gifts; for Maude could not bear to tell even papa what a dreadful man Santa Claus was, and she hugged her grief in silence. But soon all was made clear. The butler announced a man to see Mr. Page, and when he entered, Maude, who sat on her father's knee, sprang up, exclaiming, "Why, it's Santa Claus!"

"No, miss," said the man, at once; "I ain't Santa Claus."

And then, speaking rapidly, he told Mr. Page the whole story of Maggie's happy expectancy, and her empty stocking; of the open window, and the doll like the one of Maggie's fancy; how Maude's trust had shamed him; "For," he said, "I ain't no thief— leastways, not ever before"; how the thought of the empty stocking had turned the scale; and of Maggie's rapture when the doll greeted her opening eyes; and he wound up by begging Mr. Page to punish him in any way he chose, but not to take her one treasure from innocent Maggie.

And Mr. Page's eyes filled with tears as he looked at his own little daughter, and thought of the other child in the bare tenement with her one treasure.

To the man he gave work, that he might repay by honest labor the price of the doll; and to this day the crowning glory of Maggie's life is "the doll that Santa Claus brought."

A CHRISTMAS DREAM, AND HOW IT CAME TO BE TRUE

LOUISA MAY ALCOTT

"I'm so tired of Christmas I wish there never would be another one!" exclaimed a discontented-looking little girl, as she sat idly watching her mother arrange a pile of gifts two days before they were to be given.

"Why, Effie, what a dreadful thing to say! You are as bad as old Scrooge; and I'm afraid something will happen to you, as it did to him, if you don't care for dear Christmas," answered mamma, almost dropping the silver horn she was filling with delicious candies.

"Who was Scrooge? What happened to him?" asked Effie, with a glimmer of interest in her listless face, as she picked out the sourest lemon-drop she could find; for nothing sweet suited her just then.

"He was one of Dickens's best people, and you can read the charming story some day. He hated Christmas until a strange dream showed him how dear and beautiful it was, and made a better man of him."

"I shall read it; for I like dreams, and have a great many curious ones myself. But they don't keep me from being tired of Christmas," said Effie, poking discontentedly among the sweeties for something worth eating.

"Why are you tired of what should be the happiest time of all the year?" asked mamma, anxiously.

"Perhaps I shouldn't be if I had something new. But it is always the same, and there isn't any more surprise about it. I always find heaps of goodies in my stocking. Don't like some of them, and soon get tired of those I do like. We always have a great dinner, and I eat too much, and feel ill next day. Then there is a Christmas tree somewhere, with a doll on top, or a stupid old Santa Claus, and children dancing and screaming over bonbons and toys that break, and shiny things that are of no use. Really, mamma, I've had so many Christmases all alike that I don't think I *can* bear another one." And Effie laid herself flat on the sofa, as if the mere idea was too much for her.

Her mother laughed at her despair, but was sorry to see her little girl so discontented, when she had everything to make her happy, and had known but ten Christmas days.

"Suppose we don't give you *any* presents at all,—how would that suit you?" asked mamma, anxious to please her spoiled child.

"I should like one large and splendid one, and one dear little one, to remember some very nice person by," said Effie, who was a fanciful little body, full of odd whims and notions, which her friends loved to gratify, regardless of time, trouble, or money; for she was the last of three little girls, and very dear to all the family.

"Well, my darling, I will see what I can do to please you, and not say a word until all is ready. If I could only get a new idea to start with!" And mamma went on tying up her pretty bundles with a thoughtful face, while Effie strolled to the window to watch the rain that kept her in-doors and made her dismal.

"Seems to me poor children have better times than rich ones. I can't go out, and there is a girl about my age splashing along, without any maid to fuss about rubbers and cloaks and umbrellas and colds. I wish I was a beggar-girl."

"Would you like to be hungry, cold, and ragged, to beg all day, and sleep on an ash-heap at night?" asked mamma, wondering what would come next.

"Cinderella did, and had a nice time in the end. This girl out here has a basket of scraps on her arm, and a big old shawl all round her, and doesn't seem to care a bit, though the water runs out of the toes of her boots. She goes paddling along, laughing

101

at the rain, and eating a cold potato as if it tasted nicer than the chicken and ice-cream I had for dinner. Yes, I do think poor children are happier than rich ones."

"So do I, sometimes. At the Orphan Asylum today I saw two dozen merry little souls who have no parents, no home, and no hope of Christmas beyond a stick of candy or a cake. I wish you had been there to see how happy they were, playing with the old toys some richer children had sent them."

"You may give them all mine; I'm so tired of them I never want to see them again," said Effie, turning from the window to the pretty baby-house full of everything a child's heart could desire.

"I will, and let you begin again with something you will not tire of, if I can only find it." And mamma knit her brows trying to discover some grand surprise for this child who didn't care for Christmas.

Nothing more was said then; and wandering off to the library, Effie found "A Christmas Carol," and curling herself up in the sofa corner, read it all before tea. Some of it she did not understand; but she laughed and cried over many parts of the charming story, and felt better without knowing why.

All the evening she thought of poor Tiny Tim, Mrs. Cratchit with the pudding, and the stout old gentleman who danced so gayly that "his legs twinkled in the air." Presently bedtime arrived.

"Come, now, and toast your feet," said Effie's nurse, "while I do your pretty hair and tell stories."

"I'll have a fairy tale to-night, a very interesting one," commanded Effie, as she put on her blue silk wrapper and little fur-lined slippers to sit before the fire and have her long curls brushed.

So Nursey told her best tales; and when at last the child lay down under her lace curtains, her head was full of a curious jumble of Christmas elves, poor children, snow-storms, sugarplums, and surprises. So it is no wonder that she dreamed all night; and this was the dream, which she never quite forgot.

She found herself sitting on a stone, in the middle of a great field, all alone. The snow was falling fast, a bitter wind whistled by, and night was coming on. She felt hungry, cold, and tired, and did not know where to go nor what to do.

"I wanted to be a beggar-girl, and now I am one; but I don't like it, and wish somebody would come and take care of me. I don't know who I am, and I think I must be lost," thought Effie, with the curious interest one takes in one's self in dreams. But the more she thought about it, the more bewildered she felt. Faster fell the snow, colder blew the wind, darker grew the night; and poor Effie made up her mind that she was quite forgotten and left to freeze alone. The tears were chilled on her cheeks, her feet felt like icicles, and her heart died within her, so hungry, frightened, and forlorn was she. Laying her head on her knees, she gave herself up for lost, and sat there with the great flakes fast turning her to a little white mound, when suddenly the sound of music reached her, and starting up, she looked and listened with all her eyes and ears.

Far away a dim light shone, and a voice was heard singing. She tried to run toward the welcome glimmer, but could not stir, and stood like a small statue of expectation while the light drew nearer, and the sweet words of the song grew clearer.

"From our happy home
    Through the world we roam
One week in all the year,
    Making winter spring
    With the joy we bring,
For Christmas-tide is here.

    Now the eastern star
    Shines from afar
To light the poorest home;
    Hearts warmer grow,
    Gifts freely flow,
For Christmas-tide has come.

    Now gay trees rise
    Before young eyes,

Abloom with tempting cheer;
  Blithe voices sing,
  And blithe bells ring,
For Christmas-tide is here.

  Oh, happy chime,
  Oh, blessed time,
That draws us all so near!
  'Welcome, dear day,'
  All creatures say,
For Christmas-tide is here."

A child's voice sang, a child's hand carried the little candle; and in the circle of soft light it shed, Effie saw a pretty child coming to her through the night and snow. A rosy, smiling creature, wrapped in white fur, with a wreath of green and scarlet holly on its shining hair, the magic candle in one hand, and the other outstretched as if to shower gifts and warmly press all other hands.

Effie forgot to speak as this bright vision came nearer, leaving no trace of footsteps in the snow, only lighting the way with its little candle, and filling the air with the music of its song.

"Dear child, you are lost, and I have come to find you," said the stranger, taking Effie's cold hands in his, with a smile like sunshine, while every holly berry glowed like a little fire.

"Do you know me?" asked Effie, feeling no fear, but a great gladness, at his coming.

"I know all children, and go to find them; for this is my holiday, and I gather them from all parts of the world to be merry with me once a year."

"Are you an angel?" asked Effie, looking for the wings.

"No; I am a Christmas spirit, and live with my mates in a pleasant place, getting ready for our holiday, when we are let out to roam about the world, helping make this a happy time for all who will let us in. Will you come and see how we work?"

"I will go anywhere with you. Don't leave me again," cried Effie, gladly.

"First I will make you comfortable. That is what we love to do. You are cold, and you shall be warm; hungry, and I will feed you; sorrowful, and I will make you gay."

With a wave of his candle all three miracles were wrought,—for the snow-flakes turned to a white fur cloak and hood on Effie's head and shoulders, a bowl of hot soup came sailing to her lips, and vanished when she had eagerly drunk the last drop; and suddenly the dismal field changed to a new world so full of wonders that all her troubles were forgotten in a minute. Bells were ringing so merrily that it was hard to keep from dancing. Green garlands hung on the walls, and every tree was a Christmas tree full of toys, and blazing with candles that never went out.

In one place many little spirits sewed like mad on warm clothes, turning off work faster than any sewing-machine ever invented, and great piles were made ready to be sent to poor people. Other busy creatures packed money into purses, and wrote checks which they sent flying away on the wind,—a lovely kind of snow-storm to fall into a world below full of poverty. Older and graver spirits were looking over piles of little books, in which the records of the past year were kept, telling how different people had spent it, and what sort of gifts they deserved. Some got peace, some disappointment, some remorse and sorrow, some great joy and hope. The rich had generous thoughts sent them; the poor, gratitude and contentment. Children had more love and duty to parents; and parents renewed patience, wisdom, and satisfaction for and in their children. No one was forgotten.

"Please tell me what splendid place this is?" asked Effie, as soon as she could collect her wits after the first look at all these astonishing things.

"This is the Christmas world; and here we work all the year round, never tired of getting ready for the happy day. See, these are the saints just setting off; for some have far to go, and the children must not be disappointed."

As he spoke the spirit pointed to four gates, out of which four great sleighs were just driving, laden with toys, while a jolly old Santa Claus sat in the middle of each, drawing on his mittens and tucking up his wraps for a long cold drive.

"Why, I thought there was only one Santa Claus, and even he was a humbug," cried Effie, astonished at the sight.

"Never give up your faith in the sweet old stories, even after you come to see that they are only the pleasant shadow of a lovely truth."

Just then the sleighs went off with a great jingling of bells and pattering of reindeer hoofs, while all the spirits gave a cheer that was heard in the lower world, where people said, "Hear the stars sing."

"I never will say there isn't any Santa Claus again. Now, show me more."

"You will like to see this place, I think, and may learn something here perhaps."

The spirit smiled as he led the way to a little door, through which Effie peeped into a world of dolls. Baby-houses were in full blast, with dolls of all sorts going on like live people. Waxen ladies sat in their parlors elegantly dressed; black dolls cooked in the kitchens; nurses walked out with the bits of dollies; and the streets were full of tin soldiers marching, wooden horses prancing, express wagons rumbling, and little men hurrying to and fro. Shops were there, and tiny people buying legs of mutton, pounds of tea, mites of clothes, and everything dolls use or wear or want.

But presently she saw that in some ways the dolls improved upon the manners and customs of human beings, and she watched eagerly to learn why they did these things. A fine Paris doll driving in her carriage took up a black worsted Dinah who was hobbling along with a basket of clean clothes, and carried her to her journey's end, as if it were the proper thing to do. Another interesting china lady took off her comfortable red cloak and put it round a poor wooden creature done up in a paper shift, and so badly painted that its face would have sent some babies into fits.

"Seems to me I once knew a rich girl who didn't give her things to poor girls. I wish I could remember who she was, and tell her to be as kind as that china doll," said Effie, much touched at the sweet way the pretty creature wrapped up the poor fright, and then ran off in her little gray gown to buy a shiny fowl stuck on a wooden platter for her invalid mother's dinner.

"We recall these things to people's minds by dreams. I think the girl you speak of won't forget this one." And the spirit smiled, as if he enjoyed some joke which she did not see.

A little bell rang as she looked, and away scampered the children into the red-and-green school-house with the roof that lifted up, so one could see how nicely they sat at their desks with mites of books, or drew on the inch-square blackboards with crumbs of chalk.

"They know their lessons very well, and are as still as mice. We make a great racket at our school, and get bad marks every day. I shall tell the girls they had better mind what they do, or their dolls will be better scholars than they are," said Effie, much impressed, as she peeped in and saw no rod in the hand of the little mistress, who looked up and shook her head at the intruder, as if begging her to go away before the order of the school was disturbed.

Effie retired at once, but could not resist one look in at the window of a fine mansion, where the family were at dinner, the children behaved so well at table, and never grumbled a bit when their mamma said they could not have any more fruit.

"Now, show me something else," she said, as they came again to the low door that led out of Doll-land.

"You have seen how we prepare for Christmas; let me show you where we love best to send our good and happy gifts," answered the spirit, giving her his hand again.

"I know. I've seen ever so many," began Effie, thinking of her own Christmases.

"No, you have never seen what I will show you. Come away, and remember what you see to-night."

Like a flash that bright world vanished, and Effie found herself in a part of the city she had never seen before. It was far away from the gayer places, where every store was brilliant with lights and full of pretty things, and every house wore a festival air, while people hurried to and fro with merry greetings. It was down among the dingy streets where the poor lived, and where there was no making ready for Christmas.

Hungry women looked in at the shabby shops, longing to buy meat and bread, but empty pockets forbade. Tipsy men drank up their wages in the bar-rooms; and in many cold dark chambers little children huddled under the thin blankets, trying to forget their misery in sleep.

No nice dinners filled the air with savory smells, no gay trees dropped toys and bonbons into eager hands, no little stockings hung in rows beside the chimney-piece ready to be filled, no happy sounds of music, gay voices, and dancing feet were heard; and there were no signs of Christmas anywhere.

"Don't they have any in this place?" asked Effie, shivering, as she held fast the spirit's hand, following where he led her.

"We come to bring it. Let me show you our best workers." And the spirit pointed to some sweet-faced men and women who came stealing into the poor houses, working such beautiful miracles that Effie could only stand and watch.

Some slipped money into the empty pockets, and sent the happy mothers to buy all the comforts they needed; others led the drunken men out of temptation, and took them home to find safer pleasures there. Fires were kindled on cold hearths, tables spread as if by magic, and warm clothes wrapped round shivering limbs. Flowers suddenly bloomed in the chambers of the sick; old people found themselves remembered; sad hearts were consoled by a tender word, and wicked ones softened by the story of Him who forgave all sin.

But the sweetest work was for the children; and Effie held her breath to watch these human fairies hang up and fill the little stockings without which a child's Christmas is not perfect, putting in things that once she would have thought very humble presents, but which now seemed beautiful and precious because these poor babies had nothing.

"That is so beautiful! I wish I could make merry Christmases as these good people do, and be loved and thanked as they are," said Effie, softly, as she watched the busy men and women do their work and steal away without thinking of any reward but their own satisfaction.

"You can if you will. I have shown you the way. Try it, and see how happy your own holiday will be hereafter."

As he spoke, the spirit seemed to put his arms about her, and vanished with a kiss.

"Oh, stay and show me more!" cried Effie, trying to hold him fast.

"Darling, wake up, and tell me why you are smiling in your sleep," said a voice in her ear; and opening her eyes, there was mamma bending over her, and morning sunshine streaming into the room.

"Are they all gone? Did you hear the bells? Wasn't it splendid?" she asked, rubbing her eyes, and looking about her for the pretty child who was so real and sweet.

"You have been dreaming at a great rate,—talking in your sleep, laughing, and clapping your hands as if you were cheering some one. Tell me what was so splendid," said mamma, smoothing the tumbled hair and lifting up the sleepy head. Then, while she was being dressed, Effie told her dream, and Nursey thought it very wonderful;

but mamma smiled to see how curiously things the child had thought, read, heard, and seen through the day were mixed up in her sleep.

"The spirit said I could work lovely miracles if I tried; but I don't know how to begin, for I have no magic candle to make feasts appear, and light up groves of Christmas trees, as he did," said Effie, sorrowfully.

"Yes, you have. We will do it! we will do it!" And clapping her hands, mamma suddenly began to dance all over the room as if she had lost her wits.

"How? how? You must tell me, mamma," cried Effie, dancing after her, and ready to believe anything possible when she remembered the adventures of the past night.

"I've got it! I've got it!—the new idea. A splendid one, if I can only carry it out!" And mamma waltzed the little girl round till her curls flew wildly in the air, while Nursey laughed as if she would die.

"Tell me! tell me!" shrieked Effie.

"No, no; it is a surprise,—a grand surprise for Christmas day!" sung mamma, evidently charmed with her happy thought. "Now, come to breakfast; for we must work like bees if we want to play spirits tomorrow. You and Nursey will go out shopping, and get heaps of things, while I arrange matters behind the scenes."

They were running downstairs as mamma spoke, and Effie called out breathlessly,—

"It won't be a surprise; for I know you are going to ask some poor children here, and have a tree or something. It won't be like my dream; for they had ever so many trees, and more children than we can find anywhere."

"There will be no tree, no party, no dinner, in this house at all, and no presents for you. Won't that be a surprise?" And mamma laughed at Effie's bewildered face.

"Do it. I shall like it, I think; and I won't ask any questions, so it will all burst upon me when the time comes," she said; and she ate her breakfast thoughtfully, for this really would be a new sort of Christmas.

All that morning Effie trotted after Nursey in and out of shops, buying dozens of barking dogs, woolly lambs, and squeaking birds; tiny tea-sets, gay picture-books, mittens and hoods, dolls and candy. Parcel after parcel was sent home; but when Effie returned she saw no trace of them, though she peeped everywhere. Nursey chuckled, but wouldn't give a hint, and went out again in the afternoon with a long list of more things to buy; while Effie wandered forlornly about the house, missing the usual merry stir that went before the Christmas dinner and the evening fun.

As for mamma, she was quite invisible all day, and came in at night so tired that she could only lie on the sofa to rest, smiling as if some very pleasant thought made her happy in spite of weariness.

"Is the surprise going on all right?" asked Effie, anxiously; for it seemed an immense time to wait till another evening came.

"Beautifully! better than I expected; for several of my good friends are helping, or I couldn't have done it as I wish. I know you will like it, dear, and long remember this new way of making Christmas merry."

Mamma gave her a very tender kiss, and Effie went to bed.

The next day was a very strange one; for when she woke there was no stocking to examine, no pile of gifts under her napkin, no one said "Merry Christmas!" to her, and the dinner was just as usual to her. Mamma vanished again, and Nurse kept wiping her eyes and saying: "The dear things! It's the prettiest idea I ever heard of. No one but your blessed ma could have done it."

"Do stop, Nursey, or I shall go crazy because I don't know the secret!" cried Effie, more than once; and she kept her eye on the clock, for at seven in the evening the surprise was to come off.

The longed-for hour arrived at last, and the child was too excited to ask questions when Nurse put on her cloak and hood, led her to the carriage, and they drove away, leaving their house the one dark and silent one in the row. "I feel like the girls in the fairy tales who are led off to strange places and see fine things," said Effie, in a whisper, as they jingled through the gay streets.

"Ah, my deary, it *is* like a fairy tale, I do assure you, and you will see finer things than most children will tonight. Steady, now, and do just as I tell you, and don't say one word whatever you see," answered Nurse, quite quivering with excitement as she patted a large box in her lap, and nodded and laughed with twinkling eyes.

They drove into a dark yard, and Effie was led through a back door to a little room, where Nurse coolly proceeded to take off not only her cloak and hood, but her dress and shoes also. Effie stared and bit her lips, but kept still until out of the box came a little white fur coat and boots, a wreath of holly leaves and berries, and a candle with a frill of gold paper round it. A long "Oh!" escaped her then; and when she was dressed and saw herself in the glass, she started back, exclaiming, "Why, Nursey, I look like the spirit in my dream!"

"So you do; and that's the part you are to play, my pretty! Now whist, while I blind your eyes and put you in your place."

"Shall I be afraid?" whispered Effie, full of wonder; for as they went out she heard the sound of many voices, the tramp of many feet, and, in spite of the bandage, was sure a great light shone upon her when she stopped.

"You needn't be; I shall stand close by, and your ma will be there."

After the handkerchief was tied about her eyes, Nurse led Effie up some steps, and placed her on a high platform, where something like leaves touched her head, and the soft snap of lamps seemed to fill the air. Music began as soon as Nurse clapped her hands, the voices outside sounded nearer, and the tramp was evidently coming up the stairs.

"Now, my precious, look and see how you and your dear ma have made a merry Christmas for them that needed it!"

Off went the bandage; and for a minute Effie really did think she was asleep again, for she actually stood in "a grove of Christmas trees," all gay and shining as in her vision. Twelve on a side, in two rows down the room, stood the little pines, each on its low table; and behind Effie a taller one rose to the roof, hung with wreaths of popcorn, apples, oranges, horns of candy, and cakes of all sorts, from sugary hearts to gingerbread Jumbos. On the smaller trees she saw many of her own discarded toys and those Nursey bought, as well as heaps that seemed to have rained down straight from that delightful Christmas country where she felt as if she was again.

"How splendid! Who is it for? What is that noise? Where is mamma?" cried Effie, pale with pleasure and surprise, as she stood looking down the brilliant little street from her high place.

Before Nurse could answer, the doors at the lower end flew open, and in marched twenty-four little blue-gowned orphan girls, singing sweetly, until amazement changed the song to cries of joy and wonder as the shining spectacle appeared. While they stood staring with round eyes at the wilderness of pretty things about them, mamma stepped up beside Effie, and holding her hand fast to give her courage, told the story of the dream in a few simple words, ending in this way:—

"So my little girl wanted to be a Christmas spirit too, and make this a happy day for those who had not as many pleasures and comforts as she has. She likes surprises, and we planned this for you all. She shall play the good fairy, and give each of you something from this tree, after which every one will find her own name on a small tree, and can go to enjoy it in her own way. March by, my dears, and let us fill your hands."

Nobody told them to do it, but all the hands were clapped heartily before a single child stirred; then one by one they came to look up wonderingly at the pretty giver of the feast as she leaned down to offer them great yellow oranges, red apples, bunches of grapes, bonbons, and cakes, till all were gone, and a double row of smiling faces turned toward her as the children filed back to their places in the orderly way they had been taught.

Then each was led to her own tree by the good ladies who had helped mamma with all their hearts; and the happy hubbub that arose would have satisfied even Santa Claus himself,—shrieks of joy, dances of delight, laughter and tears (for some tender little things could not bear so much pleasure at once, and sobbed with mouths full of candy and hands full of toys). How they ran to show one another the new treasures! how they peeped and tasted, pulled and pinched, until the air was full of queer noises, the floor covered with papers, and the little trees left bare of all but candles!

"I don't think heaven can be any gooder than this," sighed one small girl, as she looked about her in a blissful maze, holding her full apron with one hand, while she luxuriously carried sugar-plums to her mouth with the other.

"Is that a truly angel up there?" asked another, fascinated by the little white figure with the wreath on its shining hair, who in some mysterious way had been the cause of all this merry-making.

"I wish I dared to go and kiss her for this splendid party," said a lame child, leaning on her crutch, as she stood near the steps, wondering how it seemed to sit in a mother's lap, as Effie was doing, while she watched the happy scene before her. Effie heard her, and remembering Tiny Tim, ran down and put her arms about the pale child, kissing the wistful face, as she said sweetly, "You may; but mamma deserves the thanks. She did it all; I only dreamed about it."

Lame Katy felt as if "a truly angel" was embracing her, and could only stammer out her thanks, while the other children ran to see the pretty spirit, and touch her soft dress, until she stood in a crowd of blue gowns laughing as they held up their gifts for her to see and admire.

Mamma leaned down and whispered one word to the older girls; and suddenly they all took hands to dance round Effie, singing as they skipped.

It was a pretty sight, and the ladies found it hard to break up the happy revel; but it was late for small people, and too much fun is a mistake. So the girls fell into line, and marched before Effie and mamma again, to say goodnight with such grateful little faces that the eyes of those who looked grew dim with tears. Mamma kissed every one; and many a hungry childish heart felt as if the touch of those tender lips was their best gift. Effie shook so many small hands that her own tingled; and when Katy came she pressed a small doll into Effie's hand, whispering, "You didn't have a single present, and we had lots. Do keep that; it's the prettiest thing I got."

"I will," answered Effie, and held it fast until the last smiling face was gone, the surprise all over, and she safe in her own bed, too tired and happy for anything but sleep.

"Mamma, it *was* a beautiful surprise, and I thank you so much! I don't see how you did it; but I like it best of all the Christmases I ever had, and mean to make one every year. I had my splendid big present, and here is the dear little one to keep for love of poor Katy; so even that part of my wish came true."

And Effie fell asleep with a happy smile on her lips, her one humble gift still in her hand, and a new love for Christmas in her heart that never changed through a long life spent in doing good.

OLD CHRISTMAS

WASHINGTON IRVING

A man might then behold
  At Christmas, in each hall
Good fires to curb the cold,
  And meat for great and small.
The neighbors were friendly bidden,
  And all had welcome true,
The poor from the gates were not chidden
  When this old cap was new.

Old Song

Nothing in England exercises a more delightful spell over my imagination than the lingerings of the holiday customs and rural games of former times. They recall the pictures my fancy used to draw in the May morning of life, when as yet I only knew

the world through books, and believed it to be all that poets had painted it; and they bring with them the flavor of those honest days of yore, in which, perhaps with equal fallacy, I am apt to think the world was more homebred, social, and joyous than at present. I regret to say that they are daily growing more and more faint, being gradually worn away by time, but still more obliterated by modern fashion. They resemble those picturesque morsels of Gothic architecture which we see crumbling in various parts of the country, partly dilapidated by the waste of ages and partly lost in the additions and alterations of latter days. Poetry, however, clings with cherishing fondness about the

rural game and holiday revel from which it has derived so many of its themes, as the ivy winds its rich foliage about the Gothic arch and mouldering tower, gratefully repaying their support by clasping together their tottering remains, and, as it were, embalming them in verdure.

Of all the old festivals, however, that of Christmas awakens the strongest and most heartfelt associations. There is a tone of solemn and sacred feeling that blends with our conviviality and lifts the spirit to a state of hallowed and elevated enjoyment. The services of the Church about this season are extremely tender and inspiring. They dwell on the beautiful story of the origin of our faith and the pastoral scenes that accompanied its announcement. They gradually increase in fervor and pathos during the season of Advent, until they break forth in full jubilee on the morning that brought peace and good-will to men. I do not know a grander effect of music on the moral feelings than to hear the full choir and the pealing organ performing a Christmas anthem in a cathedral, and filling every part of the vast pile with triumphant harmony.

It is a beautiful arrangement, also, derived from days of yore, that this festival, which commemorates the announcement of the religion of peace and love, has been made the season for gathering together of family connections, and drawing closer again those bands of kindred hearts which the cares and pleasures and sorrows of the world are continually operating to cast loose; of calling back the children of a family who have launched forth in life and wandered widely asunder, once more to assemble about the paternal hearth, that rallying-place of the affections, there to grow young and loving again among the endearing mementos of childhood.

There is something in the very season of the year that gives a charm to the festivity of Christmas. At other times we derive a great portion of our pleasures from the mere beauties of Nature. Our feelings sally forth and dissipate themselves over the sunny landscape, and we "live abroad and everywhere." The song of the bird, the murmur of the stream, the breathing fragrance of spring, the soft voluptuousness of summer, the golden pomp of autumn, earth with its mantle of refreshing green, and heaven with it deep delicious blue and its cloudy magnificence,—all fill us with mute but exquisite delight, and we revel in the luxury of mere sensation. But in the depth of winter, when Nature lies despoiled of every charm and wrapped in her shroud of sheeted snow, we turn for our gratifications to moral sources. The dreariness and desolation of the landscape, the short gloomy days and darksome nights, while they circumscribe our wanderings, shut in our feelings also from rambling abroad, and make us more keenly disposed for the pleasure of the social circle. Our thoughts are more concentrated; our friendly sympathies more aroused. We feel more sensibly the charm of each other's society, and are brought more closely together by dependence on each other for enjoyment. Heart calleth unto heart, and we draw our pleasures from the deep wells of loving-kindness which lie in the quiet recesses of our bosoms, and which, when resorted to, furnish forth the pure element of domestic felicity.

The pitchy gloom without makes the heart dilate on entering the room filled with the glow and warmth of the evening fire. The ruddy blaze diffuses an artificial summer and sunshine through the room, and lights up each countenance in a kindlier welcome. Where does the honest face of hospitality expand into a broader and more cordial smile, where is the shy glance of love more sweetly eloquent, than by the winter fireside? and as the hollow blast of wintry wind rushes through the hall, claps the distant door, whistles about the casement, and rumbles down the chimney, what can be more grateful than that feeling of sober and sheltered security with which we look round upon the comfortable chamber and the scene of domestic hilarity?

The English, from the great prevalence of rural habit throughout every class of society, have always been found of those festivals and holidays, which agreeably interrupt the stillness of country life, and they were, in former days, particularly observant of the religious and social rites of Christmas. It

is inspiring to read even the dry details which some antiquaries have given of the quaint humors, the burlesque pageants, the complete abandonment to mirth and good-fellowship with which this festival was celebrated. It seemed to throw open every door and unlock every heart. It brought the peasant and the peer together, and blended all ranks in one warm, generous flow of joy and kindness. The old halls of castles and manor-houses resounded with the harp and the Christmas carol, and their ample boards groaned under the weight of hospitality. Even the poorest cottage welcomed the festive season with green decorations of bay and holly—the cheerful fire glanced its rays through the lattice, inviting the passengers to raise the latch and join the gossip knot huddled round the hearth beguiling the long evening with legendary jokes and oft-told Christmas tales.

One of the least pleasing effects of modern refinement is the havoc it has made among the hearty old holiday customs. It has completely taken off the sharp touchings and spirited reliefs of these embellishments of life, and has worn down society into a more smooth and polished, but certainly a less characteristic, surface. Many of the games and ceremonials of Christmas have entirely disappeared, and, like the sherris sack of old Falstaff, are become matters of speculation and dispute among commentators. They flourished in times full of spirit and lustihood, when men enjoyed life roughly, but heartily and vigorously—times wild and picturesque, which have furnished poetry with its richest materials and the drama with its most attractive variety of characters and manners. The world has become more worldly. There is more of dissipation, and less of enjoyment. Pleasure has expanded into a broader, but a shallower stream, and has forsaken many of those deep and quiet channels where it flowed sweetly through the calm bosom of domestic life. Society has acquired a more enlightened and elegant tone, but it has lost many of its strong local peculiarities, its homebred feelings, its honest fireside delights. The traditionary customs of golden-hearted antiquity, its feudal hospitalities, and lordly wassailings, have passed away with the baronial castles and stately manor-houses in which they were celebrated. They comported with the shadowy hall, the great oaken gallery, and the tapestried parlor, but are unfitted to the light showy saloons and gay drawing-rooms of the modern villa.

Shorn, however, as it is, of its ancient and festive honors, Christmas is still a period of delightful excitement in England. It is gratifying to see that home-feeling completely aroused which holds so powerful a place in every English bosom. The preparations making on every side for the social board that is again to unite friends and kindred; the presents of good cheer passing and repassing, those tokens of regard and quickeners of kind feelings; the evergreens distributed about houses and churches, emblems of peace and gladness,—all these have the most pleasing effect in producing fond associations and kindling benevolent sympathies. Even the sound of the Waits, rude as may be their minstrelsy, breaks upon the mid-watches of a winter night with the effect of perfect harmony. As I have been awakened by them in that still and solemn hour "when deep sleep falleth upon man," I have listened with a hushed delight, and, connecting them with the sacred and joyous occasion, have almost fancied them into another celestial choir announcing peace and good-will to mankind.

How delightfully the imagination, when wrought upon by these moral influences, turns everything to melody and beauty! The very crowing of the cock, heard sometimes in the profound repose of the country, "telling the night-watches to his feathery dames," was thought by the common people to announce the approach of this sacred festival:—

Some say that ever 'gainst that season comes
Wherein our Saviour's birth is celebrated,
This bird of dawning singeth all night long;
And then, they say, no spirit dares stir abroad,
The nights are wholesome—then no planets strike,
No fairy takes, no witch hath power to charm,
So hallow'd and so gracious is the time.

Amidst the general call to happiness, the bustle of the spirits, and stir of the affections which prevail at this period what bosom can remain insensible? It is, indeed, the season of regenerated feeling—the season for kindling not merely the fire of hospitality in the hall, but the genial flame of charity in the heart.

The scene of early love again rises green to memory beyond the sterile waste of years; and the idea of home, fraught with the fragrance of home-dwelling joys, reanimates the drooping spirit, as the Arabian breeze will sometimes waft the freshness of the distant fields to the weary pilgrim of the desert.

Stranger and sojourner as I am in the land, though for me no social hearth may blaze, no hospitable roof throw open its doors, nor the warm grasp of friendship welcome me at the threshold, yet I feel the influence of the season beaming into my soul from the happy looks of those around me. Surely happiness is reflective, like the light of heaven, and every countenance, bright with smiles and glowing with innocent enjoyment, is a mirror transmitting to others the rays of a supreme and ever-shining benevolence. He who can turn churlishly away from contemplating the felicity of his fellow-beings, and can sit down darkling and repining in his loneliness when all around is joyful, may have his moments of strong excitement and selfish gratification, but he wants the genial and social sympathies which constitute the charm of a merry Christmas.

THE STAGE COACH

Omne bene
Sine poena
Tempua est ludendi.
Venit hora
Absque mora
Libros deponendi.

Old Holiday School-Song

In the preceding paper I have made some general observations on the Christmas festivities of England, and am tempted to illustrate them by some anecdotes of a Christmas passed in the country; in perusing which I would most courteously invite my reader to lay aside the austerity of wisdom, and to put on that genuine holiday spirit which is tolerant of folly and anxious only for amusement.

In the course of a December tour in Yorkshire, I rode for a long distance in one of the public coaches on the day preceding Christmas. The coach was crowded, both inside and out, with passengers who, by their talk, seemed principally bound to the mansions of relations or friends to eat the Christmas dinner. It was loaded also with hampers of game and baskets and boxes of delicacies, and hares hung dangling their long ears about the coachman's box, presents from distant friends for the impending feast. I had three fine rosy-cheeked school boys for my fellow-passengers inside, full of the buxom health and manly spirit which I have observed in the children of this country. They were returning home for the holidays in high glee, and promising themselves a world of enjoyment. It was delightful to hear the gigantic plans of the little rogues, and the impracticable feats they were to perform during their six weeks' emancipation from the abhorred thraldom of book, birch, and pedagogue. They

were full of anticipations of the meeting with the family and household, down to the very cat and dog, and of the joy they were to give their little sisters by the presents with which their pockets were crammed; but the meeting to which they seemed to look forward with the greatest impatience was with Bantam, which I found to be a pony, and, according to their talk, possessed of more virtues than any steed since the days of Bucephalus. How he could trot! how he could run! and then such leaps as he would take!—there was not a hedge in the whole country that he could not clear.

They were under the particular guardianship of the coachman, to whom, whenever an opportunity presented, they addressed a host of questions, and pronounced him one of the best fellows in the world. Indeed, I could not but notice the more than ordinary air of bustle and importance of the coachman, who wore his hat a little on one side and had a large bunch of Christmas greens stuck in the buttonhole of his coat. He is always a personage full of mighty care and business, but he is particularly so during this season, having so many commissions to execute in consequence of the great interchange of presents. And here, perhaps, it may not be unacceptable to my untravelled readers to have a sketch that may serve as a general representation of this very numerous and important class of functionaries, who have a dress, a manner, a language, an air peculiar to themselves and prevalent throughout the fraternity; so that wherever an English stage-coachman may be seen he cannot be mistaken for one of any other craft or mystery.

He has commonly a broad, full face, curiously mottled with red, as if the blood had been forced by hard feeding into every vessel of the skin; he is swelled into jolly dimensions by frequent potations of malt liquors, and his bulk is still further increased by a multiplicity of coats, in which he is buried like a cauliflower, the upper one reaching to his heels. He wears a broad-brimmed, low-crowned hat; a huge roll of colored handkerchief about his neck, knowingly knotted and tucked in at the bosom; and has in summer-time a large bouquet of flowers in his buttonhole, the present, most probably, of some enamored country lass. His waistcoat is commonly of some bright color, striped, and his small-clothes extend far below the knees, to meet a pair of jockey boots which reach about halfway up his legs.

All this costume is maintained with much precision; he has a pride in having his clothes of excellent materials, and, notwithstanding the seeming grossness of his appearance, there is still discernible that neatness and propriety of person which is almost inherent in an Englishman. He enjoys great consequence and consideration along the road; has frequent conferences with the village housewives, who look upon him as a man of great trust and dependence; and he seems to have a good understanding with every bright-eyed country lass. The moment he arrives where the horses are to be changed, he throws down the reins with something of an air and abandons the cattle to the care of the ostler, his duty being merely to drive from one stage to another. When off the box his hands are thrust into the pockets of his great coat, and he rolls about the inn-yard with an air of the most absolute lordliness. Here he is generally surrounded by an admiring throng of ostlers, stableboys, shoeblacks, and those nameless hangers-on that infest inns and taverns, and run errands and do all kind of odd jobs for the privilege of battening on the drippings of the kitchen and the leakage of the tap-room. These all look up to him as to an oracle, treasure up his cant phrases, echo his opinions about horses and other topics of jockey lore, and, above all, endeavor to imitate his air and carriage. Every ragamuffin that has a coat to his back thrusts his hands in the pockets, rolls in his gait, talks slang, and is an embryo Coachey.

Perhaps it might be owing to the pleasing serenity that reigned in my own mind that I fancied
I saw cheerfulness in every countenance
throughout the journey. A stage-coach,
however, carries animation always with it,
and puts the world in motion as it whirls
along. The horn, sounded at the entrance
of the village, produces a general bustle.
Some hasten forth to meet friends; some
with bundles and bandboxes to secure
places, and in the hurry of the moment can
hardly take leave of the group that accom-
panies them. In the meantime the coachman
has a world of small commissions to execute.
Sometimes he delivers a hare or pheasant;
sometimes jerks a small parcel or newspaper to
the door of a public house; and sometimes, with

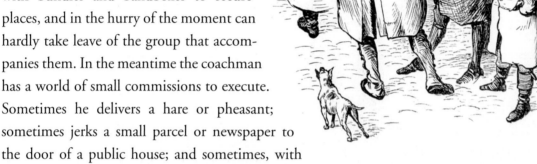

knowing leer and words of sly import, hands to some half-blushing, half-laughing
house-maid an odd-shaped billet-doux from some rustic admirer. As the coach rattles
through the village every one runs to the window, and you have glances on every side
of fresh country faces and blooming giggling girls. At the corners are assembled juntos of village idlers and wise men, who take their stations there for the
important purpose of seeing company pass; but the sagest knot is generally
at the blacksmith's, to whom the passing of the coach is an event fruitful of
much speculation. The smith, with the horse's heel in his lap, pauses
as the vehicle whirls by; the cyclops round the anvil suspend their
ringing hammers and suffer the iron to grow cool; and the sooty
spectre in brown paper cap laboring at the bellows leans on the
handle for a moment, and permits the asthmatic engine to heave
a long-drawn sigh, while he glares through the murky smoke and
sulphurous gleams of the smithy.

Perhaps the impending holiday might have given a more than usual animation to the country, for it seemed to me as if everybody was in good looks and good spirits. Game, poultry, and other luxuries of the table were in brisk circulation in the villages; the grocers', butchers', and fruiterers' shops were thronged with customers. The housewives were stirring briskly about, putting their dwellings in order, and the glossy branches of holly with their bright-red berries began to appear at the windows. The scene brought to mind an old writer's account of Christ-

mas preparation: "Now capons and hens, besides turkeys, geese, and ducks, with beef and mutton, must all die, for in twelve days a multitude of people will not be fed with a little. Now plums and spice, sugar and honey, square it among pies and broth. Now or never must music be in tune, for the youth must dance and sing to get them a heat, while the aged sit by the fire. The country maid leaves half her market, and must be sent again if she forgets a pack of cards on Christmas Eve. Great is the contention of holly and ivy whether master or dame wears the breeches. Dice and cards benefit the butler; and if the cook do not lack wit, he will sweetly lick his fingers."

I was roused from this fit of luxurious meditation by a shout from my little trav-elling companions. They had been looking out of the coach-windows for the last few miles, recognizing every tree and cottage as they approached home, and now there was a general burst of joy. "There's John! and there's old Carlo! and there's Bantam!" cried the happy little rogues, clapping their hands.

At the end of a lane there was an old sober-looking servant in livery waiting for them; he was accompanied by a superannuated pointer and by the redoubtable Ban-tam, a little old rat of a pony with a shaggy mane and long rusty tail, who stood dozing quietly by the roadside, little dreaming of the bustling times that awaited him.

I was pleased to see the fondness with which the little fellows leaped about the steady old footman and hugged the pointer, who wriggled his whole body for joy. But Bantam was the great object of interest; all wanted to mount at once, and it was with some difficulty that John arranged that they should ride by turns and the eldest should ride first.

Off they set at last, one on the pony, with the dog bounding and barking before him, and the others holding John's hands, both talking at once and overpowering him with questions about home and with school anecdotes. I looked after them with a feeling in which I do not know whether pleasure or melancholy predominated; for I was reminded of those days when, like them, I had known neither care nor sorrow and a holiday was the summit of earthly felicity. We stopped a few moments afterwards to water the horses, and on resuming our route a turn of the road brought us in sight of a neat country-seat. I could just distinguish the forms of a lady and two young girls in the portico, and I saw my little comrades, with Bantam, Carlo, and old John, trooping along the carriage-road. I leaned out of the coach-window, in hopes of witnessing the happy meeting, but a grove of trees shut it from my sight.

In the evening we reached a village where I had determined to pass the night. As we drove into the great gateway of the inn, I saw on one side the light of a rousing kitchen-fire beaming through a window. I entered, and admired, for the hundredth time, that picture of convenience, neatness,

and broad honest enjoyment, the kitchen of an English inn. It was of spacious dimensions, hung round with copper and tin vessels highly polished, and decorated here and there with a Christmas green. Hams, tongues, and flitches of bacon were suspended from the ceiling; a smoke-jack made its ceaseless clanking beside the fireplace, and a clock ticked in one corner. A well-scoured deal table extended along one side of the kitchen, with a cold round of beef and other hearty viands upon it, over which two foaming tankards of ale seemed mounting guard. Travellers of inferior order were preparing to attack this stout repast, while others sat smoking and gossiping over their ale on two high-backed oaken settles beside the fire. Trim housemaids were hurrying backwards and forwards under the directions of a fresh bustling landlady, but still seizing an occasional moment to exchange a flippant word and have a rallying laugh with the group round the fire. The scene completely realized Poor Robin's humble idea of the comforts of midwinter:

Now trees their leafy hats do bare
To reverence Winter's silver hair;
A handsome hostess, merry host,
A pot of ale now and a toast,
Tobacco and a good coal fire,
Are things this season doth require.
Poor Robin's Almanack

I had not been long at the inn when a post-chaise drove up to the door. A young gentleman stept out, and by the light of the lamps I caught a glimpse of a countenance which I thought I knew. I moved forward to get a nearer view, when his eye caught mine. I was not mistaken; it was Frank Bracebridge, a sprightly, good-humored young fellow with whom I had once travelled on the Continent. Our meeting was extremely cordial, for the countenance of an old fellow-traveller always brings up the recollection of a thousand pleasant scenes, odd adventures, and excellent jokes. To discuss all these in a transient interview at an inn was impossible; and, finding that I was not pressed for time and was merely making a tour of observation, he insisted that I should give him a day or two at his father's country-seat, to which he was going to pass the holidays and which lay at a few miles' distance. "It is better than eating a solitary Christmas dinner at an inn," said he, "and I can assure you of a hearty welcome in something of the old-fashioned style." His reasoning was cogent, and I must confess the preparation I had seen for universal festivity and social enjoyment had made me feel a little impatient of my loneliness. I closed, therefore, at once with his invitation; the chaise drove up to the door, and in a few moments I was on my way to the family mansion of the Bracebridges.

CHRISTMAS EVE

Saint Francis and Saint Benedight
Blesse this house from wicked wight;
From the night-mare and the goblin,
That is hight good fellow Robin;
Keep it from all evil spirits,
Fairies, weezels, rats, and ferrets:
From curfew time
To the next prime.

CARTWRIGHT

It was a brilliant moonlight night, but extremely cold; our chaise whirled rapidly over the frozen ground; the postboy smacked his whip incessantly, and a part of the time his horses were on a gallop. "He knows where he is going," said my companion, laughing, "and is eager to arrive in time for some of the merriment and good cheer of the servants' hall. My father, you must know, is a bigoted devotee of the old school, and prides himself upon keeping up something of old English hospitality. He is a tolerable specimen of what you will rarely meet with nowadays in its purity, the old English country gentleman; for our men of fortune spend so much of their time in town, and fashion is carried so much

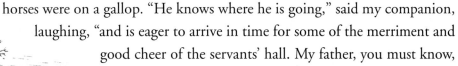

into the country, that the strong rich peculiarities of ancient rural life are almost polished away. My father, however, from early years, took honest Peacham (*Peacham's Complete Gentleman,* 1622) for his textbook, instead of Chesterfield; he determined in his own mind that there was no condition more truly honorable and enviable than that of a country gentleman on his paternal lands, and therefore passes the whole of his time on his estate. He is a strenuous advocate for the revival of the old rural games and holiday observances, and is deeply read in the writers, ancient and modern, who have treated on the subject. Indeed, his favorite range of reading is among the authors who flourished at least two centuries since, who, he insists, wrote and thought more like true Englishmen than any of their successors. He even regrets sometimes that he had not been born a few centuries earlier, when England was itself and had its peculiar manners and customs. As he lives at some distance from the main road, in rather a lonely part of the country, without any rival gentry near him, he has that most enviable of all blessings to an Englishman—an opportunity of indulging the bent of his own humor without molestation. Being representative of the oldest family in the neighborhood, and a great part of the peasantry being his tenants, he is much looked up to, and in general is known simply by the appellation of 'The Squire'—a title which has been accorded to the head of the family since time immemorial. I think it best to give you these hints about my worthy old father, to prepare you for any eccentricities that might otherwise appear absurd."

We had passed for some time along the wall of a park, and at length the chaise stopped at the gate. It was in a heavy, magnificent old style, of iron bars fancifully wrought at top into flourishes and flowers. The huge square columns that supported the gate were surmounted by the family crest. Close adjoining was the porter's lodge, sheltered under dark fir trees and almost buried in shrubbery.

The postboy rang a large porter's bell, which resounded though the still frosty air, and was answered by the distant barking of dogs, with which the mansion-house seemed garrisoned. An old woman immediately appeared at the gate. As the moonlight fell strongly upon her, I had a full view of a little primitive dame, dressed very much in the antique taste, with a neat kerchief and stomacher, and her silver hair peeping from under a cap of snowy whiteness. She came curtseying forth, with many expressions of simple joy at seeing her young master. Her husband, it seemed, was up at the house keeping Christmas Eve in the servants' hall; they could not do without him, as he was the best hand at a song and story in the household.

My friend proposed that we should alight and walk through the park to the hall, which was at no great distance, while the chaise should follow on. Our road wound through a noble avenue of trees, among the naked branches of which the moon glittered as she rolled through the deep vault of a cloudless sky. The lawn beyond was sheeted with a slight covering of snow, which here and there sparkled as the moonbeams caught a frosty crystal, and at a distance might be seen a thin transparent vapor stealing up from the low grounds and threatening gradually to shroud the landscape.

My companion looked around him with transport:—"How often," said he, "have I scampered up this avenue on returning home on school vacations! How often have I played under these trees when a boy! I feel a degree of filial reverence for them, as we look up to those who have cherished us in childhood. My father was always scrupulous in exacting our holidays and having us around him on family festivals. He used to direct and superintend our games with the strictness that some parents do the studies of their children. He was very particular that we should play the old English games according to their original form, and consulted old books for precedent and authority for every 'merrie disport'; yet I assure you there never was pedantry so delightful. It was the policy of the good old gentleman to make his children feel that home was the happiest place in the world; and I value this delicious home-feeling as one of the choicest gifts a parent could bestow."

We were interrupted by the clamor of a troop of dogs of all sorts and sizes, "mongrel, puppy, whelp, and hound, and curs of lower degree," that disturbed by the ring of the porter's bell and the rattling of the chaise, came bounding, open-mouthed, across the lawn.

> ——"The little dogs and all,
> Tray, Blanch, and Sweetheart, see, they bark at me!'"

cried Bracebridge, laughing. At the sound of his voice the bark was changed into a yelp of delight, and in a moment he was surrounded and almost overpowered by the caresses of the faithful animals.

We had now come in full view of the old family mansion, partly thrown in deep shadow and partly lit up by the cold moonshine. It was an irregular building of some magnitude, and seemed to be of the architecture of different periods. One wing was evidently very ancient, with heavy stone-shafted bow windows jutting out and overrun with ivy, from among the foliage of which the small diamond-shaped panes of glass glittered with the moonbeams. The rest of the house was in the French taste of Charles the Second's time, having been repaired and altered, as my friend told me, by one of his ancestors who returned with that monarch at the Restoration. The grounds about the house were laid out in the old formal manner of artificial flower-beds, clipped shrubberies, raised terraces, and heavy stone balustrades, ornamented with urns, a leaden statue or two, and a jet of water. The old gentleman, I was told, was extremely careful to preserve this obsolete finery in all its original state. He admired this fashion in gardening; it had an air of magnificence, was courtly and noble, and befitting good old family style. The boasted imitation of Nature in modern gardening had sprung up with modern republican notions, but did not suit a monarchical government; it smacked of the leveling system. I could not help smiling at this introduction of politics into gardening, though I expressed some apprehension that I should find the old gentleman rather intolerant in his creed. Frank assured me, however, that it was almost the only instance in which he had ever heard his father meddle with politics; and he believed that he had got this notion from a member of Parliament who once passed a few weeks with him. The Squire was glad of any argument to defend his clipped yew trees and formal terraces, which had been occasionally attacked by modern landscape gardeners.

As we approached the house we heard the sound of music, and now and then a burst of laughter from one end of the building. This, Bracebridge said, must proceed from the servants' hall, where a great deal of revelry was permitted, and even encouraged, by the Squire throughout the twelve days of Christmas, provided everything was done conformably to ancient usage. Here were kept up the old games of hoodman blind, shoe the wild mare, hot cockles, steal the white loaf, bob apple, and snap dragon; the Yule-clog and Christmas candle were regularly burnt, and the mistletoe with its white berries hung up, to the imminent peril of all the pretty housemaids.

So intent were the servants upon their sports that we had to ring repeatedly before we could make ourselves heard. On our arrival being announced the Squire came out to receive us, accompanied by his two other sons—one a young officer in the army, home on a leave of absence; the other an Oxonian, just from the university. The Squire was a fine healthy-looking old gentleman, with silver hair curling lightly round an open florid countenance, in which the physiognomist, with the advantage, like myself, of a previous hint or two, might discover a singular mixture of whim and benevolence.

The family meeting was warm and affectionate; as the evening was far advanced, the Squire would not permit us to change our travelling dresses, but ushered us at once

to the company, which was assembled in a large old-fashioned hall. It was composed of different branches of a numerous family connection, where there were the usual proportion of old uncles and aunts, comfortable married dames, superannuated spinsters, blooming country cousins, half-fledged striplings, and bright-eyed boarding-school hoydens. They were variously occupied—some at a round game of cards; others conversing around the fireplace; at one end of the hall was a group of the young folks, some nearly grown up, others of a more tender and budding age, fully engrossed by a merry game; and a profusion of wooden horses, penny trumpets, and tattered dolls about the floor showed traces of a troop of little fairy beings who, having frolicked through a happy day, had been carried off to slumber through a peaceful night.

While the mutual greetings were going on between young Bracebridge and his relatives I had time to scan the apartment. I have called it a hall, for so it had certainly been in old times, and the Squire had evidently endeavored to restore it to something of its primitive state. Over the heavy projecting fireplace was suspended a picture of a warrior in armor, standing by a white horse, and on the opposite wall hung a helmet, buckler, and lance. At one end an enormous pair of antlers were inserted in the wall, the branches serving as hooks on which to suspend hats, whips, and spurs, and in the corners of the apartment

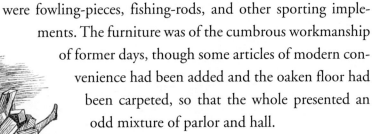

were fowling-pieces, fishing-rods, and other sporting implements. The furniture was of the cumbrous workmanship of former days, though some articles of modern convenience had been added and the oaken floor had been carpeted, so that the whole presented an odd mixture of parlor and hall.

The grate had been removed from the wide overwhelming fireplace to make way for a fire of wood, in the midst of which was an enormous log glowing and blazing, and sending forth a vast volume of light and heat: this, I understood, was the Yule-log, was particular in having brought in and illumined on a Christmas Eve, according to ancient custom.

It was really delightful to see the old Squire seated in his hereditary elbow-chair by the hospitable fireside of his ancestors, and looking around him like the sun of a system, beaming warmth and gladness to every heart. Even the very dog that lay stretched at his feet, as he lazily shifted his position and yawned would look fondly up in his master's face, wag his tail against the floor, and stretch himself again to sleep, confident of kindness and protection. There is an emanation from the heart in genuine hospitality which cannot be described, but is immediately felt and puts the stranger at once at his ease. I had not been seated many minutes by the comfortable hearth of the worthy old cavalier before I found myself as much at home as if I had been one of the family.

Supper was announced shortly after our arrival. It was served up in a spacious oaken chamber, the panels of which shone with wax, and around which were several family portraits decorated with holly and ivy. Besides the accustomed lights, two great wax tapers, called Christmas candles, wreathed with greens, were placed on a highly-polished buffet among the family plate. The table was abundantly spread with substantial fare; but the Squire made his supper of frumenty, a dish made of wheat cakes boiled in milk with rich spices, being a standing dish in old times for Christmas Eve. I was happy to find my old friend, minced pie, in the retinue of the feast and, finding him to be perfectly orthodox, and that I need not be ashamed of my predilection, I greeted him with all the warmth wherewith we usually greet an old and very genteel acquaintance.

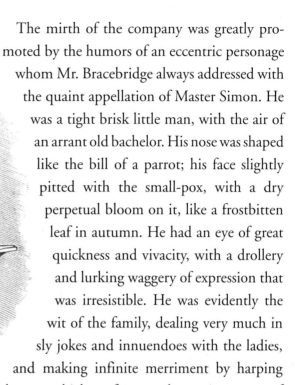

The mirth of the company was greatly promoted by the humors of an eccentric personage whom Mr. Bracebridge always addressed with the quaint appellation of Master Simon. He was a tight brisk little man, with the air of an arrant old bachelor. His nose was shaped like the bill of a parrot; his face slightly pitted with the small-pox, with a dry perpetual bloom on it, like a frostbitten leaf in autumn. He had an eye of great quickness and vivacity, with a drollery and lurking waggery of expression that was irresistible. He was evidently the wit of the family, dealing very much in sly jokes and innuendoes with the ladies, and making infinite merriment by harping upon old themes, which, unfortunately, my ignorance of the family chronicles did not permit me to enjoy. It seemed to be his great delight during supper to keep a young girl next to him in a continual agony of stifled laughter, in spite of her awe of the reproving looks of her mother, who sat opposite. Indeed, he was the idol of the younger part of the company, who laughed at everything he said or did and at every turn of his countenance. I could not wonder at it; for he must have been a miracle of accomplishments in their eyes. He could imitate Punch and Judy; make an old woman of his hand, with the assistance of a burnt cork and pocket-handkerchief; and cut an orange into such a ludicrous caricature that the young folks were ready to die with laughing.

I was let briefly into his history by Frank Bracebridge. He was an old bachelor, of a small independent income, which by careful management was sufficient for all his wants. He revolved through the family system like a vagrant comet in its orbit, sometimes visiting one branch, and sometimes another quite remote, as is often the case with gentlemen of extensive connections and small fortunes in England. He had a chirping, buoyant disposition, always enjoying the present moment; and his frequent change of scene and company prevented his acquiring those rusty, unaccommodating habits with which old bachelors are so uncharitably charged. He was a complete family chronicle, being versed in the genealogy, history, and intermarriages of the whole house of Bracebridge, which made him a great favorite with the old folks; he was a beau of all the elder ladies and superannuated spinsters, among whom he was habitually considered rather a young fellow; and he was master of the revels among the children, so that there was not a more popular being in the sphere in which he moved than Mr. Simon Bracebridge. Of late years he had resided almost entirely with the Squire, to whom he had become a factotum, and whom he particularly delighted by jumping with his humor in respect to old times and by having a scrap of an old song to suit every occasion. We had presently a specimen of his last-mentioned talent, for no sooner was supper removed and spiced wines and other beverages peculiar to the season introduced, than Master Simon was called on for a good old Christmas song. He bethought himself for a moment, and then, with a sparkle of the eye and a voice that was by no means bad, excepting that it ran occasionally into a falsetto like the notes of a split reed, he quavered forth a quaint old ditty:

"Now Christmas is come,
Let us beat up the drum,
And call all our neighbors together;
And when they appear,
Let us make them such cheer,
As will keep out the wind and the weather, etc."

The supper had disposed every one to gayety, and an old harper was summoned from the servants' hall, where he had been strumming all the evening, and to all appearance comforting himself with some of the Squire's home-brewed. He was a kind of hanger-on, I was told, of the establishment, and, though ostensibly a resident of the village, was oftener to be found in the Squire's kitchen than his own home, the old gentleman being fond of the sound of "harp in hall."

The dance, like most dances after supper, was a merry one: some of the older folks joined in it, and the Squire himself figured down several couple with a part-ner with whom he affirmed he had danced at every Christmas for nearly half a century. Master Simon, who seemed to be a kind of connecting link between the old times and

the new, and to be withal a little antiquated in the taste of his accomplishments, evidently piqued himself on his dancing, and was endeavoring to gain credit by the heel and toe, rigadoon, and other graces of the ancient school; but he had unluckily assorted himself with a little romping girl from boarding-school, who by her wild vivacity kept him continually on the stretch and defeated all his sober attempts at elegance: such are the ill-sorted matches to which antique gentlemen are unfortunately prone.

The young Oxonian, on the contrary, had led out one of his maiden aunts, on whom the rogue played a thousand little knaveries with impunity: he was full of practical jokes, and his delight was to tease his aunts and cousins, yet, like all madcap youngsters, he was a universal favorite among the women. The most interesting couple in the dance was the young officer and a ward of the Squire's, a beautiful blushing girl of seventeen. From several shy glances which I had noticed in the course of the evening I suspected there was a little kindness growing up between them; and indeed the young soldier was just the hero to captivate a romantic girl. He was tall, slender, and handsome, and, like most young British officers of late years, had picked up various small accomplishments on the Continent: he could talk French and Italian, draw landscapes, sing very tolerably, dance divinely, but, above all, he had been wounded at Waterloo. What girl of seventeen, well read in poetry and romance, could resist such a mirror of chivalry and perfection?

The moment the dance was over he caught up a guitar, and, lolling against the old marble fireplace in an attitude which I am half inclined to suspect was studied, began the little French air of the Troubadour. The Squire, however, exclaimed against having anything on Christmas Eve but good old English; upon which the young minstrel, casting up his eye for a moment as if in an effort of memory, struck into another strain, and with a charming air of gallantry gave Herrick's "Night-Piece to Julia":—

"Her eyes the glow-worm lend thee,
The shooting stars attend thee,
And the elves also,
Whose little eyes glow
Like the sparks of fire, befriend thee.

No Will-o'-the-Wisp mislight thee;
Nor snake nor slow-worm bite thee;
But on thy way,
Not making a stay,
Since ghost there is none to affright thee,

Then let not the dark thee cumber;
What though the moon does slumber,
The stars of the night
Will lend thee their light,
Like tapers clear without number.

Then, Julia, let me woo thee,
Thus, thus to come unto me,
And when I shall meet
Thy silvery feet,
My soul I'll pour into thee."

The song might or might not have been intended in compliment to the fair Julia, for so I found his partner was called; she, however, was certainly unconscious of any such application, for she never looked at the singer, but kept her eyes cast upon the floor. Her face was suffused, it is true, with a beautiful blush, and there was a gentle heaving of the bosom, but all that was doubtless caused by the exercise of the dance; indeed, so great was her indifference that she amused herself with plucking to pieces

a choice bouquet of hot-house flowers, and by the time the song was concluded the nosegay lay in ruins on the floor.

The party now broke up for the night with the kind-hearted old custom of shaking hands. As I passed through the hall on my way to my chamber, the dying embers of the *Yule-clog* still sent forth a dusky glow, and had it not been the season when "no spirit dares stir abroad," I should have been half tempted to steal from my room at midnight and peep whether the fairies might not be at their revels about the hearth.

My chamber was in the old part of the mansion, the ponderous furniture of which might have been fabricated in the days of the giants. The room was panelled, with cornices of heavy carved work, in which flowers and grotesque faces were strangely intermingled, and a row of black-looking portraits stared mournfully at me from the walls. The bed was of rich though faded damask, with a lofty tester, and stood in a niche opposite a bow window. I had scarcely got into bed when a strain of music seemed to break forth in the air just below the window. I listened, and found it proceeded from a band which I concluded to be the Waits from some neighboring village. They went round the house, playing under the windows. I drew aside the curtains to hear them more distinctly. The moonbeams fell through the upper part of the casement; partially lighting up the antiquated apartment. The sounds, as they receded, became more soft and aerial, and seemed to accord with the quiet and moonlight. I listened and listened—they became more and more tender and remote, and, as they gradually died away, my head sunk upon the pillow and I fell asleep.

CHRISTMAS DAY

Dark and dull night, flie hence away,
And give the honor to this day
That sees December turn'd to May.

. . . .

Why does the chilling winter's morne
Smile like a field beset with corn?
Or smell like to a meade new-shorne,
Thus on the sudden?—come and see
The cause why things thus fragrant be.

HERRICK

When I woke the next morning it seemed as if all the events of the preceding evening had been a dream, and nothing but the identity of the ancient chamber convinced me of their reality. While I lay musing on my pillow I heard the sound of little feet pattering outside of the door, and a whispering consultation. Presently a choir of small voices chanted forth an old Christmas carol, the burden of which was—

"Rejoice, our Saviour he was born
On Christmas Day in the morning."

I rose softly, slipt on my clothes, opened the door suddenly, and beheld one of the most beautiful little fairy groups that a painter could imagine. It consisted of a boy and two girls, the eldest not more than six, and lovely as seraphs. They were going the rounds of the house and singing at every chamber door, but my sudden appearance frightened them into mute bashfulness. They remained for a moment playing on their lips with their fingers, and now and then stealing a shy glance from under their eyebrows, until, as if by one impulse, they scampered away, and as they turned an angle of the gallery I heard them laughing in triumph at their escape.

Everything conspired to produce kind and happy feelings in this stronghold of old-fashioned hospitality. The window of my chamber looked out upon what in summer would have been a beautiful landscape. There was a sloping lawn, a fine stream winding at the foot of it, and a tract of park beyond, with noble clumps of trees and herds of deer. At a distance was a neat hamlet, with the smoke from the cottage chimneys hanging over it, and a church with its dark spire in strong relief against the clear cold sky. The house was surrounded with evergreens, according to the English custom, which would have given almost an appearance of summer; but the morning was extremely frosty; the light vapor of the preceding evening had been precipitated by the cold, and covered all the trees and every blade of grass with its fine crystalizations. The rays of a bright morning sun had a dazzling effect among the glittering foliage. A robin, perched upon the top of a mountain-ash that hung its clusters of red berries just before my window, was basking himself in the sunshine and piping a few querulous notes, and a peacock was displaying all the glories of his train and strutting with the pride and gravity of a Spanish grandee on the terrace walk below.

I had scarcely dressed myself when a servant appeared to invite me to family prayers. He showed me the way to a small chapel in the old wing of the house, where I found the principal part of the family already assembled

in a kind of gallery furnished with cushions, hassocks, and large prayer-books; the servants were seated on benches below. The old gentleman read prayers from a desk in front of the gallery, and Master Simon acted as clerk and made the responses; and I must do him the justice to say that he acquitted himself with great gravity and decorum.

The service was followed by a Christmas carol, which Mr. Bracebridge himself had constructed from a poem of his favorite author, Herrick, and it had been adapted to an old church melody by Master Simon. As there were several good voices among the household, the effect was extremely pleasing, but I was particularly gratified by the exaltation of heart and sudden sally of grateful feeling with which the worthy Squire delivered one stanza, his eye glistening and his voice rambling out of all the bounds of time and tune:

> "'Tis Thou that crown'st my glittering hearth
> With guiltless mirth,
> And giv'st me Wassaile bowles to drink
> Spiced to the brink;
> Lord, 'tis Thy plenty-dropping hand
> That soiles my land:
> And giv'st me for my bushell sowne,
> Twice ten for one."

I afterwards understood that early morning service was read on every Sunday and saint's day throughout the year, either by Mr. Bracebridge or by some member of the family. It was once almost universally the case at the seats of the nobility and gentry of England, and it is much to be regretted that the custom is falling into neglect; for the dullest observer must be sensible of the order and serenity prevalent in those households where the occasional exercise of a beautiful form of worship in the morning gives, as it were, the keynote to every temper for the day and attunes every spirit to harmony.

Our breakfast consisted of what the Squire denominated true old English fare. He indulged in some bitter lamentations over modern breakfasts of tea and toast, which he censured as among the causes of modern effeminacy and weak nerves and the decline of old English heartiness; and, though he admitted them to his table to suit the palates of his guests, yet there was a brave display of cold meats, wine, and ale on the sideboard.

After breakfast I walked about the grounds with Frank Bracebridge and Master Simon, or Mr. Simon, as he was called by everybody but the Squire. We were escorted by a number of gentlemanlike dogs, that seemed loungers about the establishment, from the frisking spaniel to the steady old stag-hound, the last of which was of a race that had been in the family time out of mind; they were all obedient to a dog-whistle which hung to Master Simon's buttonhole, and in the midst of their gambols would glance an eye occasionally upon a small switch he carried in his hand.

The old mansion had a still more venerable look in the yellow sunshine than by pale moonlight; and I could not but feel the force of the Squire's idea that the formal

terraces, heavily moulded balustrades, and clipped yew trees carried with them an air of proud aristocracy. There appeared to be an unusual number of peacocks about the place, and I was making some remarks upon what I termed a flock of them that were basking under a sunny wall, when I was gently corrected in my phraseology by Master Simon, who told me that according to the most ancient and approved treatise on hunting I must say a muster of peacocks. "In the same way," added he, with a slight air of pedantry, "we say a flight of doves or swallows, a bevy of quails, a herd of deer, of wrens, or cranes, a skulk of foxes, or a building of rooks." He went on to inform me that, according to Sir Anthony Fitzherbert, we ought to ascribe to this bird "both understanding and glory; for, being praised, he will presently set up his tail, chiefly against the sun, to the intent you may the better behold the beauty thereof. But at the fall of the leaf, when his tail falleth, he will mourn and hide himself in corners till his tail come again as it was."

I could not help smiling at this display of small erudition on so whimsical a subject; but I found that the peacocks were birds of some consequence at the hall, for Frank Bracebridge informed me that they were great favorites with his father, who was extremely careful to keep up the breed; partly because they belonged to chivalry, and were in great request at the stately banquets of the olden time, and partly because they had a pomp and magnificence about them highly becoming an old family mansion. Nothing, he was accustomed to say, had an air of greater state and dignity than a peacock perched upon an antique stone balustrade.

Master Simon had now to hurry off, having an appointment at the parish church with the village choristers, who were to perform some music of his selection. There was something extremely agreeable in the cheerful flow of animal spirits of the little man; and I confess I had been somewhat surprised at his apt quotations from authors who certainly were not in the range of every-day reading. I mentioned this last circumstance to Frank Bracebridge, who told me with a smile that Master Simon's whole stock of erudition was confined to some half a dozen old authors, which the Squire had put into his hands, and which he read over and over whenever he had a studious fit, as he sometimes had on a rainy day or a long winter evening. Sir Anthony Fitzherbert's Book of Husbandry, Markham's Country Contentments, the Tretyse of Hunting, by

Sir Thomas Cockayne, Knight, Isaac Walton's Angler, and two or three more such ancient worthies of the pen were his standard authorities; and, like all men who know but a few books, he looked up to them with a kind of idolatry and quoted them on all occasions. As to his songs, they were chiefly picked out of old books in the Squire's library, and adapted to tunes that were popular among the choice spirits of the last century. His practical application of scraps of literature, however, had caused him to be looked upon as a prodigy of book-knowledge by all the grooms, huntsmen, and small sportsmen of the neighborhood.

While we were talking we heard the distant toll of the village bell, and I was told that the Squire was a little particular in having his household at church on a Christmas morning, considering it a day of pouring out of thanks and rejoicing; for, as old Tusser observed,—

> At Christmas be merry, and thankful withal,
> And feast thy poor neighbors, the great with the small.

"If you are disposed to go to church," said Frank Bracebridge, "I can promise you a specimen of my cousin Simon's musical achievements. As the church is destitute of an organ, he has formed a band from the village amateurs, and established a musical club for their improvement; he has also sorted a choir, as he sorted my father's pack of hounds, according to the directions of Jervaise Markham in his Country Contentments: for the bass he has sought out all the 'deep, solemn mouths,' and for the tenor the 'loud-ringing mouths,' among the country bumpkins, and for 'sweet-mouths,' he has culled-with curious taste among the prettiest lasses in the neighborhood; though these last, he affirms, are the most difficult to keep in tune, your pretty female singer being exceedingly wayward and capricious, and very liable to accident."

As the morning, though frosty, was remarkably fine and clear, the most of the family walked to the church, which was a very old building of gray stone, and stood near a village about half a mile from the park gate. Adjoining it was a low snug parsonage which seemed coeval with the church. The front of it was perfectly matted with a yew tree that had been trained against its walls, through the dense foliage of which apertures had been formed to admit light into the small antique lattices. As we passed this sheltered nest the parson issued forth and preceded us.

I had expected to see a sleek well-conditioned pastor, such as is often found in a snug living in the vicinity of a rich patron's table, but I was disappointed. The parson was a little, meagre, black-looking man, with a grizzled wig that was too wide and stood off from each ear; so that his head seemed to have shrunk away within it, like a dried filbert in its shell. He wore a rusty coat, with great skirts and pockets that would have held the church Bible and prayer-book: and his small legs seemed still smaller from being planted in large shoes decorated with enormous buckles.

I was informed by Frank Bracebridge that the parson had been a chum of his father's at Oxford, and had received this living shortly after the latter had come to his estate. He was a complete black-letter hunter, and would scarcely read a work printed in the Roman character. The editions of Caxton and Wynkyn de Worde were his delight, and he was indefatigable in his researches after such old English writers as have fallen into oblivion from their worthlessness. In deference, perhaps, to the notions of Mr. Bracebridge he had made diligent investigations into the festive rites and holiday customs of former times, and had been as zealous in the inquiry as if he had been a boon companion; but it was merely with that plodding spirit with which men of adust temperament follow up any track of study, merely because it is denominated learning; indifferent to its intrinsic nature, whether it be the illustration of the wisdom or of the ribaldry and obscenity of antiquity. He had pored over these old volumes so intensely that they seemed to have been reflected into his countenance; which, if the face be indeed an index of the mind, might be compared to a title-page of black-letter.

On reaching the church-porch we found the parson rebuking the gray-headed sexton for having used mistletoe among the greens with which the church was decorated. It

was, he observed, an unholy plant, profaned by having been used by the Druids in their mystic ceremonies; and, though it might be innocently employed in the festive ornamenting of halls and kitchens, yet it had been deemed by the Fathers of the Church as unhallowed and totally unfit for sacred purposes. So tenacious was he on this point that the poor sexton was obliged to strip down a great part of the humble trophies of his taste before the parson would consent to enter upon the service of the day.

The interior of the church was venerable, but simple; on the walls were several mural monuments of the Bracebridges, and just beside the altar was a tomb of ancient workmanship, on which lay the effigy of a warrior in armor with his legs crossed, a sign of his having been a crusader. I was told it was one of the family who had signalized himself in the Holy Land, and the same whose picture hung over the fireplace in the hall.

During service Master Simon stood up in the pew and repeated the responses very audibly, evincing that kind of ceremonious devotion punctually observed by a gentleman of the old school and a man of old family connections. I observed too that he turned over the leaves of a folio prayer-book with something of a flourish; possibly to show off an enormous seal-ring which enriched one of his fingers and which had the look of a family relic. But he was evidently most solicitous about the musical part of the service, keeping his eye fixed intently on the choir, and beating time with much gesticulation and emphasis.

The orchestra was in a small gallery, and presented a most whimsical grouping of heads piled one above the other, among which I particularly noticed that of the village

tailor, a pale fellow with a retreating forehead and chin, who played on the clarinet, and seemed to have blown his face to a point; and there was another, a short pursy man, stooping and laboring at a bass-viol, so as to show nothing but the top of a round bald head, like the egg of an ostrich. There were two or three pretty faces among the female singers, to which the keen air of a frosty morning had given a bright rosy tint; but the gentle-men choristers had evidently been chosen, like old Cremona fiddles, more for tone than looks; and as several had to sing from the same book, there were clusterings of odd physiognomies not unlike those groups of cherubs we sometimes see on country tombstones.

The usual services of the choir were managed tolerably well, the vocal parts gen-erally lagging a little behind the instrumental, and some loitering fiddler now and then making up for lost time by travelling over a passage with prodigious celerity and clearing more bars than the keenest fox-hunter to be in at the death. But the great trial was an anthem that had been prepared and arranged by Master Simon, and on which he had founded great expectation. Unluckily, there was a blunder at the very outset: the musicians became flurried; Master Simon was in a fever; everything went on lamely and irregularly until they came to a chorus beginning, "Now let us sing with one accord," which seemed to be a signal for parting company: all became discord and confusion: each shifted for himself, and got to the end as well—or, rather, as soon—as he could, excepting one old chorister in a pair of horn spectacles bestriding and pinching a long sonorous nose, who happened to stand a little apart, and, being wrapped up in his own melody, kept on a quavering course, wriggling his head, ogling his book, and winding all up by a nasal solo of at least three bars' duration.

The parson gave us a most erudite sermon on the rites and ceremonies of Christmas, and the propriety

of observing it not merely as a day of thanksgiving but of rejoicing, supporting the correctness of his opinions by the earliest usages of the Church, and enforcing them by the authorities of Theophilus of Caesarea, St. Cyprian, St. Chrysostom, St. Augustine, and a cloud more of saints and fathers, from whom he made copious quotations. I was a little at a loss to perceive the necessity of such a mighty array of forces to maintain a point which no one present seemed inclined to dispute; but I soon found that the good man had a legion of ideal adversaries to contend with, having in the course of his researches on the subject of Christmas got completely embroiled in the sectarian controversies of the Revolution, when the Puritans made such a fierce assault upon the ceremonies of the Church, and poor old Christmas was driven out of the land by proclamation of Parliament. The worthy parson lived but with times past, and knew but little of the present.

Shut up among worm-eaten tomes in the retirement of his antiquated little study, the pages of old times were to him as the gazettes of the day, while the era of the Revolution was mere modern history. He forgot that nearly two centuries had elapsed since the fiery persecution of poor mince-pie throughout the land; when plum porridge was denounced as "mere popery," and roast beef as anti-christian, and that Christmas had been brought in again triumphantly with the merry court of King Charles at the Restoration. He kindled into warmth with the ardor of his contest and the host of imaginary foes with whom he had to combat; he had a stubborn conflict with old Prynne and two or three other forgotten champions of the Roundheads on the subject of Christmas festivity; and concluded by urging his hearers, in the most solemn and affecting manner, to stand to the traditional customs of their fathers and feast and make merry on this joyful anniversary of the Church.

I have seldom known a sermon attended apparently with more immediate effects, for on leaving the church the congregation seemed one and all possessed with the gayety of spirit so earnestly enjoined by their pastor. The elder folks gathered in knots in the churchyard, greeting and shaking hands, and the children ran about crying Ule! Ule! and repeating some uncouth rhymes, which the parson, who had joined us, informed me had been handed down from days of yore. The villagers doffed their hats to the Squire as he passed, giving him the good wishes of the season with every appearance of heartfelt sincerity, and were invited by him to the hall to take something to keep out the cold of the weather; and I heard blessings uttered by several of the poor, which convinced me that, in the midst of his enjoyments, the worthy old cavalier had not forgotten the true Christmas virtue of charity.

On our way homeward his heart seemed overflowed with generous and happy feelings. As we passed over a rising ground which commanded something of a prospect, the sounds of rustic merriment now and then reached our ears: the Squire paused for a few moments and looked around with an air of inexpressible benignity. The beauty of the day was of itself sufficient to inspire philanthropy. Notwithstanding the frostiness of the morning the sun in his cloudless journey had acquired sufficient power to melt away the thin covering of snow from every southern declivity, and to bring out the living green which adorns an English landscape even in mid-winter. Large tracts of smiling verdure contrasted with the dazzling whiteness of the shaded slopes and hollows. Every sheltered bank on which the broad rays rested yielded its silver rill of cold and limpid water, glittering through the dripping grass, and

sent up slight exhalations to contribute to the thin haze that hung just above the surface of the earth. There was something truly cheering in this triumph of warmth and verdure over the frosty thraldom of winter; it was, as the Squire observed, an emblem of Christmas hospitality breaking through the chills of ceremony and selfishness and thawing every heart into a flow. He pointed with pleasure to the indications of good cheer reeking from the chimneys of the comfortable farm-houses and low thatched cottages. "I love," said he, "to see this day well kept by rich and poor; it is a great thing to have one day in the year, at least, when you are sure of being welcome wherever you go, and of having, as it were, the world all thrown open to you; and I am almost disposed to join with Poor Robin in his malediction on every churlish enemy to this honest festival:—

> Those who at Christmas do repine,
>> And would fain hence dispatch him,
> May they with old Duke Humphry dine,
>> Or else may Squire Ketch catch'em."

The Squire went on to lament the deplorable decay of the games and amusements which were once prevalent at this season among the lower orders and countenanced by the higher, when the old halls of castles and manor-houses were thrown open at daylight; when the tables were covered with brawn and beef and humming ale; when the harp and the carol resounded all day long; and when rich and poor were alike welcome to enter and make merry. "Our old games and local customs," said he, "had a great effect in making the peasant fond of his home, and the promotion of them by the gentry made him fond of his lord. They made the times merrier and kinder and better, and I can truly say, with one of our old poets,

> I like them well: the curious preciseness
> And all-pretended gravity of those
> That seek to banish hence these harmless sports,
> Have thrust away much ancient honesty.

"The nation," continued he, "is altered; we have almost lost our simple true-hearted peasantry. They have broken asunder from the higher classes, and seem to think their interests are separate. They have become too knowing, and begin to read newspapers, listen to ale-house politicians, and talk of reform. I think one mode to keep them in good-humor in these hard times would be for the nobility and gentry to

pass more time on their estates, mingle more among the country-people, and set the merry old English games going again."

Such was the good Squire's project for mitigating public discontent: and, indeed, he had once attempted to put his doctrine in practice, and a few years before had kept open house during the holidays in the old style. The country-people, however, did not understand how to play their parts in the scene of hospitality; many uncouth circumstances occurred; the manor was overrun by all the vagrants of the country, and more beggars drawn into the neighborhood in one week than the parish officers could get rid of in a year. Since then he had contented himself with inviting the decent part of the neighboring peasantry to call at the hall on Christmas Day, and with distributing beef, and bread, and ale among the poor, that they might make merry in their own dwellings.

We had not been long home when the sound of music was heard from a distance. A band of country lads, without coats, their shirt-sleeves fancifully tied with ribbons, their hats decorated with greens, and clubs in their hands, was seen advancing up the avenue, followed by a large number of villagers and peasantry. They stopped before the hall door, where the music struck up a peculiar air, and the lads performed a curious and intricate dance, advancing, retreating, and striking their clubs together, keeping exact time to the music; while one, whimsically crowned with a fox's skin, the tail of which flaunted down his back, kept capering round the skirts of the dance and rattling a Christmas box with many antic gesticulations.

The Squire eyed this fanciful exhibition with great interest and delight, and gave me a full account of its origin, which he traced to the times when the Romans held possession of the island, plainly proving that this was a lineal descendant of the sword dance of the ancients. "It was now," he said, "nearly extinct, but he had accidentally met with traces of it in the neighborhood, and had encouraged its revival; though, to tell the truth, it was too apt to be followed up by the rough cudgel play and broken heads in the evening."

After the dance was concluded the whole party was entertained with brawn and beef and stout home-brewed. The Squire himself mingled among the rustics, and was received with awkward demonstrations of deference and regard. It is true I perceived two or three of the younger peasants, as they were raising their tankards to their mouths, when the Squire's back was turned making something of a grimace, and giving each other the wink; but the moment they caught my eye they pulled grave faces and were exceedingly demure. With Master Simon, however, they all seemed more at their ease. His varied occupations and amusements had made him well known throughout the neighborhood. He was a visitor at every farmhouse and cottage, gossiped with the farmers and their wives, romped with their daughters, and, like that type of a vagrant bachelor, the humblebee, tolled the sweets from all the rosy lips of the country round.

The bashfulness of the guests soon gave way before good cheer and affability. There is something genuine and affectionate in the gayety of the lower orders when it is excited by the bounty and familiarity of those above them; the warm glow of gratitude enters into their mirth, and a kind word or a small pleasantry frankly uttered by a patron gladdens the heart of the dependant more than oil and wine. When the Squire had retired the merriment increased, and there was much joking and laughter, particularly between Master Simon and a hale, ruddy-faced, white-headed farmer who appeared to be the wit of the village; for I observed all his companions to wait with open months for his retorts, and burst into a gratuitous laugh before they could well understand them.

The whole house indeed seemed abandoned to merriment: as I passed to my room to dress for dinner, I heard the sound of music in a small court, and, looking through a window that commanded it, I perceived a band of wandering musicians with pandean pipes and tambourine; a pretty coquettish housemaid was dancing a jig with a smart country lad, while several of the other servants were looking on. In the midst of her sport the girl caught a glimpse of my face at the window, and, coloring up, ran off with an air of roguish affected confusion.

THE CHRISTMAS DINNER

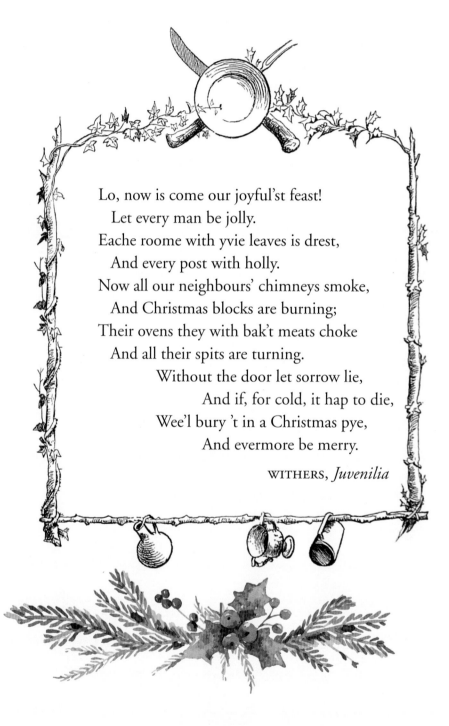

Lo, now is come our joyful'st feast!
   Let every man be jolly.
Eache roome with yvie leaves is drest,
   And every post with holly.
Now all our neighbours' chimneys smoke,
   And Christmas blocks are burning;
Their ovens they with bak't meats choke
   And all their spits are turning.
     Without the door let sorrow lie,
       And if, for cold, it hap to die,
     Wee'l bury 't in a Christmas pye,
      And evermore be merry.

WITHERS, *Juvenilia*

I had finished my toilet, and was loitering with Frank Bracebridge in the library, when we heard a distant thwacking sound, which he informed me was a signal for the serving up of the dinner. The Squire kept up old customs in kitchen as well as hall, and the rolling-pin, struck upon the dresser by the cook, summoned the servants to carry in the meats.

> Just in this nick the cook knock'd thrice,
> And all the waiters in a trice
> His summons did obey;
> Each serving-man, with dish in hand,
> March'd boldly up, like our train-band,
> Presented and away.
> SIR JOHN SUCKLING

The dinner was served up in the great hall, where the Squire always held his Christmas banquet. A blazing crackling fire of logs had been heaped on to warm the spacious apartment, and the flame went sparkling and wreathing up the wide-mouthed chimney. The great picture of the crusader and his white horse had been profusely decorated with greens for the occasion, and holly and ivy had like-wise been wreathed round the helmet and weapons on the opposite wall, which I understood were the arms of the same warrior. I must own, by the by, I had strong doubts about the authenticity of the painting and armor as having belonged to the crusader, they certainly having the stamp of more recent days; but I was told that the painting had been so considered time out of mind; and that as to the armor, it had been found in a lumber-room and ele-vated to its present situation by the Squire, who at once determined it to be the armor of the family hero; and as he was absolute authority on all such subjects in his own household, the matter had passed into current

acceptation. A sideboard was set out just under this chivalric trophy, on which was a display of plate that might have vied (at least in variety) with Belshazzar's parade of the vessels of the temple: "flagons, cans, cups, beakers, goblets, basins, and ewers," the gorgeous utensils of good companionship that had gradually accumulated through many generations of jovial housekeepers. Before these stood the two Yule candles, beaming like two stars of the first magnitude; other lights were distributed in branches, and the whole array glittered like a firmament of silver.

We were ushered into this banqueting scene with the sound of minstrelsy, the old harper being seated on a stool beside the fireplace and twanging, his instrument with a vast deal more power than melody. Never did Christmas board display a more goodly and gracious assemblage of countenances; those who were not handsome were at least happy, and happiness is a rare improver of your hard-favored visage. I always consider an old English family as well worth studying as a collection of Holbein's portraits or Albert Dürer's prints. There is much antiquarian lore to be acquired, much knowledge of the physiognomies of former times. Perhaps it may be from having continually before their eyes those rows of old family portraits, with which the mansions of this country are stocked; certain it is that the quaint features of antiquity are often most faithfully perpetuated in these ancient lines, and I have traced an old family nose through a whole picture-gallery, legitimately handed down from generation to generation almost

from the time of the Conquest. Something of the kind was to be observed in the worthy company around me. Many of their faces had evidently originated in a Gothic age, and been merely copied by succeeding generations; and there was one little girl in particular, of staid demeanor, with a high Roman nose and an antique vinegar aspect, who was a great favorite of the Squire's, being, as he said, a Bracebridge all over, and the very counterpart of one of his ancestors who figured in the court of Henry VIII.

The parson said grace, which was not a short familiar one, such as is commonly addressed to the Deity in these unceremonious days, but a long, courtly, well-worded one of the ancient school. There was now a pause, as if something was expected, when suddenly the butler entered the hall with some degree of bustle: he was attended by a servant on each side with a large wax-light, and bore a silver dish on which was an enormous pig's head decorated with rosemary, with a lemon in its mouth, which was placed with great formality at the head of the table. The moment this pageant made its appearance the harper struck up a flourish; at the conclusion of which the young Oxonian, on receiving a hint from the Squire, gave, with an air of the most comic gravity, an old carol, the first verse of which was as follows:—

"Caput apri defero
Reddens laudes Domino.
The boar's head in hand bring I,
With garlands gay and rosemary.
I pray you all synge merily
Qui estis in convivio."

Though prepared to witness many of these little eccentricities, from being apprised of the peculiar hobby of mine host, yet I confess the parade with which so odd a dish was introduced somewhat perplexed me, until I gathered from the conversation of the Squire and the parson that it was meant to represent the bringing in of the boar's head, a dish formerly served up with much ceremony and the sound of minstrelsy and song at great tables on Christmas Day. "I like the old custom," said the Squire, "not merely because it is stately and pleasing in itself, but because it was observed at the college at Oxford at which I was educated. When I hear the old song chanted it brings to mind the time when I was young and gamesome, and the noble old college hall, and my fellow-students loitering about in their black gowns; many of whom, poor lads! are now in their graves."

The parson, however, whose mind was not haunted by such associations, and who was always more taken up with the text than the sentiment, objected to the Oxonian's version of the carol, which he affirmed was different from that sung at college. He went on, with the dry perseverance of a commentator, to give the college reading, accompanied by sundry annotations, addressing himself at first to the company at large; but, finding their attention gradually diverted to other talk and other objects, he lowered his tone as his number of auditors diminished, until he concluded his remarks in an under voice to a fat-headed old gentleman next him who was silently engaged in the discussion of a huge plateful of turkey.

The table was literally loaded with good cheer, and presented an epitome of country abundance in this season of overflowing larders. A distinguished post was allotted

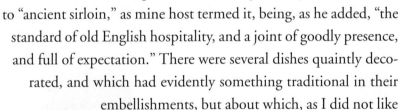

to "ancient sirloin," as mine host termed it, being, as he added, "the standard of old English hospitality, and a joint of goodly presence, and full of expectation." There were several dishes quaintly decorated, and which had evidently something traditional in their embellishments, but about which, as I did not like to appear overcurious, I asked no questions.

I could not, however, but notice a pie magnificently decorated with peacock's feathers, in imitation of the tail of that bird, which

overshadowed a considerable tract of the table. This, the Squire confessed with some little hesitation, was a pheasant pie, though a peacock pie was certainly the most authentical; but there had been such a mortality among the peacocks this season that he could not prevail upon himself to have one killed.

It would be tedious, perhaps, to my wiser readers, who may not have that foolish fondness for odd and obsolete things to which I am a little given, were I to mention the other makeshifts or this worthy old humorist, by which he was endeavoring to follow up, though at humble distance, the quaint customs of antiquity. I was pleased, however, to see the respect shown to his whims by his children and relatives; who, indeed, entered readily into the full spirit of them, and seemed all well versed in their parts, having doubtless been present at many a rehearsal. I was amused, too, at the air of profound gravity with which the butler and other servants executed the duties assigned them, however eccentric. They had an old-fashioned look, having, for the most part, been brought up in the household and grown into keeping with the antiquated mansion and the humors of its lord, and most probably looked upon all his whimsical regulations as the established laws of honorable housekeeping.

When the cloth was removed the butler brought in a huge silver vessel of rare and curious workmanship, which he placed before the Squire. Its appearance was hailed with acclamation, being the Wassail Bowl, so renowned in Christmas festivity. The contents had been prepared by the Squire himself; for it was a beverage in the skilful mixture of which he particularly prided himself, alleging that it was too abstruse and complex for the comprehension of an ordinary servant. It was a potation, indeed, that might well make the heart of a toper leap within him, being composed of the richest and raciest wines, highly spiced and sweetened, with roasted apples bobbing about the surface.

The old gentleman's whole countenance beamed with a serene look of indwelling delight as he stirred this mighty bowl. Having raised it to his lips, with a hearty wish of a merry Christmas to all present, he sent it brimming round the board, for every one to follow his example, according to the primitive style, pronouncing it "the ancient fountain of good feeling, where all hearts met together."

There was much laughing and rallying as the honest emblem of Christmas joviality circulated and was kissed rather coyly by the ladies. When it reached Master Simon, he raised it in both hands, and with the air of a boon companion struck up an old Wassail Chanson:

> "The brown bowle,
> The merry brown bowle,
> As it goes round-about-a,
>   Fill
>   Still,
> Let the world say what it will,
> And drink your fill all out-a.
>
> The deep canne,
> The merry deep canne,
> As thou dost freely quaff-a,
>   Sing
>   Fling,
> Be as merry as a king,
> And sound a lusty laugh-a."

Much of the conversation during dinner turned upon family topics, to which I was a stranger. There was, however, a great deal of rallying of Master Simon about some gay widow with whom he was accused of having a flirtation. This attack was commenced by the ladies, but it was continued throughout the dinner by the fat-headed old gentleman next the parson with the persevering assiduity of a slow hound, being one of those long-winded jokers who, though rather dull at starting game, are unrivalled for their talents in hunting it down. At every pause in the general conversation he renewed his bantering in pretty much the same terms, winking hard at me with both eyes whenever he gave Master Simon what he considered a home thrust. The latter, indeed, seemed fond of being teased on the subject, as old bachelors are apt to be, and he took occasion to inform me, in an undertone, that the lady in question was a prodigiously fine woman and drove her own curricle.

The dinner-time passed away in this flow of innocent hilarity, and, though the old hall may have resounded in its time with many a scene of broader rout and revel, yet I doubt whether it ever witnessed more honest and genuine enjoyment. How easy it is for one benevolent being to diffuse pleasure around him! and how truly is a kind heart a fountain of gladness, making everything in its vicinity to freshen into smiles! The joyous disposition of the worthy Squire was perfectly contagious; he was happy himself, and disposed to make all the world happy, and the little eccentricities of his humor did but season, in a manner, the sweetness of his philanthropy.

When the ladies had retired, the conversation, as usual, became still more animated; many good things were broached which had been thought of during dinner, but

which would not exactly do for a lady's ear; and, though I cannot positively affirm that there was much wit uttered, yet I have certainly heard many contests of rare wit produce much less laughter. Wit, after all, is a mighty tart, pungent ingredient, and much too acid for some stomachs; but honest good-humor is the oil and wine of a merry meeting, and there is no jovial companionship equal to that where the jokes are rather small and the laughter abundant. The Squire told several long stories of early college pranks and adventures, in some of which the parson had been a sharer, though in looking at the latter it required some effort of imagination to figure such a little dark anatomy of a man into the perpetrator of a madcap gambol. Indeed, the two college chums presented pictures of what men may be made by their different lots in life. The Squire had left the university to live lustily on his paternal domains in the vigorous enjoyment of prosperity and sunshine, and had flourished on to a hearty and florid old age; whilst the poor parson, on the contrary, had dried and withered away among dusty tomes in the silence and shadows of his study. Still, there seemed to be a spark of almost extinguished fire feebly glimmering in the bottom of his soul; and as the Squire hinted at a sly story of the parson and a pretty milkmaid whom they once met on the banks of the Isis, the old gentleman made an "alphabet of faces," which, as far as I could decipher his physiognomy, I verily believe was indicative of laughter; indeed, I have rarely met with an old gentleman that took absolute offence at the imputed gallantries of his youth.

I found the tide of wine and wassail fast gaining on the dry land of sober judgment. The company grew merrier and louder as their jokes grew duller. Master Simon was in as chirping a humor as a grasshopper filled with dew; his old songs grew of a warmer complexion, and he began to talk maudlin about the widow. He even gave a long song about the wooing of a widow which he informed me he had gathered from an excellent black-letter work entitled Cupid's Solicitor for Love, containing store of good advice for bachelors, and which he promised to lend me; the first verse was to effect:—

He that will woo a widow must not dally
        He must make hay while the sun doth shine;
He must not stand with her, shall I, shall I,
        But boldly say, Widow, thou must be mine.

This song inspired the fat-headed old gentleman, who made several attempts to tell a rather broad story out of Joe Miller that was pat to the purpose; but he always stuck in the middle, everybody recollecting the latter part excepting himself. The parson, too, began to show the effects of good cheer, having gradually settled down into a doze and his wig sitting most suspiciously on one side. Just at this juncture we were summoned to the drawing room, and I suspect, at the private instigation of mine host, whose joviality seemed always tempered with a proper love of decorum.

After the dinner-table was removed the hall was given up to the younger members of the family, who, prompted to all kind of noisy mirth by the Oxonian and Master Simon, made its old walls ring with their merriment as they played at romping games. I delight in witnessing the gambols of children, and particularly at this happy holiday season, and could not help stealing out of the drawing-room on hearing one of their peals of laughter. I found them at the game of blindman's-buff. Master Simon, who was the leader of their revels, and seemed on all occasions to fulfill the office of that ancient potentate, the Lord of Misrule, was blinded in the midst of the hall. The little beings were as busy about him as the mock fairies about Falstaff, pinching him, plucking at the skirts of his coat, and tickling him with straws. One fine blue-eyed girl of about thirteen, with her flaxen hair all in beautiful confusion, her frolic face in a glow, her frock half torn off her shoulders, a complete picture of a romp, was the chief tormentor; and, from the slyness with which Master Simon avoided the smaller game and hemmed this wild little nymph in corners, and obliged her to jump shrieking over chairs, I suspected the rogue of being not a whit more blinded than was convenient.

When I returned to the drawing-room I found the company seated round the fire listening to the parson, who was deeply ensconced in a high-backed oaken chair, the work of some cunning artificer of yore, which had been brought from the library for his particular accommodation. From this venerable piece of furniture, with which his

shadowy figure and dark weazen face so admirably accorded, he was dealing out strange accounts of the popular superstitions and legends of the surrounding country, with which he had become acquainted in the course of his antiquarian researches. I am half inclined to think that the old gentleman was himself somewhat tinctured with superstition, as men are very apt to be who live a recluse and studious life in a sequestered part of the country and pore over black-letter tracts, so often filled with the marvelous and supernatural. He gave us several anecdotes of the fancies of the neighboring peasantry concerning the effigy of the crusader which lay on the tomb by the church altar. As it was the only monument of the kind in that part of the country, it had always been regarded with feelings of superstition by the good wives of the village. It was said to get up from the tomb and walk the rounds of the churchyard in stormy nights, particularly when it thundered; and one old woman, whose cottage bordered on the churchyard, had seen it through the windows of the church, when the moon shone, slowly pacing up and down the aisles. It was the belief that some wrong had been left unredressed by the deceased, or some treasure hidden, which kept the spirit in a state of trouble and restlessness. Some talked of gold and jewels buried in the tomb, over which the spectre kept watch; and there was a story current of a sexton in old times who endeavored to break his way to the coffin at night, but just as he reached it received a violent blow

from the marble hand of the effigy, which stretched him senseless on the pavement. These tales were often laughed at by some of the sturdier among the rustics, yet when night came on there were many of the stoutest unbelievers that were shy of venturing alone in the footpath that led across the churchyard.

From these and other anecdotes that followed the crusader appeared to be the favorite hero of ghost-stories throughout the vicinity. His picture, which hung up in the hall, was thought by the servants to have something supernatural about it; for they remarked that in whatever part of the hall you went the eyes of the warrior were still fixed on you. The old porter's wife, too, at the lodge, who had been born and brought up in the family, and was a great gossip among the maid-servants, affirmed that in her young days she had often heard say that on Midsummer Eve, when it was well known all kinds of ghosts, goblins, and fairies become visible and walk abroad, the crusader used to mount his horse, come down from his picture, ride about the house, down the avenue, and so to the church to visit the tomb; on which occasion the church-door most civilly swung open of itself; not that he needed it, for he rode through closed gates, and even stone walls, and had been seen by one of the dairymaids to pass between two bars of the great park gate, making himself as thin as a sheet of paper.

All these superstitions I found had been very much countenanced by the Squire, who, though not superstitious himself, was very fond of seeing others so. He listened to every goblin tale of the neighboring gossips with infinite gravity, and held the porter's wife in high favor on account of her talent for the marvellous. He was himself a great reader of old legends and romances,

and often lamented that he could not believe in them; for a superstitious person, he thought, must live in a kind of fairy-land.

Whilst we were all attention to the parson's stories, our ears were suddenly assailed by a burst of heterogeneous sounds from the hall, in which were mingled something like the clang of rude minstrelsy with the uproar of many small voices and girlish laughter. The door suddenly flew open, and a train came trooping into the room that might almost have been mistaken for the breaking up of the court of Faery. That indefatigable spirit, Master Simon, in the faithful discharge of his duties as lord of misrule, had conceived the idea of a Christmas mummery or masking; and having called in to his assistance the Oxonian and the young officer, who were equally ripe for anything that should occasion romping and merriment, they had carried it into instant effect. The old housekeeper had been consulted; the antique clothespresses and wardrobes rummaged and made to yield up the relics of finery that had not seen the light for several generations; the younger part of the company had been privately convened from the parlor and hall, and the whole had been bedizened out into a burlesque imitation of an antique mask.

Master Simon led the van, as "Ancient Christmas," quaintly apparelled in a ruff, a short cloak, which had very much the aspect of one of the old housekeeper's petticoats, and a hat that might have served for a village steeple, and must indubitably have figured in the days of the Covenanters. From under this his nose curved boldly forth, flushed with a frost-bitten bloom that seemed the very trophy of a December blast. He was accompanied by the blue-eyed romp, dished up, as "Dame Mince Pie," in the venerable magnificence of a faded brocade, long stomacher, peaked hat, and high-heeled shoes. The young officer appeared as Robin Hood, in a sporting dress of Kendal green and a foraging cap with a gold tassel.

The costume, to be sure, did not bear testimony to deep research, and there was an evident eye to the picturesque, natural to a young gallant in the presence of his mistress. The fair Julia hung on his arm in a pretty rustic dress as "Maid Marian." The rest of the train had been metamorphosed in various ways; the girls trussed up in the finery of the ancient belles of the Bracebridge line, and the striplings bewhiskered with burnt cork, and gravely clad in broad skirts, hanging sleeves, and full-bottomed wigs, to represent the character of Roast Beef, Plum Pudding, and other worthies celebrated in ancient maskings. The whole was under the control of the Oxonian in the appropriate character of Misrule; and I observed that he exercised rather a mischievous sway with his wand over the smaller personages of the pageant.

The irruption of this motley crew with beat of drum, according to ancient custom, was the consummation of uproar and merriment. Master Simon covered himself with glory by the stateliness with which, as Ancient Christmas, he walked a minuet with the peerless though giggling Dame Mince Pie. It was followed by a dance of all the characters, which from its medley of costumes seemed as though the old family portraits had skipped down from their frames to join in the sport. Different centuries were figuring at cross hands and right and left; the Dark Ages were cutting pirouettes and rigadoons; and the days of Queen Bess jigging merrily down the middle through a line of succeeding generations.

The worthy Squire contemplated these fantastic sports and this resurrection of his old wardrobe with the simple relish of childish delight. He stood chuckling and rubbing his hands, and scarcely hearing a word the parson said, notwithstanding that the latter was discoursing most authentically on the ancient and stately dance of the Pavon, or peacock, from which he conceived the minuet to be derived. For my part, I was in a continual excitement from the varied scenes of whim and innocent gayety passing before me. It was inspiring to see wild-eyed frolic and warm-hearted hospitality breaking out from among the chills and glooms of winter, and old age throwing off his apathy and

catching once more the freshness of youthful enjoyment. I felt also an interest in the scene from the consideration that these fleeting customs were posting fast into oblivion, and that this was perhaps the only family in England in which the whole of them was still punctiliously observed. There was a quaintness, too, mingled with all this revelry that gave it a peculiar zest: it was suited to the time and place; and as the old manor-house almost reeled with mirth and wassail, it seemed echoing back the joviality of long departed years.

But enough of Christmas and its gambols; it is time for me to pause in this garrulity. Methinks I hear the questions asked by my graver readers, "To what purpose is all this? how is the world to be made wiser by this talk?" Alas! is there not wisdom enough extant for the instruction of the world? And if not, are there not thousands of abler pens laboring for its improvement? It is so much pleasanter to please than to instruct—to play the companion rather than the preceptor.

What, after all, is the mite of wisdom that I could throw into the mass of knowledge! or how am I sure that my sagest deductions may be safe guides for the opinions of others? But in writing to amuse, if I fail the only evil is in my own disappointment. If, however, I can by any lucky chance, in these days of evil, rub out one wrinkle from the brow of care or beguile the heavy heart of one moment of sorrow; if I can now and then penetrate through the gathering film of misanthropy, prompt a benevolent view of human nature, and make my reader more in good-humor with his fellow-beings and himself—surely, surely, I shall not then have written entirely in vain.

Christmas at Red Butte

L. M. Montgomery

"Of course Santa Claus will come," said Jimmy Martin confidently. Jimmy was ten, and at ten it is easy to be confident. "Why, he's got to come because it is Christmas Eve, and he always has come. You know that, twins."

Yes, the twins knew it and, cheered by Jimmy's superior wisdom, their doubts passed away. There had been one terrible moment when Theodora had sighed and told them they mustn't be too much disappointed if Santa Claus did not come this year because the crops had been poor, and he mightn't have had enough presents to go around.

"That doesn't make any difference to Santa Claus," scoffed Jimmy. "You know as well as I do, Theodora Prentice, that Santa Claus is rich whether the crops fail or not. They failed three years ago, before Father died, but Santa Claus came all the same. Prob'bly you don't remember it, twins, 'cause you were too little, but I do. Of course he'll come, so don't you worry a mite. And he'll bring my skates and your dolls. He knows we're expecting them, Theodora, 'cause we wrote him a letter last week, and threw it up the chimney. And there'll be candy and nuts, of course, and Mother's gone to town to buy a turkey. I tell you we're going to have a ripping Christmas."

"Well, don't use such slangy words about it, Jimmy-boy," sighed Theodora. She couldn't bear to dampen their hopes any further, and perhaps Aunt Elizabeth might manage it if the colt sold well. But Theodora had her painful doubts, and she sighed again as she looked out of the window far down the trail that wound across the prairie, red-lighted by the declining sun of the short wintry afternoon.

"Do people always sigh like that when they get to be sixteen?" asked Jimmy curiously. "You didn't sigh like that when you were only fifteen, Theodora. I wish you wouldn't. It makes me feel funny—and it's not a nice kind of funniness either."

"It's a bad habit I've got into lately," said Theodora, trying to laugh. "Old folks are dull sometimes, you know, Jimmy-boy."

"Sixteen is awful old, isn't it?" said Jimmy reflectively. "I'll tell you what I'm going to do when I'm sixteen, Theodora. I'm going to pay off the mortgage, and buy mother a silk dress, and a piano for the twins. Won't that be elegant? I'll be able to do that 'cause I'm a man. Of course if I was only a girl I couldn't."

"I hope you'll be a good kind brave man and a real help to your mother," said Theodora softly, sitting down before the cosy fire and lifting the fat little twins into her lap.

"Oh, I'll be good to her, never you fear," assured Jimmy, squatting comfortably down on the little fur rug before the stove—the skin of the coyote his father had killed four years ago. "I believe in being good to your mother when you've only got the one. Now tell us a story, Theodora—a real jolly story, you know, with lots of fighting in it. Only please don't kill anybody. I like to hear about fighting, but I like to have all the people come out alive."

Theodora laughed, and began a story about the Riel Rebellion of '85—a story which had the double merit of being true and exciting at the same time. It was quite dark when she finished, and the twins were nodding, but Jimmy's eyes were wide open and sparkling.

"That was great," he said, drawing a long breath. "Tell us another."

"No, it's bedtime for you all," said Theodora firmly. "One story at a time is my rule, you know."

"But I want to sit up till Mother comes home," objected Jimmy.

"You can't. She may be very late, for she would have to wait to see Mr. Porter. Besides, you don't know what time Santa Claus might come—if he comes at all. If he were to drive along and see you children up instead of being sound asleep in bed, he might go right on and never call at all."

This argument was too much for Jimmy.

"All right, we'll go. But we have to hang up our stockings first. Twins, get yours."

The twins toddled off in great excitement, and brought back their Sunday stockings, which Jimmy proceeded to hang along the edge of the mantel shelf. This done, they all trooped obediently off to bed. Theodora gave another sigh, and seated herself at the window, where she could watch the moonlit prairie for Mrs. Martin's homecoming and knit at the same time.

I am afraid that you will think from all the sighing Theodora was doing that she was a very melancholy and despondent young lady. You couldn't think anything more unlike the real Theodora. She was the jolliest, bravest girl of sixteen in all Saskatchewan, as her shining brown eyes and rosy, dimpled cheeks would have told you; and her sighs were not on her own account, but simply for fear the children were going to be disappointed. She knew that they would be almost heartbroken if Santa Claus did not come, and that this would hurt the patient hardworking little mother more than all else.

Five years before this, Theodora had come to live with Uncle George and Aunt Elizabeth in the little log house at Red Butte. Her own mother had just died, and Theodora had only her big brother Donald left, and Donald had Klondike fever. The Martins were poor, but they had gladly made room for their little niece, and Theodora had lived there ever since, her aunt's right-hand girl and the beloved playmate of the children. They had been very happy until Uncle George's death two years before this Christmas Eve; but since then there had been hard times in the little log house, and though Mrs. Martin and Theodora did their best, it was a woefully hard task to make both ends meet, especially this year when their crops had been poor. Theodora and her aunt had made every sacrifice possible for the children's sake, and at least Jimmy and the twins had not felt the pinch very severely yet.

At seven Mrs. Martins bells jingled at the door and Theodora flew out. "Go right in and get warm, Auntie," she said briskly. "I'll take Ned away and unharness him."

"It's a bitterly cold night," said Mrs. Martin wearily. There was a note of discouragement in her voice that struck dismay to Theodora's heart.

"I'm afraid it means no Christmas for the children tomorrow," she thought sadly, as she led Ned away to the stable. When she returned to the kitchen Mrs. Martin was sitting by the fire, her face in her chilled hand, sobbing convulsively.

"Auntie—oh, Auntie, don't!" exclaimed Theodora impulsively. It was such a rare thing to see her plucky, resolute little aunt in tears. "You're cold and tired—I'll have a nice cup of tea for you in a trice."

"No, it isn't that," said Mrs. Martin brokenly. "It was seeing those stockings hanging there. Theodora, I couldn't get a thing for the children—not a single thing. Mr. Porter would only give forty dollars for the colt, and when all the bills were paid there was barely enough left for such necessaries as we must have. I suppose I ought to feel thankful I could get those. But the thought of the children's disappointment tomorrow is more than I can bear. It would have been better to have told them long ago, but I kept building on getting more for the colt. Well, it's weak and foolish to give way like this. We'd better both take a cup of tea and go to bed. It will save fuel."

When Theodora went up to her little room her face was very thoughtful. She took a small box from her table and carried it to the window. In it was a very pretty little gold locket hung on a narrow blue ribbon. Theodora held it tenderly in her fingers, and looked out over the moonlit prairie with a very sober face. Could she give up her dear locket—the locket Donald had given her just before he started for the Klondike? She had never thought she could do such a thing. It was almost the only thing she had to remind her of Donald—handsome, merry, impulsive, warmhearted Donald, who had gone away four years ago with a smile on his bonny face and splendid hope in his heart.

"Here's a locket for you, Gift o' God," he had said gaily—he had such a dear loving habit of calling her by the beautiful meaning of her name. A lump came into Theodora's throat as she remembered it. "I couldn't afford a chain too, but when I come back I'll bring you a rope of Klondike nuggets for it."

Then he had gone away. For two years letters had come from him regularly. Then he wrote that he had joined a prospecting party to a remote wilderness. After that was silence, deepening into anguish of suspense that finally ended in hopelessness. A rumour came that Donald Prentice was dead. None had returned from the expedition he had joined. Theodora had long ago given up all hope of ever seeing Donald again. Hence her locket was doubly dear to her.

But Aunt Elizabeth had always been so good and loving and kind to her. Could she not make the sacrifice for her sake? Yes, she could and would. Theodora flung up her head with a gesture that meant decision. She took out of the locket the bits of hair—her mother's and Donald's—which it contained (perhaps a tear or two fell as she did so) and then hastily donned her warmest cap and wraps. It was only three miles to Spencer; she could easily walk it in an hour and, as it was Christmas Eve, the shops would be open late. She must walk, for Ned could not be taken out again, and the mare's foot was sore. Besides, Aunt Elizabeth must not know until it was done.

As stealthily as if she were bound on some nefarious errand, Theodora slipped downstairs and out of the house. The next minute she was hurrying along the trail in the moonlight. The great dazzling prairie was around her, the mystery and splendour of the northern night all about her. It was very calm and cold, but Theodora walked so briskly that she kept warm. The trail from Red Butte to Spencer was a lonely one. Mr. Lurgan's house, halfway to town, was the only dwelling on it.

When Theodora reached Spencer she made her way at once to the only jewellery store the little town contained. Mr. Benson, its owner, had been a friend of her uncle's, and Theodora felt sure that he would buy her locket. Nevertheless her heart beat quickly, and her breath came and went uncomfortably fast as she went in. Suppose he wouldn't buy it. Then there would be no Christmas for the children at Red Butte.

"Good evening, Miss Theodora," said Mr. Benson briskly. "What can I do for you?"

"I'm afraid I'm not a very welcome sort of customer, Mr. Benson," said Theodora, with an uncertain smile. "I want to sell, not buy. Could you—will you buy this locket?"

Mr. Benson pursed up his lips, took up the locket, and examined it. "Well, I don't often buy second-hand stuff," he said, after some reflection, "but I don't mind obliging you, Miss Theodora. I'll give you four dollars for this trinket."

Theodora knew the locket had cost a great deal more than that, but four dollars would get what she wanted, and she dared not ask for more. In a few minutes the locket was in Mr. Benson's possession, and Theodora, with four crisp new bills in her purse, was hurrying to the toy store. Half an hour later she was on her way back to Red Butte, with as many parcels as she could carry—Jimmy's skates, two lovely dolls for the twins, packages of nuts and candy, and a nice plump turkey. Theodora beguiled her lonely tramp by picturing the children's joy in the morning.

About a quarter of a mile past Mr. Lurgan's house the trail curved suddenly about a bluff of poplars. As Theodora rounded the turn she halted in amazement. Almost at her feet the body of a man was lying across the road. He was clad in a big fur coat, and had a fur cap pulled well down over his forehead and ears. Almost all of him that could be seen was a full bushy beard. Theodora had no idea who he was, or where he had come from. But she realized that he was unconscious, and that he would speedily freeze to death if help were not brought. The footprints of a horse galloping across the prairie suggested a fall and a runaway, but Theodora did not waste time in speculation. She ran back at full speed to Mr. Lurgan's, and roused the household. In a few minutes Mr. Lurgan and his son had hitched a horse to a wood-sleigh, and hurried down the trail to the unfortunate man.

Theodora, knowing that her assistance was not needed, and that she ought to get home as quickly as possible, went on her way as soon as she had seen the stranger in safe keeping. When she reached the little log house she crept in, cautiously put the children's gifts in their stockings, placed the turkey on the table where Aunt Elizabeth would see it the first thing in the morning, and then slipped off to bed, a very weary but very happy girl.

The joy that reigned in the little log house the next day more than repaid Theodora for her sacrifice.

"Whoopee, didn't I tell you that Santa Claus would come all right!" shouted the delighted Jimmy. "Oh, what splendid skates!"

The twins hugged their dolls in silent rapture, but Aunt Elizabeth's face was the best of all.

Then the dinner had to be prepared, and everybody had a hand in that. Just as Theodora, after a grave peep into the oven, had announced that the turkey was done, a sleigh dashed around the house. Theodora flew to answer the knock at the door, and there stood Mr. Lurgan and a big, bewhiskered, fur-coated fellow whom Theodora recognized as the stranger she had found on the trail. But—was he a stranger? There was something oddly familiar in those merry brown eyes. Theodora felt herself growing dizzy.

"Donald!" she gasped. "Oh, Donald!"

And then she was in the big fellow's arms, laughing and crying at the same time.

Donald it was indeed. And then followed half an hour during which everybody talked at once, and the turkey would have been burned to a crisp had it not been for the presence of mind of Mr. Lurgan who, being the least excited of them all, took it out of the oven, and set it on the back of the stove.

"To think that it was you last night, and that I never dreamed it," exclaimed Theodora. "Oh, Donald, if I hadn't gone to town!"

"I'd have frozen to death, I'm afraid," said Donald soberly. "I got into Spencer on the last train last night. I felt that I must come right out—I couldn't wait till morning. But there wasn't a team to be got for love or money—it was Christmas Eve and all the livery rigs were out. So I came on horseback. Just by that bluff something frightened my horse, and he shied violently. I was half asleep and thinking of my little sister, and I went off like a shot. I suppose I struck my head against a tree. Anyway, I knew nothing more until I came to in Mr. Lurgan's kitchen. I wasn't much hurt—feel none the worse of it except for a sore head and shoulder. But, oh, Gift o' God, how you have grown! I can't realize that you are the little sister I left four years ago. I suppose you have been thinking I was dead?"

"Yes, and, oh, Donald, where have you been?"

"Well, I went way up north with a prospecting party. We had a tough time the first year, I can tell you, and some of us never came back. We weren't in a country where post offices were lying round loose either, you see. Then at last, just as we were about giving up in despair, we struck it rich. I've brought a snug little pile home with me, and things are going to look up in this log house, Gift o' God. There'll be no more worrying for you dear people over mortgages."

"I'm so glad—for Auntie's sake," said Theodora, with shining eyes. "But, oh, Donald, it's best of all just to have you back. I'm so perfectly happy that I don't know what to do or say."

"Well, I think you might have dinner," said Jimmy in an injured tone. "The turkey's getting stone cold, and I'm most starving. I just can't stand it another minute."

So, with a laugh, they all sat down to the table and ate the merriest Christmas dinner the little log house had ever known.

KRIS KRINGLE AND HIS ELVES

B. McLoughlin

These busy and happy little Elves love the rain, ice, and snow, and when the north wind begins to blow they frolic over the mountains to help Kris Kringle. They are so eager and love the work so well that they have come too early and find old Kris Kringle, with his pipe in his hand, sound asleep in his chair. So with a merry little laugh they run off to play. Let us look for a moment at this dear old man that the children love so much. See his jovial face, his cheeks as rosy as an apple, and his hair and beard as white as the driven snow. And now that he opens his sparkling eyes, I think you will agree with me, he is the funniest little man you ever saw.

At the sound of his whistle the little Elves all appear. "I am sorry to keep my Elves waiting," he said, "but I worked all night and fell asleep in my chair. The boys and girls have been good and kind this year, and with the sick and poor I have been busier than ever before. Put your sunshine faces on, and Mr. Wind and Snow and Ice will take you where you must go."

For weeks these merry little fellows live with Kris Kringle, in his ice palace, over the mountains of snow in Kris Kringleland. They work, and sing and play, and are busy and happy the livelong day.

Let us take a peep into Kris Kringle's palace which glitters with icicles and is covered with snow. Large pine logs burn on the hearth, his furniture is soft and

easy, and his bed is of down. In his library are long rows of books that contain the records of good girls and boys.

All his land is covered with Christmas trees, and mistletoe, holly, and frost flowers grow round the door.

The shop where all the toys are made is at the side of the house. The big blazing forge stands in the room where all the iron toys are made—such as steam engines, railroad cars, swords, and guns—and in another room are all kinds of wooden toys, horses, carts, and wagons, doll's furniture, sleds, drums, and boats, and all the toys that Kris Kringle knows will please little boys.

Then comes the doll's room: in this are dolls that walk and talk, dolls that are dressed and undressed, mother dolls and baby dolls, dolls asleep and dolls awake, and as many kinds as there are little girls to suit.

Five rollicking little Elves, with paintbrushes and pots in their hands, are carrying paint to a large room in the big workshop that is used for painting toys. Here, Kris Kringle spends many happy hours, painting the sleds in browns, yellows, and reds, and the houses, trunks, and boats, and Noah's arks, in bright red colors that the good children all over the land like best.

As the toys are finished, the gay little Elves carry them to the wonderful storehouse that is crowded with all sort of interesting things.

Dear Kris Kringle, with telescope in hand and his faithful dog by his side, is at the window spying out the good children. This wonderful man knows just what sort of child every one is. No one can deceive him, for he is on watch from morning till night.

It is a busy and happy day in the Kris Kringle family. Even the dog can hardly wait. The lists are all made out, the letters are all written, the bags are all filled, and the Elves are putting the finishing touch to the silver bells.

When the twilight gathered and a hush was over all, old Kris, bundled in furs from head to foot, jumped into his great white and gold sled, that was drawn by six prancing reindeer. The happy little Elves gathered round, ringing bells and blowing horns while Kris Kringle dashed off with his lively team.

It is said that thousands of years ago, children were not always good; then Kris Kringle did such queer things for them. The boys who chased the cats and stoned the birds, and who were unkind to other animals; and the children who disobeyed the rules, and would not learn their lessons, and who were selfish and bad, found rods and empty bags and stockings filled with bran.

But in those days as now, to the children who were good, and kind, and true, Old Kris left rattles, and tops, and presents for all from a purse to a ball.

The frozen snow crackled under the reindeers' feet as they sped to reach in time the crowded towns, alleys, and lonely homes of the poor, who were to be made glad by Christmas dinners, packages of warm clothing, and toys that the faithful little Elves placed on top.

You may be sure it took a nimble little man to do all that Kris Kringle did. But his affairs always go right, and every home was visited that night.

Down the chimney he crept and with the light of his tiny lamp every room was found and every stocking was filled. Just as the last bag was emptied the sun arose.

The Elves busied themselves to put things in order while Kris was gone, for they knew he would be ready for a long sleep when he returned. Some polished and sharpened the tools and put them in their places. Two carried the important telescope to its stand, and others were kept busy answering the telephone, for messages of thanks came pouring in from far and wide.

The Elves had their trunks packed, and when they heard the bells they ran to help the weary old man out. After the reindeer were taken good care of, the Elves bade good-bye to Kris Kringle and his happy mountain. They told him they had been happy because they made someone else happy.

As they scampered off to their cozy little nooks in the woods, they shouted, "So good-bye dear old Kris, we will visit dear old Kris Kringleland again next year!"

Christmas Eve

THE NUTCRACKER AND THE MOUSE KING

E. T. A. HOFFMANN

CHRISTMAS EVE

In the 24th of December Dr. Stahlbaum's children were not allowed, on any pretext whatever, at any time of all that day, to go into the small drawing-room, much less into the best drawing-room into which it opened. Fritz and Marie were sitting cowered together in a corner of the back parlour when the evening twilight fell, and they began to feel terribly eery. Seeing that no candles were brought, as was generally the case on Christmas Eve, Fritz, whispering in a mysterious fashion, confided to his young sister (who was just seven) that he had heard rattlings and rustlings going on all day, since early morning, inside the forbidden rooms, as well as distant hammerings. Further, that a short time ago a little dark-looking man had gone slipping and creeping across the floor with a big box under his arm, though he was well aware that this little man was no other than Godpapa Drosselmeier. At this news Marie clapped her little hands for gladness, and cried:

"Oh! I do wonder what pretty things Godpapa Drosselmeier has been making for us this time!"

Godpapa Drosselmeier was anything but a nice-looking man. He was little and lean, with a great many wrinkles on his face, a big patch of black plaister where his right eye ought to have been, and not a hair on his head; which was why he wore a fine white wig, made of glass, and a very beautiful work of art. But he was a very, very clever man, who even knew and understood all about clocks and watches, and could make them himself. So that when one of the beautiful clocks that were in Dr. Stahlbaum's house was out of sorts, and couldn't sing, Godpapa Drosselmeier would come, take off his glass periwig and his little yellow coat, gird himself with a blue apron, and proceed to stick sharp-pointed instruments into the inside of the clock, in a way that made little Marie quite miserable to witness. However, this didn't really hurt the poor clock, which, on the contrary, would come to life again, and begin to whirr and sing and strike as

merrily as ever; which caused everybody the greatest satisfaction. Of course, whenever he came he always brought something delightful in his pockets for the children—perhaps a little man, who would roll his eyes and make bows and scrapes, most comic to behold; or a box, out of which a little bird would jump; or something else of the kind. But for Christmas he always had some specially charming piece of ingenuity provided; something which had cost him infinite pains and labour—for which reason it was always taken away and put by with the greatest care by the children's parents.

"Oh! what can Godpapa Drosselmeier have been making for us *this* time," Marie cried, as we have said.

Fritz was of opinion that, this time, it could hardly be anything but a great castle, a fortress, where all sorts of pretty soldiers would be drilling and marching about; and then, that other soldiers would come and try to get into the fortress, upon which the soldiers inside would fire away at them, as pluckily as you please, with cannon, till every thing banged and thundered like anything.

"No, no," Marie said. "Godpapa Drosselmeier once told me about a beautiful garden, with a great lake in it, and beautiful swans swimming about with great gold collars, singing lovely music. And then a lovely little girl comes down through the garden to the lake, and calls the swans and feeds them with shortbread and cake."

"Swans don't eat cake and shortbread," Fritz cried, rather rudely (with masculine superiority); "and Godpapa Drosselmeier couldn't make a whole garden. After all, we have got very few of his playthings; whatever he brings is always taken away from us. So I like the things papa and mamma give us much better; we keep them, all right, ourselves, and can do what we like with them."

The children went on discussing as to what he might have in store for them this time. Marie called Fritz's attention to the fact that Miss Gertrude (her biggest doll) appeared to be failing a good deal as time went on, inasmuch as she was more clumsy and awkward than ever, tumbling on to the floor every two or three minutes, a thing which did not occur without leaving very ugly marks on her face, and of course a proper condition of her clothes became out of the question altogether. Scolding was of no use. Mamma too had laughed at her for being so delighted with Miss Gertrude's little new parasol. Fritz, again, remarked that a good fox was lacking to his small zoo-logical collection, and that his army was quite without cavalry, as his papa was well aware. But the children knew that their elders had got all sorts of charming things ready for them, as also that the Child-Christ, at Christmas time, took special care for their wants. Marie sat in thoughtful silence, but Fritz murmured quietly to himself:

"All the same, I should like a fox and some hussars!"

It was now quite dark; Fritz and Marie sitting close together, did not dare to utter another syllable; they felt as if there were a fluttering of gentle, invisible wings around them, whilst a very far away, but unutterably beautiful strain of music could dimly be heard. Then a bright gleam of light passed quickly athwart the wall, and the children knew that the Child-Christ had sped away, on shining wings, to other happy children. At this moment a silvery bell said, "Kling-ling! Kling-ling!" the doors flew open, and such a brilliance of light came streaming from the drawing-room that the children stood rooted where they were with cries of "Oh! Oh!"

But papa and mamma came and took their hands, saying, "Come now, darlings, and see what the blessed Child-Christ has brought for you."

THE CHRISTMAS PRESENTS

I appeal to yourself, kind reader (or listener)—Fritz, Theodore, Ernest, or whatsoever your name may chance to be—and I would beg you to bring vividly before your mind's eye your last Christmas table, all glorious with its various delightful Christmas presents; and then perhaps you will be able to form some idea of the manner in which the two children stood speechless with brilliant glances fixed on all the beautiful things; how, after a little, Marie, with a sigh, cried, "Oh, how lovely! how lovely!" and Fritz gave several jumps of delight. The children had certainly been very, very good and well-behaved all the foregoing year to be thus rewarded; for never had so many beautiful and delightful things been provided for them as this time. The great Christmas tree on the table bore many apples of silver and gold, and all its branches were heavy with bud and blossom, consisting of sugar almonds, many-tinted bonbons, and all sorts of charming things to eat. Perhaps the prettiest thing about this wonder-tree, however, was the fact that in all the recesses of its spreading branches hundreds of little tapers glittered like stars, inviting the children to pluck its flowers and fruit. Also, all round the tree on every side everything shone and glittered in the loveliest manner. Oh, how many beautiful things there were! Who, oh who, could describe them all? Marie gazed there at the most delicious dolls, and all kinds of toys, and (what was the prettiest thing of all) a little silk dress with many-tinted ribbons was hung upon a projecting branch in such sort that she could admire it on all its sides; which she accordingly did, crying out several times, "Oh! the lovely, the lovely, darling little dress. And I suppose, I do believe, I shall really be allowed to put it on!" Fritz, in the meantime, had had two or three trials how his new fox (which he had actually found on the table) could gallop; and now stated that he seemed a wildish sort of brute; but, no matter, he felt sure he would soon get him well in order; and he set to work to muster his new squadron of hussars, admirably equipped, in red and gold uniforms, with real silver swords, and mounted on such shining white horses that you would have thought they were of pure silver too.

When the children had sobered down a little, and were beginning upon the beautiful picture books (which were open, so that you could see all sorts of most beautiful flowers and people of every hue, to say nothing of lovely children playing, all as naturally represented as if they were really alive and could speak), there came another tinkling of a bell, to announce the display of Godpapa Drosselmeier's Christmas present, which was on another table, against the wall, concealed by a curtain. When this curtain was drawn, what did the children behold?

On a green lawn, bright with flowers, stood a lordly castle with a great many shining windows and golden towers. A chime of bells was going on inside it; doors and windows opened, and you saw very small, but beautiful, ladies and gentlemen, with plumed hats, and long robes down to their heels, walking up and down in the rooms of it. In the central hall, which seemed all in a blaze, there were quantities of little candles burning in silver chandeliers; children, in little short doublets, were dancing to the chimes of the bells. A gentleman, in an emerald green mantle, came to a window, made signs thereat, and then disappeared inside again; also, even Godpapa Drosselmeier himself (but scarcely taller than papa's thumb) came now and then, and stood at the castle door, then went in again.

Fritz had been looking on with the rest at the beautiful castle and the people walking about and dancing in it, with his arms leant on the table; then he said:

"Godpapa Drosselmeier, let me go into your castle for a little."

Drosselmeier answered that this could not possibly be done. In which he was right; for it was silly of Fritz to want to go into a castle which was not so tall as himself, golden towers and all. And Fritz saw that this was so.

After a short time, as the ladies and gentlemen kept on walking about just in the same fashion, the children dancing, and the emerald man looking out at the same window, and Godpapa Drosselmeier coming to the door Fritz cried impatiently:

"Godpapa Drosselmeier, please come out at that other door!"

"That can't be done, dear Fritz," answered Drosselmeier.

"Well," resumed Fritz, "make that green man that looks out so often walk about with the others."

"And that can't be done, either," said his godpapa, once more.

"Make the children come down, then," said Fritz. "I want to see them nearer."

"Nonsense, nothing of that sort can be done," cried Drosselmeier, with impatience. "The machinery must work as it's doing now; it can't be altered, you know."

"Oh," said Fritz, "it can't be done, eh? Very well, then, Godpapa Drosselmeier, I'll tell you what it is. If your little creatures in the castle there can only always do the same thing, they're not much worth, and I think precious little of them! No, give me my hussars. They've got to manœuvre backwards and forwards just as I want them, and are not fastened up in a house."

With which he made off to the other table, and set his squadron of silver horses trotting here and there, wheeling and charging and slashing right and left to his heart's content. Marie had slipped away softly, too, for she was tired of the promenading and dancing of the puppets in the castle, though, kind and gentle as she was, she did not like to show it as her brother did. Drosselmeier, somewhat annoyed, said to the parents—"After all, an ingenious piece of mechanism like this is not a matter for children, who don't understand it; I shall put my castle back in its box again." But the mother came to the rescue, and made him show her the clever machinery which moved the figures, Drosselmeier taking it all to pieces, putting it together again, and quite recovering his temper in the process. So that he gave the children all sorts of delightful brown men and women with golden faces, hands and legs, which were made of ginger cake, and with which they were greatly content.

MARIE'S PET AND PROTÉGÉE

But there was a reason wherefore Marie found it against the grain to come away from the table where the Christmas presents were laid out; and this was, that she had just noticed a something there which she had not observed at first. Fritz's hussars having taken ground to the right at some distance from the tree, in front of which they had previously been paraded, there became visible a most delicious little man, who was standing there quiet and unobtrusive, as if waiting patiently till it should be his turn to be noticed. Objection, considerable objection, might, perhaps, have been taken to him on the score of his figure, for his body was rather too tall and stout for his legs, which were short and slight; moreover, his head was a good deal too large. But much of this was atoned for by the elegance of his costume, which showed him to be a person of taste and cultivation. He had on a very pretty violet hussar's jacket, all over knobs and braiding, pantaloons of the same, and the loveliest little boots ever seen even on a hussar officer—fitting his dear little legs just as if they had been painted on to them. It was funny, certainly, that, dressed in this style as he was, he had on a little, rather absurd, short cloak on his shoulders, which looked almost as if it were made of wood, and on his head a cap like a miner's. But Marie remembered that Godpapa Drosselmeier often appeared in a terribly ugly morning jacket, and with a frightful looking cap on his head, and yet was a very very darling godpapa.

As Marie kept looking at this little man, whom she had quite fallen in love with at first sight, she saw more and more clearly what a sweet nature and disposition was legible in his countenance. Those green eyes of his (which stuck, perhaps, a little more prominently out of his head than was quite desirable) beamed with kindliness and benevolence. It was one of his beauties, too, that his chin was set off with a well kept beard of white cotton, as this drew attention to the sweet smile which his bright red lips always expressed.

"Oh, papa, dear!" cried Marie at last, "whose is that most darling little man beside the tree?"

"Well," was the answer, "that little fellow is going to do plenty of good service for all of you; he's going to crack nuts for you, and he is to belong to Louise just as much as to you and Fritz." With which papa took him up from the table, and on his lifting the end of his wooden cloak, the little man opened his mouth wider and wider, displaying two rows of very white, sharp teeth. Marie, directed by her father, put a nut into his mouth, and—knack—he had bitten it in two, so that the shells fell down, and Marie got the kernel. So then it was explained to all that this charming little man belonged to the Nutcracker family, and was practising the profession of his ancestors. "And," said papa, "as friend Nutcracker seems to have made such an impression on you, Marie, he shall be given over to your special care and charge, though, as I said, Louise and Fritz are to have the same right to his services as you."

Marie took him into her arms at once, and made him crack some more nuts; but she picked out all the smallest, so that he might not have to open his mouth so terribly wide, because that was not nice for him. Then sister Louise came, and he had to crack some nuts for her too, which duty he seemed very glad to perform, as he kept on smiling most courteously.

Meanwhile, Fritz was a little tired, after so much drill and manœuvring, so he joined his sisters, and laughed beyond measure at the funny little fellow, who (as Fritz wanted his share of the nuts) was passed from hand to hand, and was continually snapping his mouth open and shut. Fritz gave him all the biggest and hardest nuts he could find, but all at once there was a "crack—crack," and three teeth fell out of Nutcracker's mouth, and all his lower jaw was loose and wobbly.

"Ah! my poor darling Nutcracker," Marie cried, and took him away from Fritz.

"A nice sort of chap he is!" said Fritz. "Calls himself a nutcracker, and can't give a decent bite—doesn't seem to know much about his business. Hand him over here, Marie! I'll keep

him biting nuts if he drops all the rest of his teeth, and his jaw into the bargain. What's the good of a chap like him!"

"No, no," said Marie, in tears; "you shan't have him, my darling Nutcracker; see how he's looking at me so mournfully, and showing me his poor sore mouth. But you're a hard-hearted creature! You beat your horses, and you've had one of your soldiers shot."

"Those things must be done," said Fritz; "and you don't understand anything about such matters. But Nutcracker's as much mine as yours, so hand him over!"

Marie began to cry bitterly, and wrapped the wounded Nutcracker quickly up in her little pocket-handkerchief. Papa and mamma came with Drosselmeier, who took Fritz's part, to Marie's regret. But papa said, "I have put Nutcracker in Marie's special charge, and as he seems to have need just now of her care, she has full power over him, and nobody else has anything to say in the matter. And I'm surprised that Fritz should expect further service from a man wounded in the execution of his duty. As a good soldier, he ought to know better than that."

Fritz was much ashamed, and, troubling himself no further as to nuts or nut-crackers, crept off to the other side of the table, where his hussars (having established the necessary outposts and videttes) were bivouacking for the night. Marie got Nutcracker's lost teeth together, bound a pretty white ribbon, taken from her dress, about his poor chin, and then wrapped the poor little fellow, who was looking very pale and frightened, more tenderly and carefully than before in her handkerchief. Thus she held him, rocking him like a child in her arms, as she looked at the picture-books. She grew quite angry (which was not usual with her) with Godpapa Drosselmeier because he laughed so, and kept asking how she could make such a fuss about an ugly little fellow like that. That odd and peculiar likeness to Drosselmeier, which had struck her when she saw Nutcracker at first, occurred to her mind again now, and she said, with much earnestness:

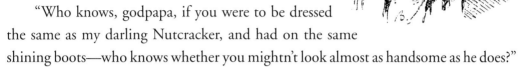

"Who knows, godpapa, if you were to be dressed the same as my darling Nutcracker, and had on the same shining boots—who knows whether you mightn't look almost as handsome as he does?"

Marie did not understand why papa and mamma laughed so heartily, nor why Godpapa Drosselmeier's nose got so red, nor why he did not join so much in the laughter as before. Probably there was some special reason for these things.

WONDERFUL EVENTS

We must now explain that, in the sitting-room, on the left-hand as you go in, there stands, against the wall, a high, glass-fronted cupboard, where all the children's Christmas presents are yearly put away to be kept. Louise, the elder sister, was still quite little when her father had this cupboard constructed by a very skilful workman, who had put in it such transparent panes of glass, and altogether made the whole affair so splendid, that the things, when inside it, looked almost more shining and lovely than when one had them actually in one's hands. In the upper shelves, which were beyond the reach of Fritz and Marie, were stowed Godpapa Drosselmeier's works of art; immediately under them was the shelf for the picture-books. Fritz and Marie were allowed to do what they liked with the two lower shelves, but it always came about that the lower one of all was that in which Marie put away her dolls, as their place of residence, whilst Fritz utilized the shelf above this as cantonments for his troops of all arms. So that, on the evening as to which we are speaking, Fritz had quartered his hussars in his—the upper—shelf of these two, whilst Marie had put Miss Gertrude rather in a corner, established her new doll in the well-appointed chamber there, with all its appropriate

Barracks.

furniture, and invited herself to tea and cakes with her. This chamber was splendidly furnished, everything on a first-rate scale, and in good and admirable style, as I have already said—and I don't know if you, my observant reader, have the satisfaction of possessing an equally well-appointed room for your dolls; a little beautifully-flowered sofa, a number of the most charming little chairs, a nice little tea-table, and, above all, a beautiful little white bed, where your pretty darling of dolls go to sleep? All this was in a corner of the shelf, the walls of which, in this part, had beautiful little pictures hanging on them; and you may well imagine that, in such a delightful chamber as this, the new doll (whose name, as Marie had discovered, was Miss Clara) thought herself extremely comfortably settled, and remarkably well off.

It was getting very late, not so very far from midnight, indeed, before the children could tear themselves away from all these Yuletide fascinations, and Godpapa Drosselmeier had been gone a considerable time. They remained riveted beside the glass cupboard, although their mother several times reminded them that it was long after bedtime. "Yes," said Fritz, "I know well enough

that these poor fellows (meaning his hussars) are tired enough, and awfully anxious to turn in for the night, though as long as I'm here, not a man-jack of them dares to nod his head." With which he went off. But Marie earnestly begged for just a little while longer, saying she had such a number of things to see to, and promising that as soon as ever she had got them all settled she would go to bed at once. Marie was a very good and reasonable child, and therefore her mother allowed her to remain for a little longer with her toys; but lest she should be too much occupied with her new doll and the other playthings so as to forget to put out the candles which were lighted all round on the wall sconces, she herself put all of them out, leaving merely the lamp which hung from the ceiling to give a soft and pleasant light. "Come soon to your bed, Marie, or you'll never be up in time in the morning," cried her mother as she went away into the bedroom.

As soon as Marie was alone, she set rapidly to work to do the thing which was chiefly at her heart to accomplish, and which, though she scarcely knew why, she somehow did not like to set about in her mother's presence. She had been holding Nutcracker, wrapped in the handkerchief, carefully in her arms all this time, and she now laid him softly down on the table, gently unrolled the handkerchief, and examined his wounds.

Nutcracker was very pale, but at the same time he was smiling with a melancholy and pathetic kindliness which went straight to Marie's heart.

"Oh, my darling little Nutcracker!" said she, very softly, "don't you be vexed because brother Fritz has hurt you so: he didn't mean it, you know; he's only a little bit hardened with his soldiering and that, but he's a good, nice boy, I can assure you:

and I'll take the greatest care of you, and nurse you, till you're quite, quite better and happy again. And your teeth shall be put in again for you, and your shoulder set right; Godpapa Drosselmeier will see to that; he knows how to do things of the kind."

Marie could not finish what she was going to say, because at the mention of Godpapa Drosselmeier, friend Nutcracker made a most horrible, ugly face. A sort of green sparkle of much sharpness seemed to dart out of his eyes. This was only for an instant, however; and just as Marie was going to be terribly frightened, she found that she was looking at the very same nice, kindly face, with the pathetic smile which she had seen before, and she saw plainly that it was nothing but some draught of air making the lamp flicker that had seemed to produce the change.

"Well!" she said, "I certainly am a silly girl to be so easily frightened, and think that a wooden doll could make faces at me! But I'm too fond, really, of Nutcracker, because he's so funny, and so kind and nice; and so he must be taken the greatest care of, and properly nursed till he's quite well."

With which she took him in her arms again, approached the cupboard, and kneeling down beside it, said to her new doll: "I'm going to ask a favour of you, Miss Clara—that you will give up your bed to this poor sick, wounded Nutcracker, and make yourself as comfortable as you can on the sofa here. Remember that you're quite well and strong yourself, or you wouldn't have such fat, red cheeks, and that there are very few dolls indeed who have as comfortable a sofa as this to lie upon."

Miss Clara, in her Christmas full-dress, looked very grand and disdainful, and said not so much as "Muck!"

"Very well," said Marie, "why should I make such a fuss, and stand on any ceremony?"—took the bed and moved it forward; laid Nutcraker carefully and tenderly down on it; wrapped another pretty ribbon, taken from her own dress, about his hurt shoulder, and drew the bedclothes up to his nose.

"But he shan't stay with that nasty Clara," she said, and moved the bed, with Nutcracker in it, up to the upper shelf, so that it was placed near the village in which

Fritz's hussars had their cantonments. She closed the cupboard, and was moving away to go to bed, when—listen, children!—there begun a low soft rustling and rattling, and a sort of whispering noise, all round, in all directions, from all quarters of the room—behind the stove, under the chairs, behind the cupboards. The clock on the wall "warned" louder and louder, but could not strike. Marie looked at it, and saw that the big gilt owl which was on the top of it had drooped its wings so that they covered the whole of the clock, and had stretched its cat-like head, with the crooked beak, a long way forward. And the "warning" kept growing louder and louder, with distinct words: "Clocks, clockies, stop ticking. No sound, but cautious 'warning.' Mousey king's ears are fine. Prr-prr. Only sing 'poom, poom'; sing the olden song of doom! prr-prr; poom, poom. Bells go chime! Soon rings out the fated time!" And then came "Poom! poom!" quite hoarsely and smothered, twelve times.

Marie grew terribly frightened, and was going to rush away as best she could, when she noticed that Godpapa Drosselmeier was up on the top of the clock instead of the owl, with his yellow coat-tails hanging down on both sides, like wings. But she manned herself, and called out in a loud voice of anguish:

"Godpapa! godpapa! what are you up there for? Come down to me, and don't frighten me so terribly, you naughty, naughty Godpapa Drosselmeier!"

But then there begun a sort of wild kickering and queaking, everywhere, all about, and presently there was a sound as of running and trotting, as of thousands of little feet behind the walls, and thousands of little lights began to glitter out between the chinks of the woodwork. But they were not lights; no, no! little glittering eyes; and Marie became aware that, everywhere, mice were peeping and squeezing themselves out through every chink. Presently they were trotting and galloping in all directions over the room; orderly bodies, continually increasing, of mice, forming themselves into regular troops and squadrons, in good order, just as Fritz's soldiers did when manoeuvres were going on. As Marie was not afraid of mice (as many children are), she could not help being amused by this, and her first alarm had nearly left her, when suddenly there came such a sharp and terrible piping noise that the blood ran cold in her veins. Ah! what did she see then? Well, truly, kind reader, I know that your heart is in the right place, just as much as my friend Field Marshal Fritz's is, itself, but if you had seen what now came before Marie's eyes, you would have made a clean pair of heels of it; nay, I consider that you would have plumped into your bed, and drawn the blankets further over your head than necessity demanded.

But poor Marie hadn't it in her power to do any such thing, because, right at her feet, as if impelled by some subterranean power, sand, and lime, and broken stone came bursting up, and then seven mouse-heads, with seven shining crowns upon them, rose through the floor, hissing and piping in a most horrible way. Quickly the body

of the mouse which had those seven crowned heads forced its way up through the floor, and this enormous creature shouted, with its seven heads, aloud to the assembled multitude, squeaking to them with all the seven mouths in full chorus; and then the entire army set itself in motion, and went trot, trot, right up to the cupboard—and, in fact, to Marie, who was standing beside it.

Marie's heart had been beating so with terror that she had thought it must jump out of her breast, and she must die. But now it seemed to her as if the blood in her veins stood still. Half fainting, she leant backwards, and then there was a "klirr, klirr, prr," and the pane of the cupboard, which she had broken with her elbow, fell in shivers to the floor. She felt, for a moment, a sharp, stinging pain in her arm, but still, this seemed to make her heart lighter; she heard no more of the queaking and piping. Everything was quiet; and though she didn't dare to look, she thought the noise of the glass breaking had frightened the mice back to their holes.

But what came to pass then? Right behind Marie a movement seemed to commence in the cupboard, and small, feint voices began to be heard, saying:

"Come, awake, measures take;
Out to the fight, out to the fight;
Shield the right, shield the right;
Arm and away, this is the night."

And harmonica-bells began ringing as prettily as you please.

"Oh! that's my little peal of bells!" cried Marie, and went nearer and looked in. Then she saw that there was bright light in the cupboard, and everything busily in motion there; dolls and little figures of various kinds all running about together, and struggling with their little arms. At this point, Nutcracker rose from his bed, cast off the bedclothes, and sprung with both feet on to the floor (of the shelf), crying out at the top of his voice:

"Knack, knack, knack,
Stupid mousey pack,
All their skulls we'll crack.
Mousey pack, knack, knack,
Mousey pack, crick and crack,
Cowardly lot of schnack!"

And with this he drew his little sword, waved it in the air, and cried:

"Ye, my trusty vassals, brethren and friends, are ye ready to stand by me in this great battle?"

Immediately three scaramouches, one pantaloon, four chimney-sweeps, two zither-players, and a drummer cried, in eager accents:

"Yes, your highness; we will stand by you in loyal duty; we will follow you to the death, the victory, and the fray!" And they precipitated themselves after Nutcracker (who, in the excitement of the moment, had dared that perilous leap) to the bottom shelf. Now they might well dare this perilous leap, for not only had they got plenty of clothes on, of cloth and silk, but besides, there was not much in their insides except cotton and sawdust, so that they plumped down like little wool-sacks. But as for poor Nutcracker, he would certainly have broken his arms and legs; for, bethink you, it was nearly two feet from where he had stood to the shelf below, and his body was as fragile as if he had been made of elm-wood. Yes, Nutcracker would have broken his arms and legs, had not Miss Clara started up, at the moment of his spring, from her sofa, and received the hero, drawn sword and all, in her tender arms.

"Oh! You dear, good Clara!" cried Marie, "how I did misunderstand you. I believe you were quite willing to let dear Nutcracker have your bed."

But Miss Clara now cried, as she pressed the young hero gently to her silken breast:

"Oh, my lord! Go not into this battle and danger, sick and wounded as you are. See how your trusty vassals, clowns and pantaloon, chimney-sweeps, zithermen and drummer, are already arrayed below; and the puzzle-figures, in my shelf here, are in motion, and preparing for the fray! Deign, then, oh my lord, to rest in these arms of mine, and contemplate your victory from a safe coign of vantage."

Thus spoke Clara. But Nutcracker behaved so impatiently, and kicked so with his legs, that Clara was obliged to put him down on the shelf in a hurry. However, he at once sank gracefully on one knee, and expressed himself as follows:

"Oh, lady! The kind protection and aid which you have afforded me, will ever be present to my heart, in battle and in victory!"

On this, Clara bowed herself so as to be able to take hold of him by his arms, raised him gently up, quickly loosed her girdle, which was ornamented with many spangles, and would have placed it about his shoulders. But the little man drew himself swiftly two steps back, laid his hand upon his heart, and said, with much solemnity:

"Oh, lady! Do not bestow this mark of your favour upon me; for—" He hesitated, gave a deep sigh, took the ribbon, with which Marie had bound him, from his shoulders, pressed it to his lips, put it on as a cognizance for the fight, and, waving his glittering sword, sprang, like a bird, over the ledge of the cupboard down to the floor.

You will observe, kind reader, that Nutcracker, even before he really came to life, had felt and understood all Marie's goodness and regard, and that it was because of his gratitude and devotion to her, that he would not take, or wear even, a ribbon of Miss Clara's, although it was exceedingly pretty and charming. This good, true-hearted Nutcracker preferred Marie's much commoner and more unpretending token.

But what is going to happen, further, now? At the moment when Nutcracker sprang down, the queaking and piping commenced again worse than ever. Alas! Under the big table, the hordes of the mouse army had taken up a position, densely massed, under the command of the terrible mouse with the seven heads. So what is to be the result?

THE BATTLE

"Beat the Generale, trusty vassal-drummer!" cried Nutcracker, very loud; and immediately the drummer began to roll his drum in the most splendid style, so that the windows of the glass cupboard rattled and resounded. Then there began a cracking and a clattering inside, and Marie saw all the lids of the boxes in which Fritz's army was quartered bursting open, and the soldiers all came out and jumped down to the bottom shelf, where they formed up in good order. Nutcracker hurried up and down the ranks, speaking words of encouragement.

"There's not a dog of a trumpeter taking the trouble to sound a call!" he cried in a fury. Then he turned to the pantaloon (who was looking decidedly pale), and, wobbling his long chin a good deal, said, in a tone of solemnity:

"I know how brave and experienced you are, General! What is essential here, is a rapid comprehension of the situation, and immediate utilization of the passing moment. I entrust you with the command of the cavalry and artillery. You can do without a horse; your own legs are long, and you can gallop on them as fast as is necessary. Do your duty!"

Immediately Pantaloon put his long, lean fingers to his mouth, and gave such a piercing crow that it rang as if a hundred little trumpets had been sounding lustily. Then there began a tramping and a neighing in the cupboard; and Fritz's dragoons and cuirassiers—but above all, the new glittering hussars—marched out, and then came to a halt, drawn up on the floor. They then marched past Nutcracker by regiments, with *guidons* flying and bands playing; after which they wheeled into line, and formed up at right angles to the line of march. Upon, this, Fritz's artillery came rattling up, and formed action front in advance of the halted cavalry. Then it went "boom-boom!" and Marie saw the sugar-plums doing terrible execution amongst the thickly-massed mouse-battalions, which were powdered quite white by them, and greatly put to shame. But a battery of heavy guns, which had taken up a strong position on mamma's footstool, was what did the greatest execution; and "poom-poom-poom!" kept up a murderous fire of gingerbread nuts into the enemy's ranks with most destructive effect, mowing the mice down in great numbers. The enemy, however, was not materially checked in his advance, and had even possessed himself of one or two of the heavy guns, when there came "prr-prr-prr!" and Marie could scarcely see what was happening, for smoke and dust; but this much is certain, that every corps engaged fought with the utmost bravery and determination, and it was for a long time doubtful which side would gain the day. The mice kept on developing fresh bodies of their forces, as they were advanced to the scene of action; their little silver balls—like pills in size—which they delivered with great precision (their musketry practice being specially fine) took effect even inside the glass cupboard. Clara and Gertrude ran up and down in utter despair, wringing their hands, and loudly lamenting.

"Must I—the very loveliest doll in all the world—perish miserably in the very flower of my youth?" cried Miss Clara.

"Oh! was it for this," wept Gertrude, "that I have taken such pains to *conserver* myself all these years? Must I be shot here in my own drawing-room after all?"

On this, they fell into each other's arms, and howled so terribly that you could hear them above all the din of the battle. For you have no idea of the hurly-burly that went on now, dear auditor! It went prr-prr-poof, pift-schnetterdeng—schnetterdeng—boom-booroom—boom-booroom—boom—all confusedly and higgledy-piggledy; and the mouse-king and the mice squeaked and screamed; and then again Nutcracker's powerful voice was heard shouting words of command, and issuing important orders, and he was seen striding along amongst his battalions in the thick of the fire.

Pantaloon had made several most brilliant cavalry charges, and covered himself with glory. But Fritz's hussars were subjected—by the mice—to a heavy fire of very evil-smelling shot, which made horrid spots on their red tunics; this caused them to hesitate, and hang rather back for a time. Pantaloon made them take ground to the left, in *echelon*, and, in the excitement of the moment, he, with his dragoons and cuirassiers, executed a somewhat analogous movement. That is to say, they brought up the right shoulder, wheeled to the left, and marched home to their quarters. Tins had the effect of bringing the battery of artillery on the footstool into imminent danger, and it was not long before a large body of exceedingly ugly mice delivered such a vigorous assault on this position that the whole of the footstool, with the guns and gunners, fell into the enemy's hands. Nutcracker seemed much disconcerted, and ordered his right wing to commence a retrograde movement. A soldier of your experience, my dear Fritz, knows well that such a movement is almost tantamount to a regular retreat, and you grieve, with me, in anticipation, for the disaster which threatens the army of Marie's beloved little Nutcracker. But turn your glance in the other direction, and look at this left wing of Nutcracker's, where all is still going well, and you will see that there is yet much hope for the commander-in-chief and his cause.

During the hottest part of the engagement masses of mouse-cavalry had been quietly debouching from under the chest of drawers, and had subsequently made a most determined advance upon the left wing of Nutcracker's force, uttering loud and horrible queakings. But what a reception they met with! Very slowly, as the nature of the *terrain* necessitated (for the ledge at the bottom of the cupboard had to be passed), the regiment of motto-figures, commanded by two Chinese Emperors, advanced, and formed square. These fine, brilliantly-uniformed troops, consisting of gardeners, Tyrolese, Tungooses, hair-dressers, harlequins, Cupids, lions, tigers, unicorns, and monkeys, fought with the utmost courage, coolness, and steady endurance. This *bataillon d'élite* would have wrested the victory from the enemy had not one of his cavalry cap-tains, pushing forward in a rash and foolhardy manner, made a charge upon one of the Chinese Emperors, and bit-ten off his head. This Chinese Emperor, in his fall, knocked over and smothered a couple of Tungooses and a unicorn, and this created a gap, through which the enemy effected a rush, which resulted in the whole battalion being bitten to death. But the enemy gained little advantage by this; for as soon as one of the mouse-cavalry soldiers bit one of these brave adversaries to death, he found that there was a small piece of printed paper sticking in his throat, of which he died in a moment. Still, this was of small advantage to Nutcracker's army, which, having once com-menced a retrograde movement, went on retreating farther

and farther, suffering greater and greater loss. So that the unfortunate Nutcracker found himself driven back close to the front of the cupboard, with a very small remnant of his army.

"Bring up the reserves! Pantaloon! Scaramouch! Drummer! where the devil have you got to?" shouted Nutcracker, who was still reckoning on reinforcements from the cupboard. And there did, in fact, advance a small contingent of brown gingerbread men and women, with gilt faces, hats, and helmets; but they laid about them so clumsily that they never hit any of the enemy, and soon knocked off the cap of their commander-in-chief, Nutcracker, himself. And the enemy's chasseurs soon bit their legs off, so that they tumbled topsy-turvy, and killed several of Nutcracker's companions-in-arms into the bargain.

Nutcracker was now hard pressed, and closely hemmed in by the enemy, and in a position of extreme peril. He tried to jump the bottom ledge of the cupboard, but his legs were not long enough. Clara and Gertrude had fainted; so they could give him no assistance. Hussars and heavy dragoons came charging up at him, and he shouted in wild despair:

"A horse! a horse! My kingdom for a horse!"

At this moment two of the enemy's riflemen seized him by his wooden cloak, and the king of the mice went rushing up to him, squeaking in triumph out of all his seven throats.

Marie could contain herself no longer. "Oh! my poor Nutcracker!" she sobbed, took her left shoe off, without very distinctly knowing what she was about, and threw it as hard as she could into the thick of the enemy, straight at their king.

Instantly everything vanished and disappeared. All was silence. Nothing to be seen. But Marie felt a more stinging pain than before in her left arm, and fell on the floor insensible.

The Invalid

When Marie awoke from a death-like sleep she was lying in her little bed; and the sun was shining brightly in at the window, which was all covered with frost-flowers. There was a stranger gentleman sitting beside her, whom she recognized as Dr. Wendelstern. "She's awake," he said softly, and her mother came and looked at her very scrutinizingly and anxiously.

"Oh, mother!" whispered Marie, "are all those horrid mice gone away, and is Nutcracker quite safe?"

"Don't talk such nonsense, Marie," answered her mother. "What have the mice to do with Nutcracker? You're a very naughty girl, and have caused us all a great deal of anxiety. See what comes of children not doing as they're told! You were playing with your toys so late last night that you fell asleep. I don't know whether or not some mouse jumped out and frightened you, though there are no mice here, generally. But, at all events, you broke a pane of the glass cupboard with your elbow, and cut your arm so badly that Dr. Wendelstern (who has just taken a number of pieces of the glass out of your arm) thinks that if it had been only a little higher up you might have had a stiff arm for life, or even have bled to death. Thank Heaven, I awoke about twelve o'clock and missed you; and I found you lying insensible in front of the glass cupboard, bleeding frightfully, with a number of Fritz's lead soldiers scattered round you, and other toys, broken motto-figures, and gingerbread men; and Nutcracker was lying on your bleeding arm, with your left shoe not far off."

"Oh, mother, mother," said Marie, "these were the remains of the tremendous battle between the toys and the mice; and what frightened me so terribly was that the mice were going to take Nutcracker (who was the commander-in-chief of the toy army) a prisoner. Then I threw my shoe in among the mice, and after that I know nothing more that happened."

Dr. Wendelstern gave a significant look at the mother, who said very gently to Marie:

"Never mind, dear, keep yourself quiet. The mice are all gone away, and Nutcracker's in the cupboard, quite safe and sound."

Here Marie's father came in, and had a long consultation with Dr. Wendelstern. Then he felt Marie's pulse, and she heard them talking about "wound-fever." She had to stay in bed, and take medicine, for some days, although she didn't feel at all ill, except that her arm was rather stiff and painful. She knew Nutcracker had got safe out of the battle, and she seemed to remember, as if in a dream, that he had said, quite distinctly, in a very melancholy tone:

"Marie! dearest lady! I am most deeply indebted to you. But it is in your power to do even more for me still."

She thought and thought what this could possibly be; but in vain; she couldn't make it out. She wasn't able to play on account of her arm; and when she tried to read, or look through the picture-books, everything wavered before her eyes so strangely that she was obliged to stop. So that the days seemed very long to her, and she could scarcely pass the time till evening, when her mother came and sat at her bedside, telling and reading her all sorts of nice stories. She had just finished telling her the story of Prince Fakardin, when the door opened and in came Godpapa Drosselmeier, saying:

"I've come to see with my own eyes how Marie's getting on."

When Marie saw Godpapa Drosselmeier in his little yellow coat, the scene of the night when Nutcracker lost the battle with the mice came so vividly back to her that she couldn't help crying out:

"Oh! Godpapa Drosselmeier, how nasty you were! I saw you quite well when you were sitting on the clock, covering it all over with your wings, to prevent it from striking and frightening the mice. I heard you quite well when you called the mouse-king. Why didn't you help Nutcracker? Why didn't you help me, you nasty godpapa? It's nobody's fault but yours that I'm lying here with a bad arm."

Her mother, in much alarm, asked what she meant. But Drosselmeier began making extraordinary faces, and said, in a snarling voice, like a sort of chant in monotone:

"Pendulums could only rattle—couldn't tick, ne'er a click; all the clockies stopped their ticking: no more clicking; then they all struck loud 'cling-clang.' Dollies! Don't your heads downhang! Hink and hank, and honk and hank. Doll-girls! don't your heads downhang! Cling and ring! The battle's over—Nutcracker all safe in clover. Comes the owl, on downy wing—Scares away the mouses' king. Pak and pik and pik and pook—clocks, bim-boom—grr-grr. Pendulums must click again. Tick and tack, grr and brr, prr and purr."

Marie fixed wide eyes of terror upon Godpapa Drosselmeier, because he was looking quite different, and far more horrid, than usual, and was jerking his right arm backwards and forwards as if he were some puppet moved by a handle. She was beginning to grow terribly frightened at him when her mother came in, and Fritz (who had arrived in the meantime) laughed heartily, crying, "Why, godpapa, you are going on funnily! You're just like my old Jumping Jack that I threw away last month."

But the mother looked very grave, and said, "This is a most extraordinary way of going on, Mr. Drosselmeier. What can you mean by it?"

"My goodness!" said Drosselmeier, laughing, "did you never hear my nice Watchmaker's Song? I always sing it to little invalids like Marie." Then he hastened to sit down beside Marie's bed, and said to her, "Don't be vexed with me because I didn't gouge out all the mouse-king's fourteen eyes. That couldn't be managed exactly; but, to make up for it, here's something which I know will please you greatly."

He dived into one of his pockets, and what he slowly, slowly brought out of it was—Nutcracker! whose teeth he had put in again quite firmly, and set his broken jaw completely to rights. Marie shouted for joy, and her mother laughed and said, "Now you see for yourself how nice Godpapa Drosselmeier is to Nutcracker."

"But you must admit, Marie," said her godpapa, "that Nutcracker is far from being what you might call a handsome fellow, and you can't say he has a pretty face. If you like I'll tell you how it was that the ugliness came into his family, and has been handed down in it from one generation to another. Did over you hear about the Princess Pirlipat, the witch Mouseyrinks, and the clever Clockmaker?"

"I say, Godpapa Drosselmeier," interrupted Fritz at this juncture, "you've put Nutcracker's teeth in again all right, and his jaw isn't wobbly as it was; but what's become of his sword? Why haven't you given him a sword?"

"Oh," cried Drosselmeier, annoyed, "you must always be bothering and finding fault with something or other, boy. What have I to do with Nutcracker's sword? I've put his mouth to rights for him; he must look out for a sword for himself."

"Yes, yes," said Fritz, "so he must, of course, if he's a right sort of fellow."

"So tell me, Marie," continued Drosselmeier, "if you know the story of Princess Pirlipat?"

"Oh no," said Marie. "Tell it me, please—do tell it me!"

"I hope it won't be as strange and terrible as your stories generally are," said her mother.

"Oh no, nothing of the kind," said Drosselmeier. "On the contrary, it's quite a funny story which I'm going to have the honour of telling this time."

"Go on then—do tell it to us," cried the children; and Drosselmeier commenced as follows:

THE STORY OF THE HARD NUT

Pirlipat's mother was a king's wife, so that, of course, she was a queen; and Pirlipat herself was a princess by birth as soon as ever she was born. The king was quite beside himself with joy over his beautiful little daughter as she lay in her cradle, and he danced round and round upon one leg, crying again and again, "Hurrah! hurrah! hip, hip, hurrah! Did anybody ever see anything so lovely as my little Pirlipat?"

And all the ministers of state, and the generals, the presidents, and the officers of the staff, danced about on one leg, as the king did, and cried as loud as they could, "No, no—never!"

Indeed, there was no denying that a lovelier baby than Princess Pirlipat was never born since the world began. Her little face looked as if it were woven of the most delicate white and rose-coloured silk; her eyes were of sparkling azure, and her hair all in little curls like threads of gold. Moreover, she had come into the world with two rows of little pearly teeth, with which, two hours after her birth, she bit the Lord High Chancellor in the fingers, when he was making a careful examination of her features, so that he cried, "Oh! Gemini!" quite loud.

There are persons who assert that "Oh Lord" was the expression he employed, and opinions are still considerably divided on this point. At all events, she bit him in the fingers; and the realm learned, with much gratification, that both intelligence and discrimination dwelt within her angelical little frame.

All was joy and gladness, as I have said, save that the queen was very anxious and uneasy, nobody could tell why. One remarkable circumstance was, that she had Pirlipat's cradle most scrupulously guarded. Not only were there lifeguardsmen always at the doors of the nursery, but—over and above the two head nurses close to the cradle—there had always to be six other nurses all round the room at night. And what seemed rather a funny thing, which nobody could understand, was that each of these six nurses had always to have a cat in her lap, and to keep on stroking it all night long, so that it might never stop purring.

It is impossible that you, my reader, should know the reason of all these precautions; but I do, and shall proceed to tell you at once.

Once upon a time, many great kings and very grand princes were assembled at Pirlipat's father's court, and very great doings were toward. Tournaments, theatricals, and state balls were going on on the grandest scale, and the king, to show that he had no lack of gold and silver, made up his mind to make a good hole in the crown revenues for once, and launch out regardless of expense. Wherefore (having previously ascertained, privately, from the state head master cook that the court astronomer had indicated a propitious hour for pork-butching), he resolved to give a grand pudding-and-sausage banquet. He jumped into a state carriage, and personally invited all the kings and the princes—to a basin of soup, merely—that he might enjoy their astonishment at the magnificence of the entertainment. Then he said to the queen, very graciously:

"My darling, *you* know exactly how I like my puddings and sausages!"

The queen quite understood what this meant. It meant that she should undertake the important duty of making the puddings and the sausages herself, which was a thing she had done on one or two previous occasions. So the chancellor of the exchequer was ordered to issue out of store the great golden sausage-kettle, and the silver *casseroles*. A great fire of sandal-wood was kindled, the queen put on her damask kitchen apron, and soon the most delicious aroma of pudding-broth rose steaming out of the kettle. This sweet smell penetrated into the very council chamber. The king could not control himself.

"Excuse me for a few minutes, my lords and gentlemen," he cried, rushed to the kitchen, embraced the queen, stirred in the kettle a little with his golden sceptre, and then went back, easier in his mind, to the council chamber.

The important juncture had now arrived when the fat had to be cut up into little square pieces, and browned on silver spits. The ladies-in-waiting retired, because the queen, from motives of

love and duty to her royal consort, thought it proper to perform this important task in solitude. But when the fat began to brown, a delicate little whispering voice made itself audible, saying, "Give me some of that, sister! I want some of it, too; I am a queen as well as yourself; give me some."

The queen knew well who was speaking. It was Dame Mouseyrinks, who had been established in the palace for many years. She claimed relationship to the royal family, and she was queen of the realm of Mousolia herself, and lived with a considerable retinue of her own under the kitchen hearth. The queen was a kind-hearted, benevolent woman; and, although she didn't exactly care to recognize Dame Mouseyrinks as a sister and a queen, she was willing, at this festive season, to spare her the tit-bits she had a mind to. So she said, "Come out, then, Dame Mouseyrinks; of course you shall taste my browned fat."

So Dame Mouseyrinks came running out as fast as she could, held up her pretty little paws, and took morsel after morsel of the browned fat as the queen held them out to her. But then all Dame Mouseyrink's uncles, and her cousins, and her aunts, came jumping out too; and her seven sons (who were terrible ne'er-do-weels) into the bargain; and they all set-to at the browned fat, and the queen was too frightened to keep them at bay. Most fortunately the mistress of the robes came in, and drove these importunate visitors away, so that a little of the browned fat was left; and this, when the court mathematician (an ex-senior wrangler of his university) was called in (which

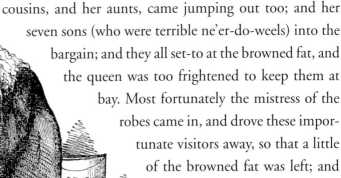

he had to be, on purpose), it was found possible, by means of skilfully devised apparatus
provided with special micrometer screws,
and so forth, to apportion and distrib-
ute amongst the whole of the sausages,
&c., under construction.

The kettledrums and the trumpets
summoned all the great princes and
potentates to the feast. They assembled
in their robes of state; some of them on
white palfreys, some in crystal coaches. The king received them with much
gracious ceremony, and took his seat at the head of the table, with his crown
on, and his sceptre in his hand. Even during the serving of the white pudding
course, it was observed that he turned pale, and raised his eyes to heaven; sighs
heaved his bosom; some terrible inward pain was clearly raging within him.
But when the black-puddings were handed round, he fell back in his seat,
loudly sobbing and groaning.

Every one rose from the table, and the court physician tried in vain to
feel his pulse. Ultimately, after the administration of most powerful reme-
dies—burnt feathers, and the like—his majesty seemed to recover his senses
to some extent, and stammered, scarce audibly, the words:
"Too little fat!"

The queen cast herself down at his feet in
despair, and cried, in a voice broken by sobs,
"Oh, my poor unfortunate royal consort!
Ah, what tortures you are doomed to
endure! But see the culprit here at your
feet. Punish her severely! Alas! Dame
Mouseyrinks, her uncles, her seven
sons, her cousins and her aunts, came
and ate up nearly all the fat—and—"

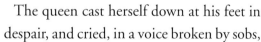

Here the queen fell back insensible.

But the king jumped up, all anger, and cried in a terrible voice, "Mistress of the robes, what is the meaning of this?"

The mistress of the robes told all she knew, and the king resolved to take revenge on Dame Mouseyrinks and her family for eating up the fat which ought to have been in the sausages. The privy council was summoned, and it was resolved that Dame Mouseyrinks should be tried for her life, and all her property confiscated. But as his majesty was of opinion that she

might go on consuming the fat, which was his appanage, the whole matter was referred to the court Clockmaker and Arcanist—whose name was the same as mine—Christian Elias Drosselmeier, and he undertook to expel Dame Mouseyrinks and all her relations from the palace precincts forever, by means of a certain politico-diplomatic procedure. He invented certain ingenious little machines, into which pieces of browned fat were

inserted; and he placed these machines down all about the dwelling of Dame Mouseyrinks. Now she herself was much too knowing not to see through Drosselmeier's artifice; but all her remonstrances and warnings to her relations were unavailing. Enticed by the fragrant odour of the browned fat, all her seven sons, and a great many of her uncles, her cousins and her aunts, walked into Drosselmeier's little machines, and were immediately taken prisoners by the fall of a small grating; after which they met with a shameful death in the kitchen.

Dame Mouseyrinks left this scene of horror with her small following. Rage and despair filled her breast. The court rejoiced greatly; the queen was very anxious, because she knew Dame Mouseyrinks's character, and knew well that she would never allow the death of her sons and other relatives to go unavenged. And, in fact, one day when the queen was cooking a fricassee of sheep's lights for the king (a dish to which he was exceedingly partial), Dame Mouseyrinks suddenly made her appearance, and said: "My sons and my uncles, my cousins and my aunts, are now no more. Have a care, lady, lest the queen of the mice bites your little princess in two! Have a care!"

With which she vanished, and was no more seen. But the queen was so frightened that she dropped the fricassee into the fire; so this was the second time Dame Mousey-rinks spoiled one of the king's favourite dishes, at which he was very irate.

But this is enough for to-night; we'll go on with the rest of it another time.

* * * * *

Sorely as Marie—who had ideas of her own about this story—begged Godpapa Drosselmeier to go on with it, he would not be persuaded, but jumped up, saying, "Too much at a time wouldn't be good for you; the rest tomorrow."

Just as Drosselmeier was going out of the door, Fritz said : "I say, God-papa Drosselmeier, was it really you who invented mousetraps?"

"How can you ask such silly questions?" cried his mother. But Drosselmeier laughed oddly, and said: "Well, you know I'm a clever clockmaker. Mousetraps had to be invented some time or other."

* * * * *

And now you know, children (said Godpapa Drosselmeier the next evening) why it was the queen took such precautions about her little Pirlipat. Had she not always the fear before her eyes of Dame Mouseyrinks coming back and carrying out her threat of biting the princess to death? Drosselmeier's ingenious machines were of no avail against the clever, crafty Dame Mouseyrinks, and nobody save the court astronomer, who was also state astrologer and reader of the stars, knew that the family of the Cat Purr had the power to keep her at bay. This was the reason why each of the lady nurses was obliged to keep one of the sons of that family (each of whom was given the honorary rank and title of "privy councillor-of-legation")

in her lap, and render his onerous duty less irksome by gently scratching his back.

One night, just after midnight, one of the chief nurses stationed close to the cradle, woke suddenly from a profound sleep. Everything lay buried in slumber. Not a purr to be heard—deep, deathlike silence, so that the death-watch ticking in the wainscot sounded quite loud. What were the feelings of this principal nurse when she saw, close beside her, a great, hideous mouse, standing on its hind legs, with its horrid head laid on the princess's face! She sprang up with a scream of terror. Everybody awoke; but then Dame

Mouseyrinks (for she was the great big mouse in Pirlipat's cradle) ran quickly away into the corner of the room. The privy councillors-of-legation dashed after her, but too late! She was off and away through a chink in the floor. The noise awoke Pirlipat, who cried terribly. "Heaven be thanked, she is still alive!" cried all the nurses; but what was their horror when they looked at Pirlipat, and saw what the beautiful, delicate little thing had turned into. An enormous bloated head (instead of the pretty little golden-haired one), at the top of a diminutive, crumpled-up body, and green, wooden-looking eyes staring, where the lovely azure-blue pair had been, whilst her mouth had stretched across from the one ear to the other.

Of course the queen nearly died of weeping and loud lamentation, and the walls of the king's study had all to be hung with padded arras, because he kept on banging his head against them, crying:

"Oh! wretched king that I am! Oh, wretched king that I am!"

Of course he might have seen, then, that it would have been much better to eat his puddings with no fat in them at all, and let Dame Mouseyrinks and her folk stay on under the hearthstone. But Pirlipat's royal father thought not of that. What he did was to lay all the blame on the court Clockmaker and Arcanist, Christian Elias Drosselmeier, of Nürnberg. Wherefore he promulgated a sapient edict to the effect that said Drosselmeier should, within the space of four weeks, restore Princess Pirlipat to her pristine condition—or, at least, indicate an unmistakable and reliable process whereby that might be accomplished—or else suffer a shameful death by the axe of the common headsman.

Drosselmeier was not a little alarmed; but he soon began to place confidence in his art, and in his luck; so he proceeded to execute the first operation which seemed to him to be expedient. He took Princess Pirlipat very carefully to pieces, screwed off her hands and her feet, and examined her interior structure. Unfortunately, he found that the bigger she got the more deformed she would be, so that he didn't see what was to be done at all. He put her carefully together again, and sank down beside her cradle—which he wasn't allowed to go away from—in the deepest dejection.

The fourth week had come, and Wednesday of the fourth week, when the king came in, with eyes gleaming with anger, made threatening gestures with his sceptre, and cried:

"Christian Elias Drosselmeier, restore the princess, or prepare for death!"

Drosselmeier began to weep bitterly. The little princess kept on cracking nuts, an occupation which seemed to afford her much quiet satisfaction. For the first time the Arcanist was struck by Pirlipat's remarkable appetite for nuts, and the circumstance that she had been born with teeth. And the fact had been that immediately after her transformation she had begun to cry, and she had gone on crying till by chance she got hold of a nut. She at once cracked it, and ate the kernel, after which she was quite quiet. From that time her nurses found that nothing would do but to go on giving her nuts.

"Oh, holy instinct of nature—eternal, mysterious, inscrutable Interdependence of Things!" cried Drosselmeier, "thou pointest out to me the door of the secret. I will knock, and it shall be opened unto me."

He at once begged for an interview with the Court Astronomer, and was conducted to him closely guarded. They embraced, with many tears, for they were great friends, and then retired into a private closet, where they referred to many books treating of sympathies, antipathies, and other mysterious subjects. Night came on. The Court Astronomer consulted the stars, and, with the assistance of Drosselmeier (himself an adept in astrology), drew the princess's horoscope. This was an exceedingly difficult operation, for the lines kept getting more and more entangled and confused for ever so long. But at last—oh what joy!—it lay plain before them that all the princess had to do to be delivered from the enchantment which made her so hideous, and get back her former beauty, was to eat the sweet kernel of the nut Crackatook.

Now this nut Crackatook had a shell so hard that you might have fired a forty-eight pounder at it without producing the slightest effect on it. Moreover, it was essential that this nut should be cracked, in the princess's presence, by the teeth of a man whose beard had never known a razor, and who had never had on boots. This man had to hand the kernel to her with his eyes closed, and he might not open them till he had made seven steps backwards without a stumble.

Drosselmeier and the astronomer had been at work on this problem uninterruptedly for three days and three nights; and on the Saturday the king was sitting at dinner, when Drosselmeier—who was to have been beheaded on the Sunday morning—burst joyfully in to announce that he had found out what had to be done to restore Princess Pirlipat to her pristine beauty. The king embraced him in a burst of rapture, and promised him a diamond sword, four decorations, and two Sunday suits.

"Set to work immediately after dinner," the monarch cried, adding, kindly, "Take care, dear Arcanist, that the young unshaven gentleman in shoes, with the nut Crackatook all ready in his hand, is on the spot; and be sure that he touches no liquor beforehand, so that he mayn't trip up when he makes his seven backward steps like a crab. He can get as drunk as a lord afterwards, if he likes."

Drosselmeier was dismayed at this utterance of the king's, and stammered out, not without trembling and hesitation, that, though the remedy was discovered, both the nut Crackatook and the young gentleman who was to crack it had still to be searched for, and that it was matter of doubt whether they ever would be got hold of at all. The king, greatly incensed, whirled his sceptre round his crowned head, and shouted, in the voice of a lion:

"Very well, then you must be beheaded!"

It was exceedingly fortunate for the wretched Drosselmeier that the king had thoroughly enjoyed his dinner that day, and was consequently in an admirable temper, and disposed to listen to the sensible advice which the queen, who was very sorry for Drosselmeier, did not spare to give him. Drosselmeier took heart, and represented that he really had fulfilled the conditions, and discovered the necessary measures, and had gained his life, consequently. The king said this was all bosh and nonsense; but at length, after two or three glasses of liqueurs, decreed that Drosselmeier and the astronomer should start off immediately, and not come back without the nut Crackatook in their pockets. The man who was to crack it (by the queen's suggestion) might be heard of by means of advertisements in the local and foreign newspapers and gazettes.

* * * * *

Godpapa Drosselmeier interrupted his story at this point, and promised to finish it on the following evening.

Next evening, as soon as the lights were brought, Godpapa Drosselmeier duly arrived, and went on with his story as follows:

* * * *

Drosselmeier and the court astronomer had been journeying for fifteen long years without finding the slightest trace of the nut Crackatook. I might go on for more than four weeks telling you where all they had been, and what extraordinary things they had seen. I shall not do so, however, but merely mention that Drosselmeier, in his profound discouragement, at last began to feel a most powerful longing to see his dear native town of Nürnberg once again. And he was more powerfully moved by this longing than usual one

day, when he happened to be smoking a pipe of kanaster with his friend in the middle of a great forest in Asia, and he cried:

"Oh, Nürnberg, Nürnberg! dear native town—he who still knows thee not, place of renown—though far he has travelled, and great cities seen—as London, and Paris, and Peterwardeen—knoweth not what it is happy to be—still must his longing heart languish for thee—for thee, O Nürnberg, exquisite town—where the houses have windows both upstairs and down!"

As Drosselmeier lamented thus dolefully, the astronomer, seized with compassionate sympathy, began to weep and howl so terribly that he was heard throughout the length and breadth of Asia. But he collected himself again, wiped the tears from his eyes, and said:

"After all, dearest colleague, why should we sit and weep and howl here? Why not come to Nürnberg? Does it matter a brass farthing, after all, where and how we search for this horrible nut Crackatook?"

"That's true, too," answered Drosselmeier, consoled. They both got up immediately, knocked the ashes out of their pipes, started off, and travelled straight on without stopping, from that forest right in the centre of Asia till they came to Nürnberg. As soon as they got there, Drosselmeier went straight

to his cousin the toymaker and doll-carver, and gilder and varnisher, whom he had not seen for a great many long years. To him he told all the tale of Princess Pirlipat, Dame Mouseyrinks, and the nut Crackatook, so that he clapped his hands repeatedly, and cried in amazement:

"Dear me, cousin, these things are really wonderful—very wonderful, indeed!"

Drosselmeier told him, further, some of the adventures he had met with on his long journey—how he had spent two years at the court of the King of Dates; how the Prince of Almonds had expelled him with ignominy from his territory; how he had applied in vain to the Natural History Society at Squirreltown—in short, how he had been everywhere utterly unsuccessful in discovering the faintest trace of the nut Crack-atook. During this narrative, Christoph Zacharias had kept frequently snapping his fingers, twisting himself round on one foot, smacking with his tongue, etc.; then he cried:

"Ee—aye—oh!—that really would be the very deuce and all."

At last he threw his hat and wig in the air, warmly embraced his cousin, and cried:

"Cousin, cousin, you're a made man—a made man you are—for either I am much deceived, or I have got the nut Crackatook myself!"

He immediately produced a little cardboard box, out of which he took a gilded nut of medium size.

"Look there!" he said, showing this nut to his cousin; "the state of matters as regards this nut is this. Several years ago, at Christmas time, a stranger man came here with a sack of nuts, which he offered for sale. Just in front of my shop he got into a quarrel, and put the sack down the better to defend himself from the nut-sellers of the place, who attacked him. Just then a heavily-loaded waggon drove over the sack, and all the nuts were smashed but one. The stranger man, with an odd smile, offered to sell me this nut for a twenty-kreuzer piece of the year 1796. This struck me as strange. I found just such a coin in my pocket, so I bought the nut, and I gilt it over, though I didn't know why I took the trouble quite, or should have given so much for it."

All question as to its being really the long-sought nut Crackatook was dispelled when the Court Astron-omer carefully scraped away the gilding, and found the word "Crackatook" graven on the shell in Chinese characters.

The joy of the exiles was great, as you may imagine; and the cousin was even happier, for Drosselmeier assured him that he was a made man too, as he was sure of a good pension, and all the gold leaf he would want for the rest of his life for his gilding, free, gratis, for nothing.

The Arcanist and the Astronomer had both got on their nightcaps, and were going to turn into bed, when the astronomer said:

"I tell you what it is, dear colleague, one piece of good fortune never comes alone. I feel convinced that we've not only found the nut, but the young gentleman who is to crack it, and hand the beauty-restoring kernel to the princess, into the bargain. I mean none other than your cousin's son here, and I don't intend to close an eye this night till I've drawn that youngster's horoscope."

With which he threw away his nightcap, and at once set to work to consult the stars. The cousin's son was a nice-looking, well-grown young fellow, had never been shaved, and had never worn boots. True, he had been a Jumping Jack for a Christmas or two in his earlier days, but there was scarcely any trace of this discoverable about him, his appearance had been so altered by his father's care. He had appeared last Christmas in a beautiful red coat with gold trimmings, a sword by his side, his hat under his arm, and a fine wig with a pigtail. Thus apparelled, he stood in his father's shop exceeding lovely to behold, and from his native *galanterie* he occupied himself in cracking nuts for the young ladies, who called him "the handsome nutcracker."

Next morning the Astronomer fell, with much emotion, into the Arcanist's arms, crying:

"This is the very man!—we have got him!—he is found! Only, dearest colleague, two things we must keep carefully in view. In the first place, we must construct a most substantial pigtail for this precious nephew of yours, which shall be connected with his lower jaw in such sort that it shall be capable of communicating a very powerful pull to it. And next, when we get back to the Residenz, we must carefully conceal the fact that we have brought the young gentleman who is to shiver the nut back with us. He must not make his appearance for a considerable time after us. I read in the horoscope that if two or three others bite at the nut unsuccessfully to begin with, the king

will promise the man who breaks it—and, as a consequence, restores the princess her good looks—the princess's hand and the succession to the crown."

The doll-maker cousin was immensely delighted with the idea of his son's marrying Princess Pirlipat, and being a prince and king, so he gave him wholly over to the envoys to do what they liked with him. The pigtail which Drosselmeier attached to him proved to be a very powerful and efficient instrument, as he exemplified by cracking the hardest of peach-stones with the utmost ease.

Drosselmeier and the Astronomer, having at once sent the news to the Residenz of the discovery of the nut Crackatook, the necessary advertisements were at once put in the newspapers, and, by the time that our travellers got there, several nice young gentlemen, among whom there were princes even, had arrived, having sufficient confidence in their teeth to try to disenchant the princess. The ambassadors were horrified when they saw poor Pirlipat again. The diminutive body with tiny hands and feet was not big enough to support the great shapeless head. The hideousness of the face was enhanced by a beard like white cotton, which had grown about the mouth and chin. Everything had turned out as the court astronomer had read it in the horoscope. One milksop in shoes after another bit his teeth and his jaws into agonies over the nut, without doing the princess the slightest good in the world. And then, when he was carried out on the verge of insensibility by the dentists who were in attendance on purpose, he would sigh:

"Ah dear, that was a hard nut."

Now when the king, in the anguish of his soul, had promised to him who should disenchant the princess his daughter and the kingdom, the charming, gentle young Drosselmeier made his appearance, and

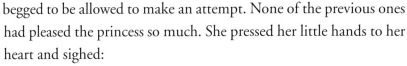

begged to be allowed to make an attempt. None of the previous ones had pleased the princess so much. She pressed her little hands to her heart and sighed:

"Ah, I hope it will be he who will crack the nut, and be my husband."

When he had politely saluted the king, the queen, and the Princess Pirlipat, he received the nut Crackatook from the hands of the Clerk of the Closet, put it between his teeth, made a strong effort with his head, and—crack—crack— the shell was shattered into a number of pieces. He neatly cleared the kernel from the pieces of husk which were sticking to it, and, making a leg, presented it courteously to the princess, after which he closed his eyes and began his backward steps. The princess swallowed the kernel, and—oh marvel!—the monstrosity vanished, and in its place there stood a wonderfully beautiful lady, with a face which seemed woven of delicate lily-white and rose-red silk, eyes of sparkling azure, and hair all in little curls like threads of gold.

Trumpets and kettledrums mingled in the loud rejoicings of the populace. The king and all his court danced about on one leg, as they had done at Pirlipat's birth, and the queen had to be treated with Eau de Cologne, having fallen into a fainting fit from joy and delight. All this tremendous tumult interfered not a little with young Drosselmeier's self-possession, for he still had to make his seven backward steps. But he collected himself as best he could, and was just stretching out his right foot to make his seventh step, when up came Dame Mouseyrinks through the floor, making a horrible weaking and squeaking, so that Drosselmeier, as he was putting his foot down, trod upon her, and stumbled so that he almost fell. Oh misery!—all in an instant he was transmogrified, just as the princess had been before: his body all shrivelled up, and could scarcely support the great shapeless head with enormous projecting eyes, and the wide gaping mouth. In the place where his pigtail used to be a scanty wooden cloak hung down, controlling the movements of his nether jaw.

The clockmaker and the astronomer were wild with terror and consternation, but they saw that Dame Mouseyrinks was wallowing in her gore on the floor. Her wickedness had not escaped punishment, for young Drosselmeier had squashed her so in the throat with the sharp point of his shoe that she was mortally hurt.

But as Dame Mouseyrinks lay in her death agony she queaked and cheeped in a lamentable style, and cried:

"Oh, Crackatook, thou nut so hard!—Oh, fate, which none may disregard!—Hee hee, pee pee, woe's me, I cry!—since I through that hard nut must die.—But, brave young Nutcracker, I see—you soon must follow after me.—My sweet young son, with sevenfold crown—will soon bring Master Cracker down.—His mother's death he will repay—so, Nutcracker, beware that day!—Oh, life most sweet, I feebly cry—I leave you now, for I must die. Queak!"

With this cry died Dame Mouseyrinks, and her body was carried out by the Court Stovelighter. Meantime nobody had been troubling themselves about young Drosselmeier. But the princess reminded the king of his promise, and he at once directed that the young hero should be conducted to his presence. But when the poor wretch came forward in his transmogrified condition the princess put both her hands to her face, and cried:

"Oh please take away that horrid Nutcracker!"

So that the Lord Chamberlain seized him immediately by his little shoulders, and shied him out at the door. The king, furious at the idea of a nutcracker being brought before him as a son-in-law, laid all the blame upon the clockmaker and the astronomer, and ordered them both to be banished for ever.

The horoscope which the astronomer had drawn in Nürnberg had said nothing about this; but that didn't hinder him from taking some fresh observations. And the stars told him that young Drosselmeier would conduct himself so admirably in his new condition that he would yet be a prince and a king, in spite of his transmogrification; but also that his deformity would only disappear after the son of Dame Mouseyrinks, the seven-headed king of the mice (whom she had born after the death of her original seven sons) should perish by his hand, and a lady should fall in love with him notwithstanding his deformity.

That is the story of the hard nut, children, and now you know why people so often use the expression "that was a hard nut," and why Nutcrackers are so ugly.

* * * * *

Thus did Godpapa Drosselmeier finish his tale. Marie thought the Princess Pirlipat was a nasty ungrateful thing. Fritz, on the other hand, was of opinion that if Nutcracker had been a proper sort of fellow he would soon have settled the mouse king's hash, and got his good looks back again.

UNCLE AND NEPHEW

Should any of my respected readers or listeners ever have happened to be cut by glass they will know what an exceedingly nasty thing it is, and how long it takes to get well. Marie was obliged to stay in bed a whole week, because she felt so terribly giddy whenever she tried to stand up; but at last she was quite well again, and able to jump about as of old. Things in the glass cupboard looked very fine indeed—everything new and shiny, trees and flowers and houses—toys of every kind. Above all, Marie found her dear Nutcracker again, smiling at her in the second shelf, with his teeth all sound and right. As she looked at this pet of hers with much fondness, it suddenly struck her that all Godpapa Drosselmeier's story had been about Nutcracker, and his family feud with Dame Mouseyrinks and her people. And now she knew that her Nutcracker was none other than young Mr. Drosselmeier, of Nürnberg, Godpapa Drosselmeier's delightful nephew, unfortunately under the spells of Dame Mouseyrinks. For whilst the story was being told, Marie couldn't doubt for a moment that the clever clockmaker at Pirlipat's father's court was Godpapa Drosselmeier himself.

"But why didn't your uncle help you? Why didn't he help you?" Marie cried, sorrowfully, as she felt more and more clearly every moment that in the battle, which she had witnessed, the question in dispute had been no less a matter than Nutcracker's crown and kingdom. Weren't all the other toys his subjects? And wasn't it clear that the astronomer's prophecy that he was to be rightful King of Toyland had come true?

Whilst the clever Marie was weighing all these things in her mind, she kept expecting that Nutcracker and his vassals would give some indications of being alive, and make some movements as she looked at them. This, however, was by no means the case. Everything in the cupboard kept quite motionless and still. Marie thought this was the effect of Dame Mouseyrinks's enchantments, and those of her seven-headed son, which still were keeping up their power.

"But," she said, "though you're not able to move, or to say the least little word to me, dear Mr. Drosselmeier, I know you understand me, and see how very well I wish you. Always reckon on my assistance when you require it. At all events, I will ask your uncle to aid you with all his great skill and talents, whenever there may be an opportunity."

Nutcracker still kept quiet and motionless. But Marie fancied that a gentle sigh came breathing through the glass cupboard, which made its panes ring in a wonderful, though all but imperceptible, manner—whilst something like a little bell-toned voice seemed to sing:

"Marie fine, angel mine! I will be thine, if thou wilt be mine!"

Although a sort of cold shiver ran through her at this, still it caused her the keenest pleasure.

Twilight came on. Marie's father came in with Godpapa Drosselmeier, and presently Louise set out the tea-table, and the family took their places round it, talking in the pleasantest and merriest manner about all sorts of things. Marie had taken her little stool, and sat down at her godpapa's feet in silence. When everybody happened to cease talking at the same time, Marie looked her godpapa full in the face with her great blue eyes, and said:

"I know now, godpapa, that my Nutcracker is your nephew, young Mr. Drosselmeier from Nürnberg. The prophecy has come true: he is a king and a prince, just as your friend the astronomer said he would be. But you know as well as I do that he is at war with Dame Mouseyrink's son—that horrid king of the mice. Why don't you help him?"

Marie told the whole story of the battle, as she had witnessed it, and was frequently interrupted by the loud laughter of her mother and sister; but Fritz and Drosselmeier listened quite gravely.

"Where in the name of goodness has the child got her head filled with all that nonsense?" cried her father.

"She has such a lively imagination, you see," said her mother; "she dreamt it all when she was feverish with her arm."

"It is all nonsense," cried Fritz, "and it isn't true! my red hussars are not such cowards as all that. If they were, do you suppose I should command them?"

But godpapa smiled strangely, and took little Marie on his knee, speaking more gently to her than ever he had been known to do before.

"More is given to you, Marie dear," he said, "than to me, or the others. You are a born princess, like Pirlipat, and reign in a bright beautiful country. But you still have much to suffer, if you mean to befriend poor transformed Nutcracker; for the king of the mice lies in wait for him at every turn. But I cannot help him; you, and you only, can do that. So be faithful and true."

Neither Marie nor any of the others knew what Godpapa Drosselmeier meant by these words. But they struck Dr. Stahlbaum—the father—as being so strange that he felt Drosselmeier's pulse, and said:

"There seems a good deal of congestion about the head, my dear sir. I'll just write you a little prescription."

But Marie's mother shook her head meditatively, and said:

"I have a strong idea what Mr. Drosselmeier means, though I can't exactly put it in words."

VICTORY

It was not very long before Marie was awakened one bright moonlight night by a curious noise, which came from one of the corners of her room. There was a sound as of small stones being thrown, and rolled here and there; and between whiles came a horrid cheeping and squeaking.

"Oh, dear me! here come these abominable mice again!" cried Marie, in terror, and she would have awakened her mother. But the noise suddenly ceased; and she could not move a muscle—for she saw the king of the mice working himself out through a hole in the wall; and at last he came into the room, ran about in it, and got on to the little table at her bed-head with a great jump.

"Hee-hehee!" he cried; "give me your sweetmeats! out with your cakes, marchpane and sugar-stick, gingerbread cakes! Don't pause to argue! If yield them you won't, I'll chew up Nutcracker! See if I don't!"

As he cried out these terrible words he gnashed and chattered his teeth most frightfully, and then made off again through the hole in the wall. This frightened Marie so that she was quite pale in the morning, and so upset that she scarcely could utter a word. A hundred times she felt impelled to tell her mother or her sister, or at all events her brother, what had happened. But she thought, "of course none of them would believe me. They would only laugh at me."

But she saw well enough that to succour Nutcracker she would have to sacrifice all her sweet things; so she laid out all she had of them at the bottom of the cupboard next evening.

"I can't make out how the mice have got into the sitting-room," said her mother. "This is something quite new. There never were any there before. See, Marie, they've eaten up all your sweetmeats."

And so it was: the epicure mouse king hadn't found the marchpane altogether to his taste, but had gnawed all round the edges of it, so that what he had left of it had to be thrown into the ash-pit. Marie never minded about her sweetmeats, being delighted to think that she had saved Nutcracker by means of them. But what were her feelings when next night there came a queaking again close by her ear. Alas! The king of the mice was there again, with his eyes glaring worse than the night before.

"Give me your sugar toys," he cried; "give them you must, or else I'll chew Nutcracker up into dust!"

Then he was gone again.

Marie was very sorry. She had as beautiful a collection of sugar-toys as ever a little girl could boast of. Not only had she a charming little shepherd, with his shepherdess, looking after a flock of milk-white sheep, with a nice dog jumping about them, but two postmen with letters in their hands, and four couples of prettily dressed young gentlemen and most beautifully dressed young ladies, swinging in a Russian swing. Then there were two or three dancers, and behind them Farmer Feldkuemmel and the Maid of Orleans. Marie didn't much care about them; but back in the corner there was a little baby with red cheeks, and this was Marie's darling. The tears came to her eyes.

"Ah!" she cried, turning to Nutcracker, "I really will do all I can to help you. But it's very hard."

Nutcracker looked at her so piteously that she determined to sacrifice everything— for she remembered the mouse king with all his seven mouths wide open to swallow the poor young fellow; so that night she set down all her sugar figures in front of the cupboard, as she had the sweetmeats the night before. She kissed the shepherd, the shepherdess, and the lambs; and at last she brought her best beloved of all, the little red-cheeked baby from its corner, but did put it a little further back than the rest. Farmer Feldkuemmel and the Maid of Orleans had to stand in the front rank of all.

"This is really getting too bad," said Marie's mother the next morning; "some nasty mouse or other must have made a hole in the glass cupboard, for poor Marie's sugar figures are all eaten and gnawed." Marie really could not restrain her tears. But she was soon able to smile again; for she thought, "What does it matter? Nutcracker is safe."

In the evening Marie's mother was telling her father and Godpapa Drosselmeier about the mischief which some mouse was doing in the children's cupboard, and her father said:

"It's a regular nuisance! What a pity it is that we can't get rid of it. It's destroying all the poor child's things."

Fritz intervened, and remarked:

"The baker downstairs has a fine grey councillors-of-legation; I'll go and get hold of him, and he'll soon put a stop to it, and bite the mouse's head off, even if it's Dame Mouseyrinks herself, or her son, the king of the mice."

"Oh, yes!" said his mother, laughing, "and jump up on to the chairs and tables, knock down the cups and glasses, and do ever so much mischief besides."

"No, no!" answered Fritz; "the baker's councillors-of-legation's a very clever fellow. I wish I could walk about on the edge of the roof, as he does."

"Don't let us have a nasty cat in the house in the night-time," said Louise, who hated cats.

"Fritz is quite right though," said the mother; "unless we set a trap. Haven't we got such a thing in the house?"

"Godpapa Drosselmeier's the man to get us one," said Fritz; "it was he who invented them, you know." Everybody laughed. And when the mother said they did not possess such a thing, Drosselmeier said he had plenty; and he actually sent a very fine one round that day. When the cook was browning the fat, Marie—with her head full of the marvels of her godpapa's tale—called out to her:

"Ah, take care, Queen! Remember Dame Mouseyrinks and her people." But Fritz drew his sword, and cried, "Let them come if they dare! I'll give an account of them." But everything about the hearth remained quiet and undisturbed. As Drosselmeier was fixing the browned fat on a fine thread, and setting the trap gently down in the glass cupboard, Fritz cried:

"Now, Godpapa Clockmaker, mind that the mouse king doesn't play you some trick!"

Ah, how did it fare with Marie that night? Something as cold as ice went tripping about on her arm, and something rough and nasty laid itself on her cheek, and cheeped and queaked in her ear. The horrible mouse king came and sat on her shoulder, foamed a blood-red foam out of all his seven mouths, and chattering and grinding his teeth, he hissed into Marie's ear:

"Hiss, hiss!—keep away—don't go in there—ware of that house—don't you be caught—death to the mouse—hand out your picture-books—none of your scornful looks!—Give me your dresses—also your laces—or, if you don't, leave you I won't—Nutcracker I'll bite—drag him out of your sight—his last hour is near—so tremble for fear!—Fee, fa, fo, fum—his last hour is come!—Hee hee, pee pee—queak—queak!"

Marie was overwhelmed with anguish and sorrow, and was looking quite pale and upset when her mother said to her next morning:

"This horrid mouse hasn't been caught. But never mind, dear, we'll catch the nasty thing yet, never fear. If the traps won't do, Fritz shall fetch the grey councillor-of-legation."

As soon as Marie was alone, she went up to the glass cupboard, and said to Nutcracker, in a voice broken by sobs:

"Ah, my dear, good Mr. Drosselmeier, what can I do for you, poor unfortunate girl that I am! Even if I give that horrid king of the mice all my picture-books, and my new dress which the Child Christ gave me at Christmas as well, he's sure to go on asking for more; so I soon shan't have anything more left, and he'll want to eat me! Oh, poor thing that I am! What shall I do? What shall I do?"

As she was thus crying and lamenting, she noticed that a great spot of blood had been left, since the eventful night of the battle, upon Nutcracker's neck. Since she had known that he was really young Mr. Drosselmeier, her godpapa's nephew, she had given up carrying him in her arms, and petting and kissing him; indeed, she felt a delicacy about touching him at all. But now she took him carefully out of his shelf, and began to wipe off this blood-spot with her handkerchief. What were her feelings when she found that Nutcracker was growing warmer and warmer in her hand, and beginning to move! She put him back into the cupboard as fast as she could. His mouth began to wobble backwards and forwards, and he began to whisper, with much difficulty:

"Ah, dearest Miss Stahlbaum—most precious of friends! How deeply I am indebted to you for everything—for everything! But don't, don't sacrifice any of your picture-books or pretty dresses for me. Get me a sword—a sword is what I want. If you get me that, I'll manage the rest—though—he may—"

There Nutcracker's speech died away, and his eyes, which had been expressing the most sympathetic grief, grew staring and lifeless again.

Marie felt no fear; she jumped for joy, rather, now that she knew how to help Nutcracker without further painful sacrifices. But where on earth was she to get hold of a sword for him? She resolved to take counsel with Fritz; and that evening, when their father and mother had gone out, and they two were sitting beside the glass cupboard, she told him what had passed between her and Nutcracker with the king of the mice, and what it was that was required to rescue Nutcracker.

The thing which chiefly exercised Fritz's mind was Marie's statement as to the unexemplary conduct of his red hussars in the great battle. He asked her once more, most seriously, to assure him if it really was the truth; and when she had repeated her statement, on her word of honour, he advanced to the cupboard, and made his hussars a most affecting address; and, as a punishment for their behaviour, he solemnly took their plumes one by one out of their busbies, and prohibited them from sounding the march of the hussars of the guard for the space of a twelvemonth. When he had performed this duty, he turned to Marie, and said:

"As far as the sword is concerned, I have it in my power to assist Nutcracker. I placed an old Colonel of Cuirassiers on retirement on a pension, no longer ago than yesterday, so that he has no further occasion for his sabre, which is sharp."

This Colonel was settled, on his pension, in the back corner of the third shelf. He was fetched out from thence, and his sabre—still a bright and handsome silver weapon—taken off, and girt about Nutcracker.

Next night Marie could not close an eye for anxiety. About midnight she fancied she heard a strange stirring and noise in the sitting-room—a rustling and a clanging—and all at once came a shrill "Queak!"

"The king of the mice! The king of the mice!" she cried, and jumped out of bed, all terror. Everything was silent; but soon there came a gentle tapping at the door of her room, and a soft voice made itself heard, saying:

"Please to open your door, dearest Miss Stahlbaum! Don't be in the least degree alarmed; good, happy news!"

It was Drosselmeier's voice—young Drosselmeier's, I mean. She threw on her dressing-gown, and opened the door as quickly as possible. There stood Nutcracker, with his sword, all covered with blood, in his right hand, and a little wax taper in his left. When he saw Marie he knelt down on one knee, and said:

"It was you, and you only, dearest lady, who inspired me with knightly valour, and steeled me with strength to do battle with the insolent caitiff who dared to insult you. The treacherous king of the mice lies vanquished and writhing in his gore! Deign, lady, to accept these tokens of victory from the hand of him who is, till death, your true and faithful knight."

With this Nutcracker took from his left arm the seven crowns of the mouse king, which he had ranged upon it, and handed them to Marie, who received them with the keenest pleasure. Nutcracker rose, and continued as follows:

"Oh! My best beloved Miss Stahlbaum, if you would only take the trouble to fol-low me for a few steps, what glorious and beautiful things I could show you, at this supreme moment when I have overcome my hereditary foe! Do—do come with me, dearest lady!"

TOYLAND

I feel quite convinced, children, that none of you would have hesitated for a moment to go with good, kind Nutcracker, who had always shown himself to be such a charming person, and Marie was all the more disposed to do as he asked her, because she knew what her just claims on his gratitude were, and was sure that he would keep his word, and show her all sorts of beautiful things. So she said:

"I will go with you, dear Mr. Drosselmeier; but it mustn't be very far, and it won't do to be very long, because, you know, I haven't had any sleep yet."

"Then we will go by the shortest route," said Nutcracker, "although it is, perhaps, rather the most difficult."

He went on in front, followed by Marie, till he stopped before the big old wardrobe. Marie was surprised to see that, though it was generally shut, the doors of it were now wide open, so that she could see her father's travelling cloak of fox-fur hanging in the front. Nutcracker clambered deftly up this cloak, by the edgings and trimmings of it, so as to get hold of the big tassel which was fastened at the back of it by a thick cord. He gave this tassel a tug, and a pretty little ladder of cedar-wood let itself quickly down through one of the arm-holes of the cloak.

"Now, Miss Stahlbaum, step up that ladder, if you will be so kind," said Nutcracker. Marie did so. But as soon as she had got up through the arm-hole, and begun to look out at the neck, all at once a dazzling light came streaming on to her, and she found herself standing on a lovely, sweet-scented meadow, from which millions of sparks were streaming upward, like the glitter of beautiful gems.

"This is Candy Mead, where we are now," said Nutcracker. "But we'll go in at that gate there."

Marie looked up and saw a beautiful gateway on the meadow, only a few steps off. It seemed to be made of white, brown, and raisin-coloured marble; but when she came close to it she saw it was all of baked sugar-almonds and raisins, which—as Nutcracker said when they were going through it—was the reason it was called "Almond and Raisin Gate." There was a gallery running round the upper part of it, apparently made of barley-sugar, and in this gallery six monkeys, dressed in red doublets, were playing on brass instruments in the most delightful manner ever heard; so that it was all that Marie could do to notice that she was walking along upon a beautiful variegated marble pavement, which, however, was really a mosaic of lozenges of all colours. Presently the sweetest of odours came breathing round her, streaming from a beautiful little wood on both sides of the way. There was such a glittering and sparkling among the dark foliage, that one could see all the gold and silver fruits hanging on the many-tinted stems, and these stems and branches were all ornamented and dressed up in ribbons and bunches of flowers, like brides and bridegrooms, and festive wedding guests. And as the orange perfume came wafted, as if on the wings of gentle zephyrs, there was a soughing among

the leaves and branches, and all the gold-leaf and tinsel rustled and tinkled like beautiful music, to which the sparkling lights could not help dancing.

"Oh, how charming this is!" cried Marie, enraptured.

"This is Christmas Wood, dearest Miss Stahlbaum," said Nutcracker.

"Ah!" said Marie, "if I could only stay here for a little! Oh, it is so lovely!"

Nutcracker clapped his little hands, and immediately there appeared a number of little shepherds and shepherdesses, and hunters and huntresses, so white and delicate that you would have thought they were made of pure sugar, whom Marie had not noticed before, although they had been walking about in the wood: and they brought a beautiful gold reclining chair, laid down a white satin cushion in it, and politely invited Marie to take a seat. As soon as she did so, the shepherds and shepherdesses danced a pretty ballet, to which the hunters and huntresses played the music on their horns, and then they all disappeared amongst the thickets.

"I must really apologize for the poor style in which this dance was executed, dearest Miss Stahlbaum," said Nutcracker. "These people all belong to our Wire Ballet Troupe, and can only do the same thing over and over again. Had we not better go on a little farther?"

"Oh, I'm sure it was all most delightful, and I enjoyed it immensely!" said Marie, as she stood up and followed Nutcracker, who was going on leading the way. They went by the side of a gently rippling brook, which seemed to be what was giving out all the perfume which filled the wood.

"This is Orange Brook," said Nutcracker; "but, except for its sweet scent, it is nothing like as fine a water as the River Lemonade, a beautiful broad stream, which falls—as this one does also—into the Almond-milk Sea."

And, indeed, Marie soon heard a louder plashing and rushing, and came in sight of the River Lemonade, which went rolling along in swelling waves of a yellowish colour, between banks covered with a herbage and underwood which shone like green carbuncles. A remarkable freshness and coolness, strengthening heart and breast, exhaled from this fine river. Not far from it a dark yellow stream crept sluggishly along, giving out a most delicious odour; and on its banks sat numbers of pretty children, angling for little fat fishes, which they ate as soon as they caught them. These fish were very much like filberts, Marie saw when she came closer. A short distance farther, on the banks of this stream, stood a nice little village. The houses of this village, and the church, the parsonage, the barns, and so forth, were all dark brown with gilt roofs, and many of the walls looked as if they were plastered over with lemon-peel and shelled almonds.

"That is Gingerthorpe on the Honey River," said Nutcracker. "It is famed for the good looks of its inhabitants; but they are very short-tempered people, because they suffer so much from tooth-ache. So we won't go there at present."

At this moment Marie caught sight of a little town where the houses were all sorts of colours and quite transparent, exceedingly pretty to look at. Nutcracker went on towards this town, and Marie heard a noise of bustle and merriment, and saw some thousands of nice little folks unloading a number of waggons which were drawn up in the market-place. What they were unloading from the waggons looked like packages of coloured paper, and tablets of chocolate.

"This is Bonbonville," Nutcracker said. "An embassy has just arrived from Paperland and the King of Chocolate. These poor Bonbonville people have been vexatiously threatened lately by the Fly-Admiral's forces, so they are covering their houses over with their presents from Paperland, and constructing fortifications with the fine pieces of workmanship which the Chocolate-King has sent them. But oh! dearest Miss Stahl-baum, we are not going to restrict ourselves to seeing the small towns and villages of this country. Let us be off to the metropolis."

He stepped quickly onwards, and Marie followed him, all expectation. Soon a beautiful rosy vapour began to rise, suffusing everything with a soft splendour. She saw that this was reflected from a rose-red, shining water, which went plashing and rushing away in front of them in wavelets of roseate silver. And on this delightful water, which kept broadening and broadening out wider and wider, like a great lake, the loveliest swans were floating, white as silver, with collars of gold. And, as if vying with each other, they were singing the most beautiful songs, at which little fish, glittering like diamonds, danced up and down in the rosy ripples.

"Oh!" cried Marie, in the greatest delight, "this must be the lake which Godpapa Drosselmeier was once going to make for me, and I am the girl who is to play with the swans."

Nutcracker gave a sneering sort of laugh, such as she had never seen in him before, and said:

"My uncle could never make a thing of this kind. You would be much more likely to do it yourself. But don't let us bother about that. Rather let us go sailing over the water, Lake Rosa here, to the metropolis."

The Metropolis

Nutcracker clapped his little hands again, and the waves of Lake Rosa began to sound louder and to plash higher, and Marie became aware of a sort of car approaching from the distance, made wholly of glittering precious stones of every colour, and drawn by two dolphins with scales of gold. Twelve of the dearest little boys, with head-dresses and doublets made of humming-birds' feathers woven together, jumped to land, and carried first Marie and then Nutcracker,

290

gently gliding above the water, into the car, which immediately began to move along over the lake of its own accord. Ah! how beautiful it was when Marie went onward thus over the waters in the shell-shaped car, with the rose-perfume breathing around her, and the rosy waves plashing. The two golden-scaled dolphins lifted their nostrils, and sent streams of crystal high in the air; and as these fell down in glittering, sparkling rainbows, there was a sound as of two delicate, silvery voices, singing, "Who comes over the rosy sea?—Fairy is she. Bim-bim—fishes; sim-sim—swans; sfa-sfa—golden birds; tratrah, rosy waves, wake you, and sing, sparkle and ring, sprinkle and kling— this is the fairy we languish to see—coming at last to us over the sea. Rosy waves dash—bright dolphins play—merrily, merrily on!"

But the twelve little boys at the back of the car seemed to take some umbrage at this song of the water-jets; for they shook the sun-shades they were holding so that the palm leaves they were made of clattered and rattled together; and as they shook them they stamped an odd sort of rhythm with their feet, and sang:

"Klapp and klipp, and klipp and klapp, and up and down."

"They are merry, amusing fellows," said Nutcracker, a little put out; "but they'll set the whole lake into a state of regular mutiny on my hands!" And in fact there did begin a confused, and confusing, noise of strange voices which seemed to be floating both in the water and in the air. However, Marie paid no attention to it, but went on looking into the perfumed rosy waves, from each of which a pretty girl's face smiled back to her.

"Oh! look at Princess Pirlipat," she cried, clapping her hands with gladness, "smiling at me so charmingly down there! Do look at her, Mr. Drosselmeier."

But Nutcracker sighed, almost sorrowfully, and said: "That is not Princess Pirlipat, dearest Miss Stahlbaum, it is only yourself; always your own lovely face smiling up from the rosy waves." At this Marie drew her head quickly back, closed her eyes as tightly as she could, and was terribly ashamed. But just then the twelve boys lifted her out of the car and set her on shore. She found herself in a small thicket or grove, almost more beautiful even than Christmas Wood, everything glittered and sparkled so in it. And the fruit on the trees was extraordinarily wonderful and beautiful, and not only of very curious colours, but with the most delicious perfume.

"Ah!" said Nutcracker, "here we are in Comfit Grove, and yonder lies the metropolis."

How shall I set about describing all the wonderful and beautiful sights which Marie now saw, or give any idea of the splendour and magnificence of the city which lay stretched out before her on a flowery plain? Not only did the walls and towers of it shine in the brightest and most gorgeous colours, but the shapes and appearance of the buildings were like nothing to be seen on earth. Instead of roofs the houses had on beautiful twining crowns, and the towers were garlanded with beautiful leaf-work, sculptured and carved into exquisite, intricate designs. As they passed in at the gateway, which looked as if it was made entirely of macaroons and sugared fruits, silver soldiers presented arms, and a little man in a brocade dressing-gown threw himself upon Nutcracker's neck, crying:

"Welcome, dearest prince! welcome to Sweetmeatburgh!"

Marie wondered not a little to see such a very grand personage recognise young Mr. Drosselmeier as a prince. But she heard such a number of small delicate voices making such a loud clamouring and talking, and such a laughing and chattering going on, and such a singing and playing, that she couldn't give her attention to anything else, but asked Drosselmeier what was the meaning of it all.

"Oh, it is nothing out of the common, dearest Miss Stahlbaum," he answered. "Sweetmeatburgh is a large, populous city, full of mirth and entertainment. This is only the usual thing that is always going on here every day. Please to come on a little farther."

After a few paces more they were in the great marketplace, which presented the most magnificent appearance. All the houses which were round it were of filagreed sugar-work, with galleries towering above galleries; and in the centre stood a lofty cake covered with sugar, by way of obelisk, with fountains round it spouting orgeade, lemonade, and other delicious beverages into the air. The runnels at the sides of the footways wore full of creams, which you might have ladled up with a spoon if you had chosen. But prettier than all this were the delightful little people who were crowding about everywhere by the thousand, shouting, laughing, playing, and singing, in short, producing all that jubilant uproar which Marie had heard from the distance. There were beautifully dressed ladies and gentlemen, Greeks and Armenians, Tyrolese and Jews, officers and soldiers, clergymen, shepherds, jack-puddings, in short, people of every conceivable kind to be found in the world.

The tumult grew greater towards one of the corners; the people streamed asunder. For the Great Mogul happened to be passing along there in his palanquin, attended by three-and-ninety grandees of the realm, and seven hundred slaves. But it chanced that the Fishermen's Guild, about five hundred strong, were keeping a festival at the opposite corner of the place; and it was rather an unfortunate coincidence that the Grand Turk took it in his head just at this particular moment to go out for a ride, and crossed the square with three thousand Janissaries. And, as if this were not enough, the grand procession of the Interrupted Sacrifice came along at the same time, marching up towards the obelisk with a full orchestra playing, and the chorus singing:

"Hail! all hail to the glorious sun!"

So there was a thronging and a shoving, a driving and a squeaking; and soon lamentations arose, and cries of pain, for one of the fishermen had knocked a Brahmin's head off in the throng, and the Great Mogul had been very nearly run down by a jack-pudding. The din grew wilder and wilder. People were beginning to shove one

another, and even to come to fisticuffs; when the man in the brocade dressing-gown who had welcomed Nutcracker as prince at the gate, clambered up to the top of the obelisk, and, after a very clear-tinkling bell had rung thrice, shouted, very loudly, three several times:

"Pastrycook! pastrycook! pastrycook!"

Instantly the tumult subsided. Everybody tried to save his bacon as quickly as he could; and, after the entangled processions had been got disentangled, the dirt properly brushed off the Great Mogul, and the Brahmin's head stuck on again all right, the merry noise went on just the same as before.

"Tell me why that gentleman called out 'Pastrycook,' Mr. Drosselmeier, please," said Marie.

"Ah! dearest Miss Stahlbaum," said Nutcracker, "in this place 'Pastrycook' means a certain unknown and very terrible Power, which, it is believed, can do with people just what it chooses. It represents the Fate, or Destiny, which rules these happy little people, and they stand in such awe and terror of it that the mere mention of its name quells the wildest tumult in a moment, as the burgomaster has just shown. Nobody thinks further of earthly matters, cuffs in the ribs, broken heads, or the like. Every one retires within himself, and says:

"What is man? and what his ultimate destiny?"

Marie could not forbear a cry of admiration and utmost astonishment as she now found herself all of a sudden before a castle, shining in roseate radiance, with a hundred beautiful towers. Here and there at intervals upon its walls were rich bouquets of violets, narcissus, tulips, carnations, whose dark, glowing colours heightened the dazzling whiteness, inclining to rose-colour, of the walls. The great dome of the central building, as well as the pyramidal roofs of the towers, were set all over with thousands of sparkling gold and silver stars.

"Aha!" said Nutcracker, "here we are at Marchpane Castle at last!"

Marie was sunk and absorbed in contemplation of this magic palace. But the fact did not escape her that the roof was wanting to one of the principal towers, and that little men, up upon a scaffold made of sticks of cinnamon, were busy putting it on again. But before she had had time to ask Nutcracker about this, he said:

"This beautiful castle was a short time since threatened with tremendous havoc, if not with total destruction. Sweet-tooth the giant happened to be passing by, and he bit off the top of that tower there, and was beginning to gnaw at the great dome. But the Sweetmeatburgh people brought him a whole quarter of the town by way of tribute, and a considerable slice of Comfit Grove into the bargain. This stopped his mouth, and he went on his way."

At this moment soft, beautiful music was heard, and out came twelve little pages with lighted clove-sticks, which they held in their little hands by way of torches. Each

of their heads was a pearl, their bodies were emeralds and rubies, and their feet were beautifully-worked pure gold. After them came four ladies about the size of Marie's Miss Clara, but so gloriously and brilliantly attired that Marie saw in a moment that they could be nothing but princesses of the blood royal. They embraced Nutcracker most tenderly, and shed tears of gladness, saying:

"Oh, dearest prince! beloved brother!"

Nutcracker seemed deeply affected. He wiped away his tears, which flowed thick and fast, and then he took Marie by the hand and said, with much pathos and solemnity:

"This is Miss Marie Stahlbaum, the daughter of a most worthy medical man, and the preserver of my life. Had she not thrown her slipper just in the nick of time—had she not procured me the pensioned Colonel's sword—I should have been lying in my cold grave at this moment, bitten to death by the accursed king of the mice. I ask you to tell me candidly, can Princess Pirlipat, princess though she be, compare for a moment with Miss Stahlbaum here in beauty, in goodness, in virtues of every kind? My answer is, emphatically 'No.' "

All the ladies cried "No"; and they fell upon Marie's neck with sobs and tears, and cried: "Ah! noble preserver of our beloved royal brother! Excellent Miss Stahlbaum!"

They now conducted Marie and Nutcracker into the castle, to a hall whose walls were composed of sparkling crystal. But what delighted Marie most of all was

the furniture. There were the most darling little chairs, bureaus, writing-tables, and so forth, standing about everywhere, all made of cedar or Brazil-wood, covered with golden flowers. The princesses made Marie and Nutcracker sit down, and said that they would themselves prepare a banquet. So they went and brought quantities of little cups and dishes of the finest Japanese porcelain, and spoons, knives and forks, graters and stew-pans, and other kitchen utensils of gold and silver. Then they fetched the most delightful fruits and sugar things—such as Marie had never seen the like of—and began to squeeze the fruit in the daintiest way with their little hands, and to grate the spices and rub down the sugar-almonds; in short, they set to work so skilfully that Marie could see very well how accomplished they were in kitchen matters, and what a magnificent banquet there was going to be. Knowing her own skill in this line, she wished, in her secret heart, that she might be allowed to go and help the princesses, and have a finger in all these pies herself. And the prettiest of Nutcracker's sisters, just as if she had read the wishes of Marie's heart, handed her a little gold mortar, saying:

"Sweet friend, dear preserver of my brother, would you mind just pounding a little of this sugar-candy?"

Now as Marie went on pounding in the mortar with good will and the utmost enjoyment—and the sound of it was like a lovely song—Nutcracker began to relate, with much minuteness and prolixity, all that had happened on the occasion of the terrible engagement between his forces and the army of the king of the mice; how he had had the worst of it on account of the bad behaviour of his troops; how the horrible mouse king had all but bitten him to death, so that Marie had had to sacrifice a number of his subjects who were in her service, etc., etc.

During all this it seemed to Marie as if what Nutcracker was saying—and even the sound of her own mortar—kept growing more and more indistinct, and going farther and farther away. Presently she saw a silver mistiness rising up all about, like clouds, in which the princesses, the pages, Nutcracker, and she herself were floating. And a curious singing and a buzzing and humming began, which seemed to die away in the distance; and then she seemed to be going up—up—up, as if on waves constantly rising and swelling higher and higher, higher and higher, higher and higher.

Conclusion

And then came a "prr-poof," and Marie fell down from some inconceivable height.

"That was a crash and a tumble!"

However, she opened her eyes, and, lo and behold, there she was in her own bed! It was broad daylight, and her mother was standing at her bedside, saying:

"Well, what a sleep you have had! Breakfast has been ready for ever so long."

Of course, dear audience, you see how it was. Marie, confounded and amazed by all the wonderful things she had seen, had fallen asleep at last in Marchpane Castle, and the boys or the pages, or perhaps the princesses themselves, had carried her home and put her to bed.

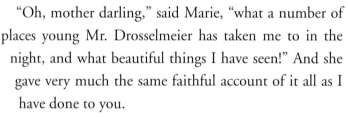

"Oh, mother darling," said Marie, "what a number of places young Mr. Drosselmeier has taken me to in the night, and what beautiful things I have seen!" And she gave very much the same faithful account of it all as I have done to you.

Her mother listened, looking at her with much astonishment, and, when she had finished, said:

"You have had a long, beautiful dream, Marie; but now you must put it all out of your head."

Marie firmly maintained that she had not been dreaming at all; so her mother took her to the glass cupboard, lifted out Nutcracker from his usual position on the third shelf, and said:

"You silly girl, how can you believe that this wooden figure can have life and motion?"

"Ah, mother," answered Marie, "I know perfectly well that Nutcracker is young Mr. Drosselmeier from Nürnberg, Godpapa Drosselmeier's nephew."

Her father and mother both burst out into ringing laughter.

"It's all very well your laughing at poor Nutcracker, father," cried Marie, almost weeping; "but he spoke very highly of you; for when we arrived at Marchpane Castle, and he was introducing me to his sisters, the princesses, he said you were a most worthy medical man."

The laughter grew louder, and Louise, and even Fritz, joined in it. Marie ran into the next room, took the mouse king's seven crowns from her little box, and handed them to her mother, saying:

"Look there, then, dear mother; those are the mouse king's seven crowns which young Mr. Drosselmeier gave me last night as a proof that he had got the victory."

Her mother gazed in amazement at the little crowns, which were made of some very brilliant, wholly unknown metal, and worked more beautifully than any human hands could have worked them. Dr. Stahlbaum could not cease looking at them with admiration and astonishment either, and both the father and the mother enjoined Marie most earnestly to tell them where she really had got them from. But she could only repeat what she had said before; and when her father scolded her, and accused her of untruthfulness, she began to cry bitterly, and said:

"Oh, dear me; what can I tell you except the truth, poor unfortunate girl that I am!"

At this moment the door opened, and Godpapa Drosselmeier came in, crying:

"Hullo! hullo! What's all this? My little Marie crying? What's all this? what's all this?"

Dr. Stahlbaum told him all about it, and showed him the crowns. As soon as he had looked at them, however, he cried out:

"Stuff and nonsense! stuff and nonsense! These are the crowns I used to wear on my watch-chain. I gave them as a present to Marie on her second birthday. Do you mean to tell me you don't remember?"

None of them did remember anything of the kind. But Marie, seeing that her father and mother's faces were clear of clouds again, ran up to her godpapa, crying:

"You know all about the affair, Godpapa Drosselmeier; tell it to them then. Let them know from your own lips that my Nutcracker is your nephew, young Mr. Drosselmeier from Nürnberg, and that it was he who gave me the crowns."

But Drosselmeier made a very angry face, and muttered, "Stupid stuff and nonsense!" upon which Marie's father took her in front of him, and said, with much earnestness:

"Now just look here, Marie; let there be an end of all this foolish trash and absurd nonsense for once and for all; I'm not going to allow any more of it; and if ever I hear you say again that that idiotic, misshapen Nutcracker is your godpapa's nephew, I shall shy, not only Nutcracker, but all your other playthings—Miss Clara not excepted—out of the window."

Of course poor Marie dared not utter another word concerning that which her whole mind was full of, for you may well suppose that it was impossible for anyone who had seen all that she had seen to forget it. And I regret to say that even Fritz himself at once turned his back on his sister whenever she wanted to talk to him about the wondrous realm in which she had been so happy. Indeed, he is said to have frequently murmured, "Stupid goose!" between his teeth, though I can scarcely think this compatible with his proved kindness of heart. This much, however, is matter of certainty, that, as he no longer believed what his sister said, he now, on a public parade, formally recanted what he had said to his red hussars, and, in the place of the plumes he had deprived them of, gave them much taller and finer ones of goose quills, and allowed them to sound the march of the hussars of the guard as before.

Marie did not dare to say anything more of her adventures. But the memories of that fairy realm haunted her with a sweet intoxication, and the music of that delightful, happy country still rang sweetly in her ears. Whenever she allowed her thoughts to dwell

on all those glories she saw them again, and so it came about that, instead of playing as she used to do, she sat quiet and meditative, absorbed within herself. Everybody found fault with her for being this sort of little dreamer.

It chanced one day that Godpapa Drosselmeier was repairing one of the clocks in the house, and Marie was sitting beside the glass cupboard, sunk in her dreams and gazing at Nutcracker. All at once she said, as if involuntarily:

"Ah, dear Mr. Drosselmeier, if you really were alive, I shouldn't be like Princess Pirlipat, and despise you because you had had to give up being a nice handsome gentleman for my sake!"

"Stupid stuff and nonsense!" cried Godpapa Drosselmeier.

But, as he spoke, there came such a tremendous bang and shock that Marie fell from her chair insensible.

When she came back to her senses her mother was busied about her and said:

"How could you go and tumble off your chair in that way, a big girl like you? Here is Godpapa Drosselmeier's nephew come from Nürnberg. See how good you can be."

Marie looked up. Her godpapa had got on his yellow coat and his glass wig, and was smiling in the highest good-humour. By the hand he was holding a very small but very handsome young gentleman. His little face was red and white; he had on a beautiful red coat trimmed with gold lace, white silk stockings and shoes, with a lovely bouquet of flowers in his shirt frill. He was beautifully frizzed and powdered, and had a magnificent queue hanging down his back. The little sword at his side seemed to be made entirely of jewels, it sparkled and shone so, and the little hat under his arm was woven of flocks of silk. He gave proof of the fineness of his manners in that he had brought for Marie a quantity of the most delightful toys—above all, the very same figures as those which the mouse king had eaten up—as well as a beautiful sabre for Fritz. He cracked nuts at table for the whole party; the very hardest did not withstand him. He placed them in his mouth with his left hand, tugged at his pigtail with his right, and crack! they fell in pieces.

Marie grew red as a rose at the sight of this charming young gentleman; and she grew redder still when, after dinner, young Drosselmeier asked her to go with him to the glass cupboard in the sitting-room.

"Play nicely together, children," said Godpapa Drosselmeier; "now that my clocks are all nicely in order, I can have no possible objection."

But as soon as young Drosselmeier was alone with Marie, he went down on one knee, and spake as follows:

"Ah! my most dearly-beloved Miss Stahlbaum! see here at your feet the fortunate Drosselmeier, whose life you saved here on this very spot. You were kind enough to say, plainly and unmistakably, in so many words, that you would not have despised me, as Princess Pirlipat did, if I had been turned ugly for your sake. Immediately I ceased to be a contemptible Nutcracker, and resumed my former not altogether ill-looking person and form. Ah! most exquisite lady! bless me with your precious hand; share with me my crown and kingdom, and reign with me in Marchpane Castle, for there I now am king."

Marie raised him, and said gently:

"Dear Mr. Drosselmeier, you are a kind, nice gentleman; and as you reign over a delightful country of charming, funny, pretty people, I accept your hand."

So then they were formally betrothed; and when a year and a day had come and gone, they say he came and fetched her away in a golden coach, drawn by silver horses. At the marriage there danced two-and-twenty thousand of the most beautiful dolls and other figures, all glittering in pearls and diamonds; and Marie is to this day the queen of a realm where all kinds of sparkling Christmas Woods, and transparent Marchpane Castles—in short, the most wonderful and beautiful things of every kind—are to be seen—by those who have the eyes to see them.

So this is the end of the tale of the Nutcracker and the Mouse King.

POEMS

A VISIT FROM ST. NICHOLAS

CLEMENT CLARKE MOORE

'Twas the night before Christmas, when all through the house
Not a creature was stirring, not even a mouse;
The stockings were hung by the chimney with care,
In hopes that St. Nicholas soon would be there.

The children were nestled all snug in their beds
While visions of sugar-plums danced through their heads;
And Mamma in her 'kerchief, and I in my cap,
Had just settled our brains for a long winter's nap.
When out on the lawn there arose such a clatter,
I sprang from my bed to see what was the matter.

Away to the window I flew like a flash,

Tore open the shutters and threw up the sash.

The moon on the breast of the new-fallen snow

Gave the lustre of mid-day to objects below,

When, what to my wondering eyes did appear,

But a miniature sleigh and eight tiny rein-deer,

With a little old driver, so lively and quick,

I knew in a moment he must be St. Nick.

More rapid than eagles his coursers they came,
And he whistled, and shouted, and called them by name:
"Now, *Dasher!* Now, *Dancer!* now *Prancer* and *Vixen!*
On *Comet!* on, *Cupid!* on, *Donder* and *Blitzen!*
To the top of the porch! to the top of the wall!
Now dash away! dash away! dash away, all!"

As leaves that before the wild hurricane fly,
When they meet with an obstacle, mount to the sky,
So up to the house-top the coursers they flew,
With the sleigh full of toys, and St. Nicholas too.
And then, in a twinkling, I heard on the roof
The prancing and pawing of each little hoof.

As I drew in my head, and was turning around,
Down the chimney St. Nicholas came with a bound,
He was dressed all in fur, from his head to his foot,
And his clothes were all tarnished with ashes and soot;
A bundle of toys he had flung on his back,
And he looked like a peddler just opening his pack.

His eyes—how they twinkled! his dimples how merry!
His cheeks were like roses, his nose like a cherry!
His droll little mouth was drawn up like a bow,
And the beard of his chin was as white as the snow;
The stump of a pipe he held tight in his teeth,
And the smoke it encircled his head like a wreath;

He had a broad face and a little round belly
That shook when he laughed, like a bowl-ful of jelly.
He was chubby and plump, a right jolly old elf,
And I laughed when I saw him, in spite of myself;
A wink of his eye and a twist of his head
Soon gave me to know I had nothing to dread;
He spoke not a word, but went straight to his work,
And filled all the stockings; then turned with a jerk,

And laying his finger aside of his nose,
And giving a nod, up the chimney he rose;
He sprang to his sleigh, to his team gave a whistle,
And away they all flew like the down of a thistle.
But I heard him exclaim, ere he drove out of sight

"Happy Christmas to all
And to all a Good Night!"

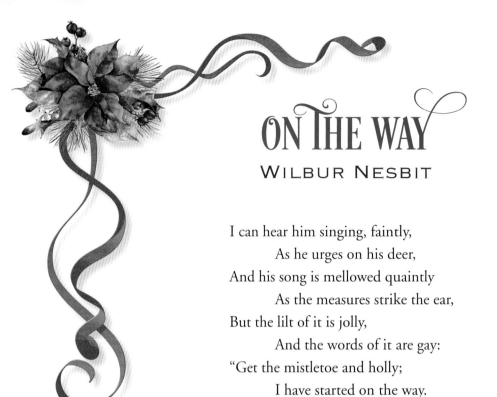

ON THE WAY
WILBUR NESBIT

I can hear him singing, faintly,
    As he urges on his deer,
And his song is mellowed quaintly
    As the measures strike the ear,
But the lilt of it is jolly,
    And the words of it are gay:
"Get the mistletoe and holly;
    I have started on the way.

"Little fellow, little fellow, with the doubting in your eyes,
I have started on my journey, 'neath the mystic northern skies.
And I see you building fancies in the flicker of the grate—
Little fellow, little fellow, while you wonder and you wait."

I can hear the hoof-beats thudding.
    As the snow is flung behind.
While the laden sleigh is scudding
    With the swiftness of the wind;
And the echoes now are flinging
    Broken murmurs of the song
That old Santa Claus is singing
    While the reindeer speed along:

"Little fellow, little fellow, for the faith that still you hold,
I am speeding down the windings of the trail I've known of old—
And I know the deepest wishes in the golden heart of you.
And the dreams you have and cherish are the dreams that must come true."

Ho, the gleaming holly berry.
          And the branches of the tree,
And the measures mad and merry
          Of the song for you and me!
Far and faint, but waxing clearer,
          Comes the whirring of the whip,
While the good old Saint draws nearer
          With this ballad on his lip:

"Little fellow, little fellow, while you sit and dream of me,
And the marvel of the morning that shall show the wondrous tree,
For your trust in all the fancies of the shadow and the gleam,
I am starting on my journey down the highway of your dream."

SANTA'S SURPRISE PARTY

GLADYS HYATT SINCLAIR

'Twas a glad Christmas Eve, and all over the world,
With reindeer and sleigh dear old Santa had whirled.
No one was forgotten or slighted by him;
Each stocking was bulging and crammed to the brim.
"There!" cried the old saint as he stopped at his door,
"I've made all the little ones happy once more!
But the rest of the night will be lonely, I fear;
Why, what is this wonderful racket I hear?"
He bounded down nimbly, so great his surprise,
But stopped just inside, scarce believing his eyes;
For here were the children that he had supposed
Were sleeping down yonder with eyes tightly closed;
Here singing and dancing and frisking in glee
Around a most dazzling and beautiful tree!
"Oh, Santa," they cried "We have found you at last!
How tired you must be! You have journeyed so fast
To take us good gifts; but now, Santa Claus, see!
We have brought *you* some gifts and this splendid, big tree!
We want you to know, just for once in a way,
How happy you make us, each new Christmas Day.
These gifts did not grow in your Christmas tree grove;
We brought them for you, with our very best love!"
Then I wish you had seen them lead Santa about
To examine his gifts—heard him laugh and his shout
When he found a fur coat with a collar so wide,
When he read the gay note that was fastened inside!

There were bells for the reindeer, a pipe
　　and red mittens
And one little girl had brought Santa her
　　kittens.
He'd a brush for his clothes and a brush for
　　his hair,
He'd had pictures and books and a great
　　easy chair

Where a good saint might nap it and sit
　　at his ease,
While presents grew ripe on his evergreen
　　trees.
He'd a pair of new spectacles, shining and
　　bright,
To help him to fill little stockings aright.
There were cushions so soft for the magi-
　　cal sleigh,
A cap trimmed with fur and a dressing-
　　gown gay,

And stockings so long and so warm and so thick,
Jack Frost can no more play his favorite trick
Of blowing a blast upon Santa Claus's toes
As over the steeples, at Christmas, he goes.
"Please wear this red scarf," whispered one little elf;
"I made it, dear Santa; I worked it myself!"
He caught up the girlie and gave her a kiss.
He hugged them and thanked them—not one did he miss;
Then, "laying his finger aside of his nose,"
He twinkled his eyes—and what do you suppose?
Such visions of stockings, filled up to the top,
Bedazzled those children, they scarcely could stop
To cry "Merry Christmas! Good night, Santa dear!"
And to wish him a glorious "Happy New Year!"

Then home o'er the cloud hills they scampered and ran;
Now guess all the gifts that they found—if you can!

THE CHRISTMAS TREE

HARRIET PRESCOTT SPOFFORD

"Oh," sighed the little Christmas tree,
"How sad my fortune seems to be!
    Here in the dim wood might I stay,
    Where the great boughs swing low all day,
    And the green shadows round me play,
And all my brothers sing with me!"

But to the city, wiping tears
Of crystal gum, with many fears,
    The small tree journeyed, and was kept
    Where the little light about him crept;
    And there, it seems to him, he slept
It might be days, it might be years.

Then, at last, pleasant people stirred,
And took him where he gladly heard
    Sweet voices, and saw lovely hands
    Wreathe him with tufted snow, and bands
    Of gold, and things from foreign lands,
With many a song and joyous word.

And he had gifts to give, the shout
Of happy children all about;
    And one day, when his boughs were bare,
    They laid him in the chimney there,
    And with great crackling and a flare
His sparks among the stars fled out!

THAT LITTLE CHRISTMAS TREE

HELEN STANDISH PERKINS

It was a little Christmas tree, with candles all aglow,
And golden balls and silver stars, a bright and shining row.
The children danced around it, and clapped their hands with glee;
And not a child was happier than the little Christmas tree.

But next week, stripped of all its gifts and cast into the yard
It murmured with a little sigh: "Now, surely this is hard!
To give delight for but that night,
And then to be forgot,
Would seem to be for any tree
A most unhappy lot!"

But Ned and Ted and Little Fred
soon spied it where it lay.
"Hurrah!" they cried, "A mast! A mast!
We'll sail and sail away,
And far across the Arctic seas
Our gallant ship shall go
To find the seals and polar bears
And jolly Esquimaux."

A plank their ship, a sheet their sail, the happy
    tree their mast,
These bold explorers northward turned, and sailed
    away so fast
      That soon o'er unknown lands there waved
          The banner of the free.
      The staff that proudly bore it
          Was the little Christmas tree.

What afterward befell it would take me long to tell:
It once became a fairy wood, where elves and dryads dwell;
    And once a prancing, coal-black steed,
      With a noble knight astride;
    And once a dark and gloomy cave
      Where bears and lions hide.

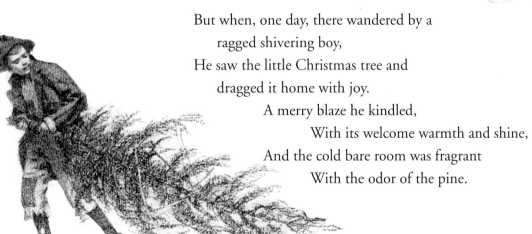

      But when, one day, there wandered by a
        ragged shivering boy,
      He saw the little Christmas tree and
        dragged it home with joy.
        A merry blaze he kindled,
          With its welcome warmth and shine,
      And the cold bare room was fragrant
        With the odor of the pine.

The children crowded round it with happy eyes so bright;
The tree thought of the glittering star and candles all alight.
The firelight shone upon the floor
And danced upon the wall.
"Ah," sighed the little Christmas tree,
"*This* is the best of all."

The tale, dear little children,
Is true as it can be;
For I saw all these thing happen
To that little Christmas tree.

Signs of the Times

Gladys Hyatt Sinclair

Smiles on the faces as people go past,
Squeaks in the snow where they hurry so fast;
Meetings and greetings, so merry and glad,
Wishings and winkings—all "Santa Claus mad";
Laughter that bubbles, and dancing wee feet;
Holly wreaths hung all the way down the street;
See the green Christmas trees, frostily pearled—
Christmas is coming, there's joy in the world!

Loving hands busy by day and by night;
Loving hearts beating, all buoyant and light;
Secrets and whispers and mystery rife,
Doors that dare close e'en between man and wife;
Parcels and packages, bundle and box;
Can't someone hurry these stupid old clocks?
Santa Claus waits on his trip to be whirled—
Christmas is coming, there's joy in the world!

SANTA CLAUS AND HIS WORKS

GEORGE P. WEBSTER

This nice little story for girls and for boys,
Is all about Santa Claus, Christmas, and toys
So listen my children, to what you shall hear,
For I know, to each little one, Santa is dear.

In a nice little village called Santa Claus-ville,
With its houses and church at the foot of the hill,
Lives jolly old Santa Claus—day after day,
He works and he whistles the moments away.

For he knows that in labor is happiness found,
And a merrier fellow was never around:
So fat and good natured this jolly old chap
Will never be idle except for a nap.

His house in fair Santa Claus-ville as you know,
Is near the North Pole, in the ice and the snow;
But clothed all in fur from his head to his toes,
Not a feeling of coldness the old fellow knows.

He has the most beautiful long snowy hair,
Tho' the top of his head is quite shiny and bare;
His dear little eyes how they twinkle and shine,
But he never was known to drink brandy or wine.

'Tis only because he is merry and bright
That they sparkle like two little stars of the night,
And perhaps 'tis his kindness of heart showing through,
While he's planning and working dear children for you.

334

For good little children he's working away,
Making the toys which he'll bring them some day;
And busy all day, while he whistles and sings,
He's planning and making the funniest things.

From houses and furniture, dishes and pans,
To bracelets and brooches, and bright-colored fans,
And soldiers and pop-guns, and trumpets and drums,
To baby's tin rattle, and a bright top which hums.

And oh, the gay dollies with long curling hair,
That open their eyes and sit up in a chair.
There old Santa will sit with his specs on his nose
And work all the day making pretty new clothes;

Such as dresses and sashes, and hats for the head,
And night-gowns to wear when they jump into bed;
And garters and socks, and the tiniest shoes,
And lots of nice things such as doll-babies use.

Then he makes with his tools many wonderful things,
Such as monkeys and acrobats jumping on strings,
With many things more for I cannot tell half—
But just look at his picture I'm sure you will laugh.

And a very wise fellow is Santa Claus, too,
He is jolly and kind but he knows what to do;
And after his work for the day is all done,
As he sees the long rays of the bright setting sun,

He climbs to his turret, way up near the sky,
And looks o'er the world with his keen searching eye;
Peeps into the cities, the towns, great and small,
And villages too, for he's sure to see all.

He looks into homes of the rich and the poor,
Of those who have plenty, and those who endure;
For God's little children he finds everywhere,
The rich and the poor are alike in his care.

With his dog standing by him and spy-glass in hand,
He looks for good children all over the land:
And whenever he sees them, at work or at play,
The old fellow listens to hear what they say.

And if they are gentle, and loving, and kind,
To give them a present he makes up his mind;
And when Christmas time comes he will surely be there,
To leave of his treasure a bountiful share.

Oh, a jolly good sight is this funny old chap
When he's robed in his bear-skin and fur-bordered cap,
All ready to start on his way through the cold,
In a sleigh covered over with jewels and gold.

While his deer from the mountains all harnessed with care,
Like race-horses prance through the clear, frosty air;
'Tis fun just to watch them and hear the bells ring,
E'n the stars seem to think it a comical thing.

For old Santa is bundled so close to the chin,
That there isn't a chance for the cold to get in.
His cheeks are so rosy, his eyes are so bright,
That truly he makes quite a comical sight.

He cracks his long whip, and he whistles a tune,
While he winks at the stars, and he bows to the moon;
And over the tree-tops he drives like the wind,
Leaving the birds of the night far behind.

And his deers speed away on their journey so fleet,
That they seem to have wing to their swift flying feet;
For there's work to be done by the cheery old man,
And his coursers are speeding as fast as they can.

Ah! here is a picture, oh, children just look
At the names of the good little girls in his book!
And a long list of names of the good little boys,
Who are careful and never disturb with their noise.

There is Tommy, who tended the baby with care,
He shall have beautiful books for his share;
And how happy Eliza will be when she looks
For her present and, too, finds some beautiful books.

For dear little Mary, a doll there will be,
And for little Alice, a gay Christmas-tree;
And wee little Georgie, the baby, will find
A big stick of candy, just suiting his mind.

There, the old fellow stands, with a queer knowing look,
'Till he has in his mind every name in the book;
And he would be kind to them all, if he could,
But he only gives presents to those who are good.

An army he gives to the boy who is neat,
And never is rude, in the house or the street;
And a farm to the boy who goes smiling to school,
Who knows all his lessons and minds every rule.

For old Santa knows well, who the good children are,
And through his good telescope sees them afar;
And he never is known to forget, or pass by,
No matter how many his searching may spy.

When Christmas Eve comes, into bed you must creep,
And late in the night when you all are asleep
He is certain to come, so your stocking prepare,
And hang them all close to the chimney with care.

How funny he looks as he stands on the round,
And gathers the toys that are far from the ground;
He is large round the waist, but what care we for that—
Like the good-natured people who always are fat.

The lank grumbling wolf, who lies hidden all day,
And the fox who at midnight goes out for his prey,
And the serpent who hides in the foliage green,
Are all of them ugly, ill-tempered, and lean.

But Santa Claus comes, in his queer-looking hat,
And we know he's good-humored because he is fat.
So when you grow up, I would not have you slim,
But plump and good-natured, and merry like him.

Should he need for his breakfast, some fish or some veal,
The sea-calves are his, and the whale, and the seal.
Where he lives there is always a cool pleasant air,
Last summer, oh! didn't we wish we were there?

He's a funny old chap and quite shy, it would seem,
For I never but once caught a glimpse of his team:
'Twas a bright moonlight night, and it stood in full view,
So seeing it, I can describe it to you.

When Christmas time comes, he will toil like a Turk,
For the cheery old fellow is happy at work.
With his queer-looking team through the air he will go,
And alight on the houses, all white with the snow;

And into the chimney will dart in a thrice,
When all are asleep, but the cat and the mice;
And he has to be quick, to be through in a night,
For his work must be done ere the coming of light.

Then he'll fill up the stockings with candy and toys,
And all without making a bit of a noise,
There'll be presents for Julia, and Bettie, and Jack,
And plenty more left in the old fellow's sack.

And if Evrie behaves well, and minds what is said,
Quits teasing the cat, and goes early to bed,
He'll find for his present a sled, or a gun,
A ready companion in frolic and fun.

When Christmas is over old Santa Claus goes,
Straight home and then takes a full week of repose,
And when all the holiday frolics are o'er,
He goes to his shop, and his labors once more.

And all the long years, with his paint and his glue,
He is making new toys, little children, for you.
So be glad, and remember to do what you can,
To please and make happy this good little man,

And now ere the story is ended we'll give
Three cheers for old Santa Claus, long may he live!
To work for good children, and long may they try
To be good, that he never may pass any by.

Three cheers! For the hero of Santa Claus-ville;
Let us echo them now, with a hearty good will
A cleverer fellow no man ever saw,
So hail to old Santa Claus! Hip, Hip, Hurrah!

KRIS KRINGLE'S TRAVELS

SUSIE M. BEST

A jolly old fellow
    Is Mr. Kris Kringle!
He's coming! he's coming!
    Just hear his bells jingle!

The fleetest of reindeer
    Are drawing his sleigh
Because he must travel
    So far before day.

The keen wind of water
    Is biting his nose;
Ho! ho! In the moonlight
    It looks like a rose!

His bright blue eyes twinkle
    Like stars in the skies;
His snowy white whiskers
    Float out as he flies.

He comes to a housetop—
    His reindeer he halts;
From the seat where he's sitting
    All lightly he vaults.

He runs to the chimney—
    Oh, dear! he jumps in.
It's strange how he does it,
    Because he's not thin!

Down, down he is slipping,
    He knows where to go,—
To the room where the stockings
    Are hung in a row.

He feels in his pockets,
    He opens his sack;
He empties them quickly,
    And then he runs back.

Up the chimney he hurries,
    The housetop he gains,
Once more in his carriage,
    He catches the reins.

Again the bells jingle,
    And fill him with mirth;
And this way Kris Kringle
    Goes over the earth!

MEASURED FOR CHRISTMAS

EGBERT L. BANGS

Ugh! there's a worm upon your dress
Said little Caroline to Bess.

"It drags its tail up to its head,
And then takes one long step," she said.

"It is a measuring worm," said Bess.
"I want a pretty, new silk dress."

A father's ear drank in each word
That in his chair he overheard.

When Christmas came, oh, joy for Bess,
There came for her a new silk dress.

A pleasant note was pinned to it;
It said, "I hope this dress will fit.

"I've cut it by its measure true
Sent by the worm that measured you,

So, merry Christmas, darling Bess!
Who sent your gift? Now, can you guess?"

Of course dear Bess could have no doubt
How what she wished had come about.

354

Her faith in Santa Claus was firm;
And how she blessed the fairy worm

That took her measure, with such skill!
While good old Santa paid the bill.

Now, that's the way that little Bess
Believes her pretty, new silk dress

Was made and sent; let her believe;
The passing years will undeceive

The little girl who shakes her curls,
And says that worms do measure girls

For dresses that kind Santa brings,
With lots of other precious things.

IMAGE CREDITS